What People Are Saying

'*believe*' makes for a fabulous read. I did not want to put it down. It's like dessert without all the calories. I savored every morsel. I was intrigued at every turn. When I came to the last page it was bittersweet. I was loving curling up with it so much that I hated for it to end. The characters stepped off the pages and into my heart. I hope Karen writes a sequel. ~*Karen M. O'Leary author of Do Your Tears Belong To Me? Xulon Press*

The mental imagery is vivid... In '*believe,*' we become part of a connection to souls that spans across time...at the same time real in this material world and imagined in the mind of a seer. As happiness and tragedy commingle in our own life and in the lives of loved ones, we strive to remain hopeful and to believe. '*believe*' fuels that hope no matter what kismet presents. Read and believe. ~ *Kamal Kalia, M.D. New England Neurosurgical Associates, LLC*

Filled with intrigue, readers will flip through the pages to uncover the secret between the covers of '*believe.*' Karen Biery weaves a distinctive tale packed with fully-developed characters overshadowed by a puzzling history that grabs the reader from the first page. In the end, readers *believe.* ~ *Mary Jo Rulnick, author of The Frantic Woman's Guide to Feeding Family and Friends (Grand Central, formerly Warner Books*)

believe

believe

by

Karen Biery

River Road Press
Branson, Missouri

Published by **River Road Press**

Library of Congress Control Number: 2009933471

ISBN: 978-0-9800332-5-0

Edited by Pat McGrath Avery

Printed in the United States of America

Quantity discounts are available on bulk purchases of this book for educational institutions or social organizations. For information, please contact the publisher.

www.RiverRoadPress.org

To All

who have

longed and lost

ACKNOWLEDGEMENTS

As my first novel, the list to thank is a long one. How to list is the question. I guess I should start at the beginning.

Thank you to my friend, Carolyn Piampiano who started me on this path with the introduction to SQuire Rushnell's when GOD winks. Thank you SQuire for your words of wisdom and guidance.

Thank you to my parents, Max and Evelyn Newton for their encouragement, love and support. To my in laws, Bob and Laura Biery for their kind words and excitement. To my sister, Tracy for the myriad of times she asked to read, read and re-read the novel. To Kamal and Kellie Kalia for giving me Madeline's medical conditions and issues. To my stepdaughter, Anne for the sparkle in her eyes, skip in her voice and true excitement during the process. To my dear friends, Pat Riley and Sue Forkel, for their willingness to listen to unending issues and for offering solid advice without prejudice (well maybe just a bit).

Many thanks to Dr. Craig Paulenich for making me fall in love with the English language and for giving me my own voice and belief. To Joyce, Pat and John at River Road Press whom without their knowledge and months of handholding and guidance this book would not have happened. To Bill and Jean Esposito for their keen eye and red (or black) pen who also said they would be upset if this novel sat in a desk drawer. To my sister-in-laws, Barb and Denise Biery, for their willingness to read and critique. To Jen Lanza-Linn whose encouragement meant more than she could know. To the Canasta Queen, Sue Stitle, for her expert pencil, enthusiasm, and efficiency.

To Tom McNickle for his inspiration and encouragement to pick up my first watercolor sable and advice on how to improve. And to the last two people whose help and encouragement is very humbling: To Sandy Copeland for her network of people, hours of advice, unending willingness to help, and years of friendship and last but far from least, my husband, Jeff, who without all the pushing, prodding, support and love none of these pages would have ever been written. He is my gathering of flowers.

1

Her schedule was tight, and she found it difficult to wander. She read each name as she rushed by the headstones. She clutched the crumpled paper in her pocket that had directed her to the north end of Hope Cemetery. According to the groundskeeper's records, her mother was laid to rest in that area. She refused to stop until her eyes found her name. Her racing mind exhausted her. She glanced at her timepiece. It read 12:30 p.m. A rush of nerves flashed through her. Her time was limited. She drew her face heavenward and prayed for more time.

It was then Suzie saw her, a little child carved in stone -- her innocence wrapped in charm yet filled with sadness. Suzie stared at the skillfully carved image. The statue's eyes shone of caring beauty and wonder beyond her young years. They spoke of silent thoughtfulness that engulfs one's waking hours and steals the evening's dreams - a mystery hardened in stone.

Her thoughts trailed off to the upcoming events: an art show, a book signing, and the annoying deadline that loomed over her head. Her chest tightened from thoughts of her schedule. She willed herself to move, but her body was held fast to this statue before her. The song of a wood thrush calmed her agitation.

Suzie's eyes worked their way downward, drinking in every detail - the ribbons in her hair, a collar of lace, the ruffled bodice, and the exquisite detail of her dress. Her hands rested on her lap and held a gathering of early spring flowers. Two pink hyacinths were encircled by daffodils and laced with forget-me-nots. The flowers were fresh. Suzie moved her hand toward the bouquet. With the slightest touch, a daffodil tumbled to the ground. She bent to pick it up. Her eyes read:

Goldie Bell
Daughter of Jacob and Lizzie Taylor
Born August 22, 1884. Died Sept 8, 1886.

She drew in her breath. Her eyes widened. A rush of blood warmed her. Her face flushed and tingled. She looked at the date again and spoke out loud, "September eighth. That's my birthday!" The flower's life moisture dripped from her hand as she squeezed its stem.

She jumped at the sound of footsteps behind her. She held her breath and spun around. She saw nothing. She felt the veil of time lifted from her vision. She stared in disbelief at her timepiece. It read 1:34 p.m.

"1:34!" she exclaimed out loud. "I have a book signing at 1:30 downtown."

The magic was stolen. The moment lost. If only she had known how close she was, she would have lingered a bit longer. The desires of her heart were within her grasp and she let them slip away, unaware of the stranger clad in a long black coat who stood a few feet from her.

Her destiny would have to wait.

When Suzie arrived at the Downtown Café, it was 1:47 p.m. She chastised herself for losing track of time. She was unaware of the crowd. The applause brought her thoughts back to the present. Her faced flushed. She had an easier time accepting criticism than praise.

The crowd parted. Suzie sat down at the table with stacks of books at both ends. At her feet were two more. She knew her editor expected a big show from this small town.

The café owner smiled from behind the counter. She excused herself and walked to the table. "Welcome to Salem, Patricia. It is so nice to have you here." Kathy extended her hand. "Can I get you something to drink?" She placed the daffodil in a bud vase.

"Coffee, black, would be great."

The outside world knew her as Patricia Charlotte DuVeau. Since high school, the only people who called her Suzie were close friends and family. Her father gave her that nickname many years ago shortly after her adoption. He used to tell her she was his little flower, his black-eyed Susan, because of her blonde hair and dark brown eyes. The memory brought a smile to her face.

The café was located on a side street off the downtown shopping district. Decorated with the rich colors of an English pub, it featured strategically placed leather sofas and brass lighting that accented the grids in the ceiling. They added warmth to the natural charm and gave a feeling of calm in a hectic society.

The Quakers founded the city of Salem in 1806. Salem played an important role in the Women's Rights Movement and the Anti-Slavery Society in the mid-to-late 1800s. Many of the city's homes boasted of their secret rooms and hidden passages for slave smuggling. The buildings were beautiful in structure, rich in detail and filled with whispers of times past.

The city also claimed its own martyr, Edwin Coppoc, a twenty-four-year-old who followed John Brown to Harper's Ferry, Virginia, and participated in the raid to liberate the slaves on October 17 and 18, 1859. Coppoc was captured, tried for treason, and given a sentence of death by hanging. His body was moved three times from fear of discovery by grave robbers. He was finally laid to rest on December 30, 1859 in Hope Cemetery's east side, the same cemetery as Suzie's mother.

She had scheduled the book signing from 1:30 until 5:00 p.m. This was a bit long for such an event, but she was grateful for several reasons. It allowed her free time away from the distractions of home life and the studio. It gave her uninterrupted driving time to plan her next book. Most important, it presented an opportunity to find her birth mother's grave.

Around four o'clock, Suzie received a well-deserved break from the crowd. She rose from the table to stretch her legs. As she walked around the café, she noticed a poster with information about the annual candlelight graveyard tour of Hope Cemetery. Her thoughts wandered to Goldie Bell, the statue she encountered earlier that day. She was lost in thought and did not notice the woman next to her.

"Ms. DuVeau?"

The soft voice seemed strangely familiar. She turned to see an aging woman smiling at her.

"Hello," Suzie returned the smile.

"Suzie, I wondered if you would sign my book."

"Of course I will." She motioned for the woman to follow her to the table. "Who would you like me to address this to?"

The woman smiled. Suzie noticed the kindness in her eyes. There was something familiar about this woman, the softness of her facial features, her smile, the way she tipped her head when she listened. Suzie felt an immediate connection.

"Madeline P. Crory."

Suzie signed: 'To Madeline Crory, May you be as touched by this book as I am from our meeting. Patricia DuVeau.' It was then it dawned on her. This woman called her by her nickname. No one in this town knew her by that name. Stunned, she searched her memory for clues. As she extended her hand to this woman, Madeline took Suzie's hand in both of hers.

"The pleasure is mine," Madeline said as she smiled.

"Do I know you?" Suzie could not contain her anticipation.

"Not in the sense you are thinking." At that remark, she turned to go.

"Wait!" Suzie called out, but another line had formed.

Suzie returned to the task of autographing her books. She felt imprisoned as she watched the woman walk through the door.

From outside the window, Madeline watched Suzie. She stood behind the table with a puzzled look on her face. Madeline thought her sister, Charlotte, would have been furious with her, but she didn't care.

It had been years since Madeline was under her sibling's control, and she enjoyed the freedom. When she heard Suzie was coming to town, she knew she had to see her. Her only regret was not saying more.

"I hope you won't think of me as unfair for not opening the flood gates. Perhaps there will be a better time. This is not the place." She blew Suzie a kiss, smiled, and walked away.

Suzie had signed her third book when she saw Madeline through the window. The display of affection warmed her with feelings of love and acceptance. She wanted to run after her, but the voice of her editor resonated. "The success of your book lies with how you are received by the public. If they like you, they will buy your next book. It's all PR, kid. Do it well."

She forced herself to stay past five o'clock. Perhaps tomorrow, at her watercolor premier, the atmosphere would be less tense. Today was for the editor. Tomorrow is all hers.

Suzie pulled her daffodil from its vase and left the Downtown Café at 5:40 p.m. She was exhausted. Not only from the mental anguish of being "in the limelight," but from the restless drive. Her original plan was an overnight stop in New York to visit an old friend, Carolyn, and to continue her drive to Salem the following morning.

A knock spoiled her intentions of a leisurely drive. She opened the door to find a messenger from her editor, Paul. His outstretched hand begged for the promised outline of her next book. After a myriad of lame excuses and lies, Suzie closed the door with disgust. She glanced at her laptop and imagined it covered with an inch of dust. She lost days preparing a bogus outline and was faced with the reality of a sixteen hour drive to Salem.

She tried to focus on the drive to the inn. Her cell phone rang. It was Paul. She was expecting this. When she pressed the talk button, it was silent.

"Paul? Are you there? In case you can hear me, I can't hear you. All went well. There were well over two hundred fifty people there. We sold all of the books except one. My cell phone service is limited here. I'm exhausted. I'll call you tomorrow after the art show."

She hung up, unsure if he heard a word she said. Before she set the phone down, it beeped. She only had one bar of service. "Well, I can't listen to his message anyway." She turned off her phone. Incommunicado. What a great place to be.

2

Living in New England had given her a greater appreciation for historical places. When she knew she was coming to Salem, she researched the area to find a quiet bed and breakfast. She found The Spread Eagle Tavern twelve miles south in Hanoverton. It was a full service inn and sounded charming, so she made the necessary arrangements.

As she turned off the main road, she caught a glimpse of the inn. It was a three story, red brick building with a beautiful sign of an eagle in flight hanging out front. So majestic and free, she thought. She rounded the corner and parked in the rear.

The tang of wood smoke from multiple fireplaces permeated the air. The innkeeper, David Peterson, took her bag and escorted her to her room. The sign on the door read the Lincoln Suite.

"Would there be anything you will be requiring before dinner, Ms. DuVeau?"

"A glass of wine would be great."

"Red or white?"

The question took her by surprise. "Cabernet," she said, trying to suppress a giggle.

"I'll bring it right up. Welcome to the Spread Eagle Tavern."

Suzie was pleased with the detail of the Lincoln Suite. The floral window treatment matched the dust ruffle as well as the fabric draped behind the flat canopy bed. When she tossed herself on the duvet cover, she noticed the canopy was covered with coordinating fabric and drawn to the center by a rosette. The period fireplace mantle was painted white and had a verdant arrangement in the center. Logs were stacked on the andirons waiting for a match.

"This is beautiful!" She drew in a deep breath and felt herself relax for the first time in days.

A knock on the door startled her from sleep. David presented a tray with a glass of Cabernet, a small plate of grapes and wedges of aged cheese. A crystal bud vase held a small cluster of daffodils. Beside it, was a copy of her book. She picked up the book and penned: 'To David, I found my home away from home. Thank you, Patricia DuVeau.' He smiled.

"Dinner at 7:30 still satisfactory?"

"That sounds perfect. Thank you."

He nodded and closed the door.

She took her first sip. "Umm...that's good." She swirled the burgundy liquid around in the glass and laughed out loud. "Who would have thought three years ago that I would be here today. I am so blessed."

She added her flower to the vase and pulled the bouquet to her nose. It reminded her of an experience at her studio apartment. She loved to garden. She had been disappointed that no one prior had planted any spring bulbs. Her intentions had been to plant some hyacinths, tulips, and daffodils in the upcoming fall as a complement to the tierella and daylilies, but the days passed with incredible speed. That winter, she found herself standing on frozen ground wishing she had made the time to plant. The second spring came early, and much to Suzie's surprise, she noticed tiny shoots push through the ground. Daffodils found their way to her doorstep without any effort on her part. She was elated.

"Somehow life found a way to bless me when I did not deserve it," she exclaimed out loud and then laughed to herself. "Odd," she thought. "The same thing happened in my last house."

She drew a hot bath and placed her wine glass beside the tub. She picked up a pack of matches on the antique candle stand, lit the vanilla wick, and turned off the lights. To her, this was the perfect way to unwind and reflect. She did some of her best thinking in this atmosphere, so she did it as often as possible.

As she slipped off her clothes, she caught a glimpse of herself in the mirror. There was always room for improvement, but overall she was comfortable with her appearance. She tested the water and slipped into the suds.

Under the flicker of candlelight, the bathroom took on a different feeling. Little shadows danced across the walls and ceiling as the flame swayed with the slightest breeze. She heard the distant clang of silverware in symphonic rhythm. An occasional eruption of laughter made her smile. She closed her eyes and released the day's hustle and worries. When the water cooled, she dried herself with one Turkish towel and wrapped her hair in another. Finally, she thought, her life had turned down the right path, one where she found peace and comfort. She was unaware how her life was about to change.

The Spread Eagle Tavern boasts of its own smoke house in the center courtyard, and many different savory meats peppered the menu. She had a difficult time choosing but finally decided on the crab cakes the waitress had suggested. Her dinner was succulent. Not a single disappointment from the Sierra salad to the crème brulee. After she finished her meal, Suzie carried her cup of coffee and followed David for a private tour of the inn.

"A Hanoverton resident named Will Rhodes built the inn in 1837." David pointed to a tile scene behind the bar. "It was built near the Sandy and Beaver Canal, which linked Cleveland to Pittsburgh through a series of locks. It brought much prosperity and many travelers to the small town of Hanoverton."

"I can just imagine how busy this area must have been back then," Suzie said.

He sighed. "Due to the change in transportation from canals to railroad, the inn closed in the late 1800s and became a private home. The Johnson family of Salem bought the home in 1988 and spent two years completing the extensive renovation."

They walked together through the tavern. "They spared no expense to restore and recreate the luster from the past. Every piece of woodwork was removed, numbered, restored, and replaced. The sagging floors were replaced with poplar planks and secured with hand-forged square nails." He pointed to the floors as he spoke. "The rathskeller boasts of a twelve foot vaulted ceiling with bricks used from a local 190-year-old home after it was demolished." He tapped his fingers on the framed photograph of the triple-brick house. "It was quite an undertaking."

"How did they do that?" Suzie wondered.

"They tore the bricks from the house and chipped the old mortar from its surface. Then they re-fired each brick at their Summitville Tile plant. They hand dug the floor of the rathskeller and built it from scratch." His hand waved in the air, "All of this masonry work you see is from that house." He pointed to a narrowed hallway. "The vaulted ceiling is mirrored in there." Suzie peered at five tables placed in an intimate setting. She noted to herself that she would dine there next.

They walked up the staircase to the main floor. "Original windowpanes were retained and fitted to replace damaged or broken ones. Another building was moved and attached to the existing building here." He pointed to a brick wall and waved his hands in the air. "It resulted in a void perfect for a courtyard." He pointed out of the window from the Taft Room to a small wood building in the corner of the patio. "They placed the smokehouse out there -- and you have to look at the spouting. It's all copper."

They walked past the fireplace in the Barbara Bush Room. He tapped on the tile. "The hand-painted tiles were also from Summitville Tile. They were designed to fit the fireplaces and the bar areas."

They walked across the hall into the Asher Benjamin room. "This was the original tavern." He pointed to the threshold of the exterior door. "Look at the wear. I guess there were a lot of thirsty visitors by the looks of it!" He chuckled.

Most of the guest and dining areas were named for either past presidents or their wives. McKinley, Lincoln, Washington, Taft, Bush, Jefferson, and even Dolley Madison were among some of the names. The walls boasted many current presidential photographs with the owners and members of their families. Some were taken on the grounds while others were in the White House. David explained with pride about many of the important occasions represented by the collection. He waited patiently while Suzie examined each image.

When she was finished, he led her through the rest of the Inn. He paused at several antique pieces on their tour. Suzie was impressed with their taste. Each room displayed a hanging bread cupboard. The hallways proudly exhibited tavern tables and linen presses. Antiques filled all of the guest rooms.

The tour lasted for nearly an hour and ended outside of the Lincoln Suite. Suzie felt the weight of the day as well as the meal on her body.

"Here we are."

"This room is beautiful."

"Did you notice its special antique?"

Suzie looked over his shoulder to the interior of her room. She named a few pieces then shrugged her shoulders in surrender.

David walked her over to a narrow wall by the fireplace and pointed to a small frame. It was a ticket stub. "It's from the Ford Theatre."

Suzie opened her mouth in surprise. "That's amazing. I guess it's in the perfect room!" They both laughed.

"Shall we give you a wakeup call?"

"Yes. 7:30 should be fine."

"Breakfast is served from 7:00 until 9:00. You may dine in any of the dining rooms you prefer."

She noticed a table for two placed by a window at the top of the staircase directly outside of her room. Making a hand motion toward the table, she asked, "Would this be available?"

"Absolutely, this table would be perfect. What time would suit you?"

'8:30?"

"Okay, 8:30 it is. Enjoy your rest. Good night and sleep well."

When Suzie opened the door to her room, her fireplace had been lit. A mint punctuated the turndown service. She walked to the window and drew her curtains. It was nearly 11:00 p.m. It threatened rain all day but only a few scattered drops fell. The temperature peaked at 48 degrees. For the most part, it was a dreary, damp day, the kind when one never feels warm.

The glow of the fireplace was a welcomed sight. She placed another log on the fire, changed into her pajamas, and slipped under the covers. She chased thoughts from the day. She needed her rest. Tomorrow was too important.

She watched the flames flicker in the fireplace. The logs cracked, popped, and sizzled as the new wood caught. The warm glow cast an inviting blanket over the entire room as the flames danced. She tried to enjoy this moment but her eyes were heavy, and the sounds enveloped her like a mother's lullaby. She was lulled to sleep by the sounds of the roaring fire and the silence of a quiet, sleeping inn.

Lightning flashed with a loud crack of thunder. The violent sound shook the room. Suzie jumped out of bed and ran to the window. It was difficult to see. The only light came from the intermittent lightning flashes. The wind howled and the rain pounded against the windows. The lightning flashed again. Her eyes fell on a man in a long black coat standing on the lawn. He struggled against the wind to maintain his balance.

With another flash of lightning, it was apparent his gaze was fixed on her window. The brim of his hat shadowed his face, yet she felt his eyes on her. He stood still with an upturned face. Another flash. The wind grew stronger. He moved one hand to hold his hat. The wind pulled at his coat and revealed a spark of color.

"Something in his hands," Suzie whispered to herself. "...something," she strained her eyes to see. "...Something yellow..." The lightning was so frequent that it appeared as daylight. Suzie placed her face close to the rain-soaked window. She felt her warm breath return to her skin. "Yellow...yellow... can't see... what does he have... it's yellow...yellow…flowers!"

Her breath fogged the window. Frantic, she wiped the moisture away. He was gone. Vanished, and with him the wind.

The night became eerily still. Shivers ran down her spine. She started to quiver. Her jaw twitched. Her legs tingled. She fell back against the armchair and collapsed.

"Who was that?"

She fumbled for her timepiece. 1:34 a.m. She had barely slept. Trying to put the vision of the man behind her, she glanced at the glowing embers. She placed two more logs on the fire and crawled back into bed. The feather tick was still warm and her position of comfort was easy to resume. The flames leapt furiously over the logs. A warm glow filled the room, yet she was restless. Her heart pumped in her throat. She wanted to race to the window to catch another glimpse of her black clad stranger, but fear kept her covered.

"I am safe here," she whispered again and again.

Overcome by the desire, she crept to the window. Her room was lit with firelight and she would be easily spotted from the outside, but she didn't care. She had to see if he was standing there. Her breath came in quick, heavy bursts. She felt her muscles tighten as she scanned the landscape. The grounds were empty. Relieved, she turned to climb back into bed. Something out of the corner of her eye made her stop. She stood frozen with her mouth agape. The electricity had returned and the lamplights burned once again. She saw a long black coat caught on a tree limb.

After she was certain of what her tired eyes were seeing, she slid between the sheets. She drew a deep breath as she covered herself and exhaled slowly. After a few deep breaths, she felt herself relax. She knew no more until she heard a rap on the door.

"Ms. DuVeau. It's 7:30. This is your wake up call."

She looked around the room. Early sunlight streamed in her window from the open curtain.

"Thank you," she said, now fully awake. She looked around the room for something she hadn't noticed the night before. The room did not have a telephone or television. She showered without thought, nearly in denial of her looming schedule. She pulled her favorite suit from the dry cleaner's plastic bag and slipped it on. She admired her looks in the mirror -- her best suit, patterned stockings, black stiletto slides and a vintage tapestry bag.

"Ready for the show?" she asked herself.

She grabbed her favorite scarf, multi-colored with layers of lace, beads, and snippets of vintage sheer fabric, sewn to perfection by her dear friend, Sandy. She checked her appearance in the cheval mirror once again and walked out of the room.

Suzie ate her breakfast at the little table outside of her room. It was a quaint location, quiet, remote, not another table in sight. As she savored her last cup of coffee, she made mental notes of her upcoming day.

The art show of her watercolors began at noon. Her writer's cramp would return, for part of the show included personal signing of the client's paintings whether purchased there or previously. Although she found it difficult to stand before her audience of admirers, she would be lying to herself if she didn't admit a small part of her loved it.

"It is so taxing," she admitted to herself, "and two days in a row of a plastered smile on my face is about my limit."

In a fog of thought, she rose and went back to the Lincoln Suite. She forgot to close the door behind her. She walked over to the window. It was then she remembered the storm. She scanned the lawn for the tree where the coat was caught the night before. She couldn't see it. Convinced it was the other window she walked to her left. No tree. "I know it was there," she said out loud.

A young woman who cleared her table walked to the entrance of her door. “Is there something you are missing, Ms. DuVeau?”

Startled, Suzie turned to her and replied, “No. I just thought I saw something outside last night, but...” her voice trailed off to mumbles, “it’s not there.”

“I'm sorry. I didn’t hear you. Is everything okay?”

Suzie stood without movement and stared out of the window. Her mind raced as she replayed last night’s events in her mind. She thought of the man in the hat with his coat tossed by the wind. He held yellow flowers, she thought, in his hand. He looked towards her. Then later she realized the coat was stuck to a tree. Now, as she stared out the window, there was not a tree to be found. Her mouth hung open.

“Ms. DuVeau?”

The young woman’s voice intruded into her thoughts. “Yes?”

“Are you okay?”

Dismissing the thoughts as if it was a dream, she smiled, “I'm fine.” Changing the tone of the conversation, Suzie said, “That was some storm we had last night, wasn't it?” The look on the woman's face was all Suzie needed to understand.

“Storm? We didn't have a storm.”

For a moment she was paralyzed, completely lost to the conversation. Then Suzie laughed out loud. “I was so exhausted. I must have been dreaming!” She stood in the doorway, shook her head, and tried to make sense of it. “It seemed so real! I even thought I got up and looked out the window. I guess my mind was playing tricks on me.”

The young women smiled and turned to finish clearing the table. “Have a good day.”

"Thanks, I will."

Suzie closed the door. She was dumbfounded. "It seemed so real. I don't understand it."

She was lost in thought. She felt she was standing between myth and reality. She realized as she walked out of the door that her window curtain was open when she woke.

"I couldn't have dreamed it, unless I was sleepwalking and opened the curtain in my sleep -- but, I have never walked in my sleep before," she said out loud but to herself.

David brushed by her. "Good morning, Patricia."

"And to you, David."

"Did you sleep well?"

"Yes I did, except for the storm," she said testing the waters.

He looked at her puzzled, "Storm?"

She felt a bit foolish, and her face flushed to red. She waved her hand in the air as if she fanned away a bug and said, "I guess I must have dreamed it. A very vivid dream though. That's what happens when you go to bed on a full stomach I hear," she said with laughter in her voice. As she picked up her tapestry bag, her eyes settled on the bouquet of daffodils sitting on her bedside table. All were perfect except one.

A brisk wind greeted her at the back door and caressed her face. She felt focused and alert. As she drove to her show of flatwork, her thoughts drifted from reality to fantasy, intertwining the two. She was certain that what she had experienced was real.

3

The day dawned with the promise of a new beginning. The sky cleared overnight and left the rain a distant memory. The air was crisp and refreshing, pledging a warm spring. Suzie's mood soared as she drove closer to Salem.

She hoped for a successful show. Even though yesterday's book signing was a hit, her paintings were dearer. She felt that her very soul hung on a nail for all to view. To an artist, fewer things held more value than to see one's own work in the hands of another.

She parked her car, took a deep breath, and entered the front door. The Wandering Cheshire Gallerie smelled of fresh paint and new carpet. A muralist had painted a portion of Suzie's bio on the wall as part of a permanent display. Seeing her own words painted in script made her heart skip a beat.

The staff bustled while finishing the last minute details. Suzie perused the gallery. Pausing at one painting, she questioned the title. The gallery's owner, Evelyn Wynn, came up behind her.

"Patricia, you're early." Evelyn smiled, "Something to drink?"

"No. Thank you, though." Suzie replied. "Your gallery has finished brilliantly."

"It's been a life-long dream. On some days, I still have to pinch myself."

The two of them discussed at length how they would maintain a permanent display of Suzie's work. Evelyn's original thought was to purchase one and keep it for her personal collection, but Suzie presented her with another idea.

"What if we used the Cheshire as a rotating study?"

"What do you mean?"

"I would like to send a different painting every third month. We could place it by my bio. When the new painting arrives, return the previous one to me with a list of the comments. I could have a rotating market study and you could have a fresh look four times a year."

"What if I sell the painting?"

"That's even better, for both of us. Then just send me the list of comments."

"I love that idea! I wanted to purchase one for my own collection, but I am so over budget with pre-opening expenses that..." Evelyn stared at the floor.

"Then it's settled."

"I can't tell you how thrilled I am," Evelyn squealed. She tried to hide her budgetary disappointment. She had hoped to have an original PC DuVeau painting to call her own.

"Tell me, Evelyn," Suzie toyed, "which is your favorite?"

Evelyn escorted Suzie across the room. "This one," she said as she pointed to a painting named "Evening."

Suzie was surprised. "Tell me why."

"I love the colors. The way they mold and blend within each other reminds me of a hot, summer evening on the

Fourth of July. I can almost hear the boom of the fireworks as they explode and color the sky."

She loved to hear her work described through someone else's eyes almost as much as taking a brush to paper. She also liked being in control, with no one peering over her shoulder. It felt like flying.

Suzie broke the silence by saying, "Let's begin with this one." She pulled the painting from the wall. Evelyn moved her hand to gather the title card, but Suzie stopped her.

"That can stay."

Puzzled, Evelyn followed Suzie.

Suzie hung the painting under her bio. She slipped a new title card into the Lucite holder. It read 'Fourth'. She walked back to the empty space and posted the sign, 'Work in progress' above the title card 'Evening'

"It's good to keep them guessing," she winked.

Evelyn smiled, "I have never met an artist so accommodating."

Suzie explained how she questioned the title moments earlier and had decided to change it. "It was just meant to be." The corners of her mouth curled.

As noon neared, a small line formed outside. Suzie recognized a few people from yesterday. Some hands held paintings while others were empty. She felt those familiar jitters, anticipation mixed with fear.

People slowly entered the gallery. Some headed straight for Suzie, calling for her signature, while others brushed by without so much as a glance in her direction. Unlike yesterday, the crowd was a good mix of gender, age, and financial status. The attire was everything from jeans to party dresses, khakis to suits. The eclectic group was typical of a small town.

She watched a small crowd of children enter with two adults, one male, and one female. Suzie guessed them to be business associates -- although the way the woman looked at the man made Suzie think that she was interested in more than a working relationship. Several couples giggled and leaned a little too close to each other. 'Dating,' Suzie thought to herself. One woman caught her eye as she abruptly walked away from a man who had accompanied her. He turned to follow. 'Married,' she said this time. She loved to play this game. It kept her mind off of her own loneliness.

A young boy drew her attention as she watched him interact with a man, probably his father. The child looked her way and Suzie met his eyes. She smiled as he waved. She loved children, their innocence, and ability to view the world through eyes of wonder. He was about four years old and had curly blonde hair. The way that he held his father's hand made Suzie realize that they were alone. She admired the tenderness the man showed his son and how the boy's face lit when he spoke to him. She walked toward them, knelt down, and talked with the little boy.

All in all, the crowd was steady the majority of the day. She had forty-two paintings on display. By three o'clock, she sold nineteen, including 'Fourth', which Evelyn's husband bought for their personal collection, despite the overextension of the gallery's budget. Suzie signed all of the paintings for that special touch. Many potential buyers promised to think about it and come back, but with Suzie's retail experience she knew that barely 12% would return. She was pleased with the results. In one day, her sales were slightly over sixteen thousand dollars. It was enough to pay her bills for several months and help the Wynns call their first show a success.

The crowd dwindled to a few last guests. Suzie noticed a gentleman lingering by a painting entitled 'Rage'. The colors were strong, almost fierce. Bold brush strokes broken by deep scrapes exposed the gentle tones underneath. Suzie remembered this painting well. The scrapes were from her nails running over the damp colors in frustration. Not over the painting, but a conversation with her ex-husband. She remembered layering color upon color to create a torrid effect. Her brush strokes became wider, stronger, and more erratic as she rehashed the conversation in her mind.

As she walked toward this gentleman, she chuckled to herself and wondered how something so beautiful could come out of a conversation so vile.

"It's a healing thing, you know. To work through a strong emotion and make something beautiful out of it," Suzie said more to herself than to him.

To her surprise, he said nothing. He stood motionless. The moment was uncomfortable and oppressive. She thought he must detest her work. Her heart ran in the opposite direction, yet she was unable to will her body to move. With her face flushed and skin warmed, an overwhelming feeling of nausea gripped her. She took a deep breath, and managed to move away from him.

Needing a glass of ice water, she staggered to the refreshment table. Elated with the show's success, Evelyn talked in short excited phrases. After a few moments, when she looked at Suzie, her smile slid from her face.

"Your skin is pale. Are you feeling faint?"

"I just had the strangest experience," Suzie said as she clung to the table. "I was talking to a gentleman over there," she made a hand motion toward the exact location, "and..." Her voice dropped off. She scanned the room. He was gone.

"He's not here," Suzie gasped.

"He must have left," Evelyn replied nonchalantly.

"No. He couldn't have," Suzie said desperately. "The door is over there." Her hand shook as she pointed in the opposite direction. "Even if he ran, he couldn't have darted out of the door before I turned around."

Evelyn was concerned. "Where did you say he was standing?"

"By the painting 'Rage'."

Evelyn made a quick assessment of the situation and agreed with Suzie. "Did he say something that upset you?"

Suzie stared at the painting for a minute and said, "No, that's just it. He didn't say anything. He didn't move. He didn't do *anything*. However, I felt as if he read my thoughts. I didn't see his face. His hair was dark, longer, and he held a hat in his hands. He had on a long, black coat...Oh my God!" Suzie exclaimed. "A long black coat..." The rush of nerves left her chilled and nauseous. The room lost color and began to spin. Evelyn rushed Suzie to a chair and forced her to sit. She filled a glass with ice water and shooed her staff. Their eyes were full of questions.

"She's not feeling well," was her reply.

Suzie sat in silence and tried to focus, but her head felt heavy, foggy, and full of questions. She felt her life force had been removed. After a few minutes passed, the reality of the scene she just caused made her feel ridiculous. Everyone stared. Evelyn tried to keep everyone occupied. All Suzie thought about was how silly it must look to everyone but her.

She managed to stand. Evelyn made a move to run to her, but Suzie held out her hand quickly and said, "Evelyn, thank you, but I'm fine. I just felt dizzy for a while. I am much better now."

Evelyn smiled through disbelief.

"I'm fine. Really," Suzie tried to sound reassuring. "I think I'm just exhausted."

Truth be known, she did not know how she felt. She walked slowly around the room, keeping her hand on the wall.

She made her way to the painting 'Rage'. She paused, thinking again of how this man had affected her. How could she explain it when she did not understand it herself? She did not feel threatened or angry. It was a deeper emotion. She felt as if she could feel his pain, his desire, his longing to say something. He was troubled and came to her for help. Yet he was unable to communicate through words. She understood his thoughts, "How do I begin? How do I tell you? How will you understand?" No audible words, no sound communication, but Suzie knew his thoughts.

Her inner voice was apparent all of her life. She did not hear voices but had a sense of prodding from an unseen guide -- one who taught and exposed things not always understood at that moment, which became very clear in time. It was never a one-on-one conversation, or a physical body. It was circumstances that could be passed off as a coincidence, but if she was aware, she saw their hidden message. Her friends called her clairvoyant. She thought of it as gifted.

Many of her experiences came with death. She felt the lost one's presence, saw a face, or smelled a fragrance. She thought of those encounters as a way of saying goodbye. If she drove by a serious accident, she physically felt the victim's pain. When she visited people in the hospital, there was no need for words. She knew their wishes without speaking. She often felt a gentle touch to her body, an arm tug, a hand on her shoulder, or a brush against her cheek.

This experience was different. There was a physical body. She saw him. She stood beside him, and spoke to him. This was more intense. A strong desire to search for him filled her, but had no idea how.

By four o'clock the show was over. As Suzie helped Evelyn usher the last guests to the door, her foot skirted something across the floor. Lying at her feet was a single yellow daffodil. She picked it up and twirled it in her fingers. She knew what she needed to do next.

4

Madeline woke in a cold sweat. It was 1:34 a.m. Her nightgown was twisted and bunched around her hips. All she thought about was Suzie, how she looked, carried herself, her smile, her laughter, and a tenderness that shone through her soft brown eyes. Suzie's auburn hair was almost the same color as that of Madeline's sister, except it was much longer and thicker. It rested on her shoulders like an elegant silk scarf.

No longer tired, Madeline got out of bed, fixed her nightgown, grabbed her robe, and headed for the kitchen. She filled her teapot with water and stood by the stove staring into the swirling water until the steam rose. She poured herself a cup of hot water and chose a teabag from her cherry tea caddie. She held her teacup in her hands and let the steam and fragrance arouse her senses. The sound of her tea kettle startled her.

"Oops. Forgot to turn off the gas," she sang.

She allowed her mind to wander as she enjoyed her tea. She wondered about Suzie's life, her favorite food, what made her happy, and sad, but most of all she wondered about her home life. She wondered how her adoptive mother treated her, how their relationship was, and how Suzie handled her death.

After her cup was empty, she felt more relaxed, yet she was not tired. She thought of the things she needed to do when the sun woke from its slumber. It was April 9th, the tenth anniversary of her sister Charlotte's death. She needed to gather flowers from the florist. They had to be fresh or her sister would turn over in her grave. After she ran a few more errands, banking, groceries, and the dry cleaner, she wanted to stop by Suzie's premiere.

Her thoughts drifted off again to Suzie. She had kept tabs on her through several sources - friends, churches, her father, newspaper ads, and art publications - but always from a distance. Her sister made her promise to stay away, just as Charlotte herself did.

"She has an adopted family now," Charlotte would say. "It's not our place. We made a promise and it must be kept."

When Charlotte was alive, Madeline constantly suppressed the longing, but since her death, the desire had become so strong, it consumed much of Madeline's thoughts.

Madeline had been to Rockport two summers prior with a tourist group on a bus tour. It had been a grueling trip, and not very relaxing. When it was over, she assured herself she would never repeat that adventure. The highlight, as well as the reason for the trip, had been a stop in Rockport, MA. In the height of the summer tourist season, many artists sold their work by the seaside, and Madeline had only original artwork hanging on her walls. As she perused the multitude of artists' names, she found Suzie's. She carefully studied the map for her location and set out to find her.

When she arrived at the tent, she was extremely disappointed. Suzie was not there. A young brunette greeted her cheerfully.

"Hello. Are you familiar with Suzie, I mean Patricia's work?"

"Yes, I am," Madeline replied. "Although I only have a few of her pieces."

This was true. Madeline had been following Suzie's painting career for quite some time. She picked up her first piece in a New York gallery. Her second was a gift from a friend, and her third she bought herself at Suzie's studio in Ipswich. She had missed her that time too.

"I seem to always miss her," Madeline told the girl as she relayed her story.

"Her work is full of movement," said the young girl. "She's very talented."

She walked Madeline over to a painting and explained, "The jury voted this painting 'Best of Show'. Suzie doesn't know it yet. She got an emergency phone call this morning from her editor and had to meet with him immediately."

"Editor?" Madeline questioned.

"Yes, Suzie has written a book. It was to go to print last week, but the proof raised a few concerns. Suzie had to go smooth a few ruffled feathers. By the way, my name is Claire. I'm the daughter of Suzie's friend, Carolyn."

"Nice to meet you."

"Suzie asked me to watch the booth until her return."

"She is lucky to have someone like you she can count on in a pinch."

Claire smiled, "Oh I enjoy these shows. I've taken a few workshops from Suzie myself, although I'm afraid I don't have the talent." She laughed.

A few more women entered the tent, and Claire immediately excused herself to speak with them. Madeline was left standing in front of a painting entitled 'Lunar

Dream'. It was a mix of Suzie's impressionistic and abstract styles with a touch of realism. It was a newly hatched Luna moth, damp with new life, drying its wings while clinging to a blade of grass. Above the moth were faint images of a moth gaining height in flight. The background blended soft shades of moss with cerulean set apart by a touch of violet, strategically placed to represent a native wildflower. It was a long narrow painting, and Madeline had the perfect spot for it. She turned and called for Claire.

"I would like to purchase Suzie's 'Best of Show' -- and please tell her I am so sorry I missed her yet again."

Claire carefully wrapped the painting, while Madeline counted her money.

"That comes to $1860," Claire said proudly.

"Here's two thousand," Madeline said. "Please tell Suzie how much I love it."

Claire froze in amazement. No one had ever paid extra. They usually tried to barter for a better price. She put the money away and jotted Madeline's name on the journal with a little * beside it.

Madeline was excited about her purchase, but found it difficult to hide her disappointment at not having personal contact with Suzie. She carried the painting to the bus and held it on her lap. The driver was blowing his horn when she arrived. As the bus pulled out of the parking lot, Madeline turned back to look toward Suzie's tent. She thought she caught a glimpse of a young woman with auburn hair rush into the booth. She smiled to herself, pulled the painting closer, and held it on her lap the entire trip home.

Madeline had fallen back to sleep. When she woke, it was ten o'clock. She jumped from her chair, showered, dressed, and applied her make-up in record time. She ran out of the door.

She stopped at The Flower Loft at the entrance of the cemetery and drove to her sister's gravesite. She discarded the spent flowers from the previous visit and placed the fresh ones in the jardinière.

Emotion filled her when she visited Charlotte's grave. She loved her sister, but at the same time, she felt oppressed. Madeline had been her sister's caretaker since a car accident left Charlotte crippled. She was able to get around with the help of a walker or two canes, but her pain was terrific, and so was her temper.

Guilt riddled Madeline. It was apparent that Charlotte never forgave her.

It had been clear that early spring night in 1959. Madeline was sixteen, fresh with teenage excitement. She had just received her driver's license. Charlotte was two years older. They were on their way home from a movie. Madeline begged to drive. Charlotte finally conceded. Madeline was a good driver, but inexperienced. When a deer darted in front of them, she overcompensated and lost control of the car.

The car bounced and rolled before it slammed into a tree, knocking Madeline unconscious. Thrown from the car, Charlotte landed under the tree as it fell. It crushed her legs and pinned her under its weight. She vomited from the pain. To make matters worse, the dirt road was scarcely traveled.

A farmer on his tractor saw them first. He heard Charlotte's screams and ran to her. His tractor was helpless against the size of the tree. He explained he would need to return with help. He was apprehensive as he approached Madeline who was crumpled in the front seat like a pile of discarded rags. He touched her shoulder. She moaned.

The minutes seemed like hours before his return. Charlotte writhed from pain and Madeline had not moved. The ambulance came quickly. It took the entire team to remove the tree. They carefully lifted Charlotte onto the gurney. Madeline was unaware that she rode beside her sister in the ambulance. At times, in her dreams, she recalled the hateful words screamed from the gurney beside her.

The next eleven months seemed an eternity. Madeline had sustained many fractures - ribs, collarbone, and left wrist. She had severe head trauma, which led to seizures. She lost her memory for days, weeks, and months at a time. She was unable to recall anything that happened during her 'dark times' as Charlotte referred to them. Madeline's return to health was slow.

Charlotte, however, was not as fortunate. The doctors said she would never walk again, but with God's help and Charlotte's tenacity, she began to recover. She had ten surgeries in two years. Although a full recovery was unlikely, she did her best to remind Madeline of the pain she had caused. Madeline bore the responsibility for Charlotte's position. She harbored deep resentment against Madeline even though it was an accident.

Madeline accepted the responsibility as her sister's caretaker with great pride. They had been on their own for the past seven months since their parents' plane crash. The court system considered Charlotte an adult at eighteen. She became Madeline's legal guardian.

Madeline never married, but Charlotte out-lived two husbands. Some say they died of broken hearts. Her heart was crippled from hatred, but when it suited her, she could be charming. With both husbands, she rarely showed her true self until they were tangled deep in her web of deception. They refused to turn their backs on her. It was not in their character. She knew how to make them feel devoted and sorry for her until they were unable to separate the two. She worked her manipulation well, but saved the special oppression for her devoted sister. Madeline, of course, knew what her sister was doing, but her guilt was paralyzing.

Life with Charlotte was not always horrible. Because of Charlotte's choice in husbands, and their parents' assets, they were financially secure.

Madeline lived in a small suite built onto the north corner of the house, complete with a modest kitchen and a small fireside room. The oversized bedroom sported a Lincoln bed from the late 1800s made of black walnut. The auctioneer told them that a wealthy family in Canton, Ohio had commissioned it. Queen-sized, ten feet in height, and a rare find for that age, Madeline fell in love with it the first time she saw it. Charlotte was in one of her generous moods that day, so with the wave of her hand, the bed became Madeline's. It rested perfectly in the large bedroom and matched the other antique pieces. Madeline fitted it with a feather tick. Each night, when she crawled into bed, she thanked her sister for the generous gift. Although the bed had cost much more than Charlotte wanted to pay, she knew it was important for her sister to have a good night's sleep. After all, Madeline needed her strength to take good care of her crippled sister.

Madeline finished her errands as quickly as possible. Her heart raced as she opened the door of The Wandering Cheshire. She slipped into the room and easily became lost in the large crowd. She spotted Suzie as she knelt on the floor. She was talking with a young boy and his father. Madeline smiled as she watched the excited look on Suzie's face.

"It's a shame she doesn't have any children," Madeline said to herself.

"Yes, it is," came the reply from Evelyn Wynn.

The moment was uncomfortable for Madeline. Her face flushed. She felt her motives were visible. She managed a thin smile and excused herself. She drew a long breath of the cool air. She turned to go, but peered back into the window for one more glimpse of Suzie. From where she stood, she couldn't see her.

She muttered under her breath, "This just wasn't the right time." Her sigh was heavy. "I wonder if there will ever be a right time."

5

When Suzie arrived at the cemetery, she knew her time was limited. She had less than an hour to walk the cemetery before dark. She parked her car and picked up where she had left off. She passed the Sharp Mausoleum built in 1899, the Thomas Mausoleum, Strotter Brown, the ex-slave basket maker, and countless others before she came to a patch of yellow daffodils. It surrounded a cross, embellished with carved ivy. Leaning against it was an umbrella. It was Suzie's.

"How did this get here? I never came down this far. I don't even remember leaving it."

She glanced up the road and saw Goldie Bell to her far left. She froze as she watched a man in a long black coat remove pink roses from Goldie's hands and replace them with yellow daffodils. Suzie knew this was the same man who was outside her window at the inn and at the art show. She dropped her umbrella and ran up the road. She kept her eyes fixed on him and he never glanced her way. She watched him gently lay the pink roses on the ground in front of the marble statue. She felt her steps pound the road as she struggled in her heels. She was just about to yell for him to wait, when a car stopped in front of her. She slowed to a fast walk as she moved away from the car. When she looked back to Goldie, he was gone. She groaned in disgust.

"Did you lose him?" the gentleman seated in the car asked.

"Yes. Do you know him?"

"No, but I have seen him many times."

"Where, here or..." Suzie's voice trailed. Her eyes searched the cemetery.

"I always see him here. He brings flowers to Goldie every day. I think she smiles every time she sees him."

They both looked toward the statue and somehow Goldie did look a bit different. Suzie turned toward the gentleman and smiled.

"My name is Patricia DuVeau. I'm in town for my book signing and my...."

"Art show. I've seen your work. You should consider painting Goldie Bell, but please paint her with her feet. She lost them to a malicious prank several years back, and I swear she has lost some of her smile since then. I believe I have an earlier photograph of Goldie in my office. If you would like, you may look at it before you make your decision. My name is Dale Shaffer. I'm known around here as the town historian. I'm pleased to make your acquaintance."

Suzie was dumbfounded with her luck. What are the odds of this happening? Maybe he would be able to help her find her mother. Her thoughts were too narrow, but with some luck Dale Shaffer will point her in the right direction. After all, he had been waiting for her.

"The pleasure is mine, Mr. Shaffer. I have many questions for you...."

"I will try to answer them for you, but this is not the place. Darkness will soon be around us and a warm fireside conversation is exactly what we need."

"That sounds charming."

Suzie followed Dale to his home, nestled in a quaint area of town wrapped in the richest of historical places. They enjoyed a pot of hot tea together, and Dale shared many of Salem's wonderful stories - stories of sordid history from slavery to bravery, sorrow, and celebration.

Suzie was easily entertained with Dale's excitement and knowledge of Salem's rich history. He had written several books on the subject and had plans for more. She listened to his passion as he described a story in remarkable detail of the workings of the Anti-Slavery Society.

"It was in late August of 1854 that the members held their twelfth annual meeting. At three p.m. on the closing day a telegram arrived via a messenger. A slave girl, fourteen years old, was traveling on the westbound train scheduled to stop in Salem at 6 p.m. and then continue on to Tennessee. She traveled with a southern lady and gentleman.

When many of the Anti-Slavery group, as well as an officer, boarded the train, they looked for the girl. When they found her, they asked if she desired freedom. When she said 'yes', they carried her from the train, took up a collection for her care, and gave her the name of Abby Kelly Salem. They provided a place for her in the home of Joel MacMillan. She remained in Salem for several years. She gave many lectures on the steps of Liberty Hall because she was refused permission to speak in the churches."

Dale took a deep breath. Suzie listened intently. "The oldest house in Salem belonged to Jonas Cattel who built it in 1808. Jonas was a Quaker and a state senator. He built his home with a passion for freeing slaves. Upstairs there was a closet within a closet that hid many slaves. In the basement, behind a fireplace, was another place of refuge. The slaves were smuggled from the nearby railroad tracks by a false bottom buckboard when the train stopped to refuel. The path from the house to the tracks was used so often the deep impression from the wagon wheels is still visible today. To further hide the covert operation, trees were planted along the path so close together it created a visual barrier from the outside. Once the slaves were inside the house, they crawled through the back opening of the fireplace into the hidden room. If a knock came to the door, someone lit a fire. The house is still celebrated today as a historic landmark of the Underground Railroad."

"I'm curious about something," Suzie said. "Tell me about the man we saw today."

"Oh my," he sighed, "that is a long and sad tale and I'm afraid it needs to be discussed over a hot bowl of soup."

Suzie followed him into the kitchen. He set the large pot on the stove and turned the heat to simmer. As they set the bowls, napkins and silverware on the table, he turned to her and said, "I believe this story has a peculiar meaning to you somehow. Maybe after the tale is told, it will be apparent."

She felt her face flush as if she had been discovered. She wanted to tell Dale about all the times she saw this man, but she was afraid he would think her odd. Dale was so kind, she couldn't take that chance. The truth be known, she did feel a connection with this mysterious man and to Goldie Bell.

It didn't take long for the fresh vegetable soup to be piping hot. Suzie didn't think she was hungry until the steam flavored the air. He sliced a few pieces of fresh bread and placed the butter dish on the table.

"Now where were we?" he spoke out loud, almost to himself. "Ah, yes, Goldie Bell."

"Forgive me, Mr. Shaffer, but you were going to tell me about the man in the long black coat that we saw today." Suzie spoke so rapidly, so desperately, she felt light headed.

Dale chuckled loudly, "My dear, all in due time. Their stories are intertwined and a story must be told from the beginning. Sit back and enjoy your soup. Don't burn yourself, for it is a bit hot."

"Goldie died in the 1800s! How could that be the beginning?" Suzie interjected, but Dale began the tale and she didn't want to miss a word.

"The story begins in 1884. The Taylors, father Jacob and mother Lizzie, were blessed with the birth of twins on August 22. They named their son Lena and Goldie Bell was their daughter. The day after their birth was strenuous and difficult. Lena fell sick and never recovered. He died the following day, August 23rd. His father was heartbroken and vowed loyalty to Goldie Bell to ensure nothing would happen to his tiny joy. They were always together. She adored her daddy and followed him wherever he went."

He paused for a moment and drew a long, deep breath before continuing. "In the autumn of 1886, Goldie and her father had spent the day gathering elderberries to make juice. After cleaning the berries, they cooked them in a large iron kettle. When the juice was ready, they canned the winter treat and placed the mason jars in the cupboard. Lizzie and Jacob were busy cleaning up the kitchen while Goldie Bell licked the kettle clean."

Dale rose from his chair and excused himself to his study. Suzie was so entranced by his story-telling skills that she didn't move a muscle until his return. He handed her a few photographs, several of Goldie Bell's statue which had been taken over a long period of time, magnifying the decline of the fine features nature had stolen from her, and one of a farmhouse taken from the distance.

He pointed to the photograph of the farmhouse. "That was the Taylor farm before Goldie Bell's death. Jacob sold the house and the land shortly after the burial. He had the statue commissioned from an artist in Italy, made of marble in Goldie's likeness. Jacob was so distraught after losing Goldie Bell. He died in 1896. All say he died of a broken heart. His body was buried with the twins."

The heaviness of Mr. Shaffer's heart could not be mistaken in his voice. His breathing became labored. Suzie felt she had overstayed her welcome.

She was about to speak when he said weakly, "Even in death, their hearts are one."

From the magnitude of sorrow in the story, it was difficult to hold back the tears. Suzie stretched her hand across the table and placed her hand on his.

"I feel I must be going. My heart is heavy and the lump in my throat is so large, I feel I can't breathe." She squeezed his hand.

"Thank you for sharing much with me, from the tea and soup to your willingness to share your knowledge of Salem's history. You must be a great comfort to many. Please forgive me, though. Before I go, I must ask you a question. How did Goldie Bell die? "

The long pause weighed heavily on Suzie's mind, but she was patient not to speak. She knew she had worn Mr. Shaffer down and felt the need to let him rest. His face was down-turned and when he lifted his head, his eyes were red-rimmed.

"Iron poisoning. She never recovered from the sweet taste of elderberry juice from the vessel of death."

Suzie rose from her chair without a word, walked over to Dale and knelt beside him.

"You have been so kind. Before I return to New England, we will speak again." She patted his shoulder, "I'll show myself out. Thank you again for all of your help."

She walked to the door, slipped on her shoes, and turned to smile at him one more time as a show of gratitude. He was seated at the table with his head hung low, and eyes closed. His cheeks glistened with fresh tears.

As she started out the door, he said, "Suzie, he brings Goldie Bell flowers every day. She always has a fresh bouquet in her little hands. Mostly he brings daffodils, although sometimes I see a fresh bouquet of pink roses too. I don't know his name. I have never been close enough to see his face, although it is strange…from a distance, he never seems to age -- and no matter what the weather, he always wears that long black coat."

When she stepped outside, the night air was cold, but her face was warm. She stood on the front porch for a few minutes to catch her breath. She was so engrossed in the story of Goldie Bell, she forgot about the man in the coat. With Dale's final words ringing in her ears, she stepped off the porch and walked to her car. She didn't realize she clutched the photographs until she touched the car door handle. A pang of guilt traveled down her spine. She decided to return them the next time she visited. She slid into the front seat and traveled back to The Spread Eagle Tavern.

6

Her cell phone had rung nine times since early morning. Each time, it was Paul, although she never answered it once. She knew it would be difficult to hold him at bay much longer, but she needed more time. She committed to spend one week in Salem and began to feel pressured. She questioned her abilities to accomplish her list. The day before raised so many questions she spent half of the night organizing her thoughts.

She dressed quickly this morning and was out the door before the cleaning staff arrived. She grabbed her paint box and the photographs. She stopped at the Downtown Café for a muffin and cup of coffee and set out for the one thing she had in mind for the day - the cemetery.

The morning drive was misty, a change from the day before, and Suzie's heart rate quickened as she entered the gates of Hope Cemetery. Normally, the gates would not be unlocked until eight o'clock, but when she arrived they were wide open. Looking for a parking spot, she noticed that the familiar yellow daffodils in Goldie Bell's hands were now a nosegay of pink roses.

With numerous cars in the cemetery, it only meant one thing. A large crowd gathered under a tent. Dark shades shadowed their faces. She felt drawn toward the group of mourners. As she moved closer, one man in a dark coat caught her attention. He stood slightly removed from the rest of the people. The overgrown trees obscured his face, but Suzie saw his smile. He was smiling at her.

The pastor spoke and the crowd's sobs were silenced. They seemed relieved to have their attention moved from grief. He spoke of the woman with the utmost respect of her life, her faith, and the family legacy she left behind. His words moved like a soft lullaby and Suzie found herself touched by his sentiments.

Suzie lost herself in wonder of her own mother's funeral at this very cemetery ten years before. Who attended? What was said? Most important, how would she have reacted? She did not feel herself walking with the crowd, nor did she remember weeping.

With the abrupt tone of her cell phone, she excused herself. She glanced at the screen. It was Paul.

"Hello?" she whispered.

"Suzie, I have been trying to reach you all morning!"

"I'm sorry," she lied, "I've been at the library and I left my phone in the car." She could hear his smile.

"Good. How is it going?"

"The progress is slow, but I'm gaining on it."

The pause seemed to last an eternity.

"Listen, Paul. I've been thinking. The outline I gave you is weak."

She knew he agreed. He was easy to read.

"I've got an idea that I stumbled across here. The nucleus is very strong. I've spent all morning and much of last night in research. I know we discussed intertwining the first two books, but I think I can accomplish that through the next."

Stop yourself! Do you know what you are saying? You are getting in deeper! Her inner voice shouted, but she knew she was on the right path. 'Blind faith' her adoptive mother called it.

Paul remained silent so she pushed on.

"Anyway, I think this idea will please you. I'll have the outline worked up within a few days. Oh and Paul? I'll need to stay in Salem for at least another week. That is, if you like the new outline. If not I'll be on my way back to New England and will focus my efforts on the first idea."

She felt Paul's surprise. "Okay."

"Then it's settled. I'll email the outline to you as soon as I have it worked up. Oh, and Paul? Thanks."

"You're welcome," he said, but there was a touch of doubt in his voice, "Suzie, I'm going out on a limb for you. I can grant you the extra time in Salem and also the leeway to pursue a fresh idea, but I cannot give you an extension. So, don't ask." He hung up.

Suzie stared at the phone. "What have I done? I've just managed to put myself in an impossible position."

By the time she finished her conversation, the crowd had started to thin. Fresh roses covered the casket. She heard the motor of the hoist hum and took that as her cue to continue her search. She had covered most of the grounds and could not locate her. She decided to broaden her search area. Twice she returned to the record keeper's office for help, but the 'Closed for vacation' sign still hung on the door. She decided she would find it on her own. She didn't mind. She enjoyed the solitude of the cemetery.

She found herself wandering again over the north area where the burials were recent. Many of the gravesites were without headstones. Some were only a few weeks old. Others had been there for years -- and yet only a minute brass plaque marked their resting places. It was time consuming to search through the markers. After a few minutes, she stopped and looked around, scanning the area.

To her left, a delivery truck lowered a head stone into place. Another monument sat on the truck. It looked like an urn filled with flowers. The mist changed to fine droplets and quickly gathered strength. The rain soaked her hair and the chill of the damp day ran like a river down her back. She glanced at her timepiece that swung from a bar pin. It was 1:30 p.m. Her stomach growled from hunger. She nearly covered the entire cemetery and no sign of her mother.

"I'm sure the papers I received stated Hope Cemetery. It shouldn't be this difficult," she said exasperated. "I've covered every inch of this cemetery."

The rain stung as it hit her face. She tried to gather her collar around her face for protection. Her thin coat offered no shelter from the driving wind and rain.

She was about to call it quits when she remembered her umbrella by the cross monument. She looked in its direction. She shivered uncontrollably. The earlier mist created an eerie effect. She could not shake the feeling that someone was watching her. Quickly she spun around and glanced in all directions. Not a soul in sight. She ran toward the oldest gravestones hoping to find her umbrella.

Dressed in her running shoes, she covered the distance quickly. As she approached the crafted markers, their spell slowed her progress. Normally, she enjoyed walking through a century-old cemetery, but today she was cold, soaked, and discouraged. Her mind focused on a warm bath and a glowing fire.

When she reached the top of the knoll, the cross was not there. The chill she felt was not from the weather. Again, she felt watched. Her eyes searched for her car. Fear gripped her. She abandoned all thoughts of her umbrella and her mother's grave.

Seeing her car in the distance, she hurried toward it. Her heart pounded in her ears. The rain froze on her face as she ran. Gasping for air, she flung the car door open and threw herself onto the seat. The door closed on her coat, but she didn't care. She locked the door, started the car, and spun on the wet blacktop. As she drove past Goldie Bell, she noticed a splash of yellow in her hands. She slammed on the brakes and looked in her rear-view mirror. She was certain Goldie held pink roses, but now they sat on the ground.

Again, she shuddered and wondered why she lingered. The windshield wipers froze in mid-position. She fumbled with the wand. When she looked up, he stood in front of her. He held her umbrella in his hands. The rain dripped from his hat and shielded his eyes from view. The wind whipped his coat around his hips. All moisture left her mouth. Her breaths came in short gasps. Her heart raced. Their stares locked.

She jumped at the sound of a horn and looked into her rear-view mirror. She shouted, "I can't move! He's in my way!"

The agitated driver held his horn. She looked through her windshield. He was gone. Her umbrella rested against the statue. She opened the door and grabbed it. Again, her tires spun toward the entrance.

A few miles south of Salem, she remembered to take her first breath. Nervous laughter came from her throat. Her eyes settled on the daffodil lying on the seat next to her. It dripped with rain.

She heard the sound of a horn. She looked up in horror. A truck's grill was all she saw. She jerked the steering wheel hard to the right. The car tumbled over the embankment.

Her world moved in slow motion. Tree saplings slapped the windshield and shattered the glass. Her body rolled with the car as it thumped along the ground. Her shoulders were tense. Her knuckles, bonded to the steering wheel, were void of color. Her car slammed to a stop.

Debris covered her windshield. She groaned with movement. The car roof rested an inch from her head.

A fist on the side window broke her trance. "Miss... are you okay? Can you hear me? Turn the ignition off. Your engine is racing."

She looked through the shattered window and saw a black coat thrown by the wind. Her warm breath had created a thin film of moisture on the inside. She froze.

"Miss...are you all right?"

He tried to open the door. Suzie panicked. She tried to scream but couldn't make a sound. He rattled the door. It was jammed. Smoke poured from under the hood.

He pounded on the window. "Suzie, get out of the car! It's going to blow!" His hands shook violently. His voice was forceful and tense. "Suzie...get out now! Suzie...."

With his last burst of energy, he pulled again. The door flew open. For the first time, Suzie saw his face, fierce with determination, yet somehow gentle and full of concern. She had a fleeting thought of familiarity, but was unable to move. Her joints were rigid, stiff with adrenaline, and paralyzed from fear. He reached in the car and pulled her from it. She tried to scream. Nothing would come.

Her body was rag doll limp, but her mind ablaze with panic. He placed her on the ground and ran toward the car. A loud roar exploded into a ball of melted metal. His body was engulfed in flames. She screamed in horror. Pieces of burnt metal fell around her. She buried her face and sobbed.

7

When she woke, she was lying on her bed in the Lincoln Suite. The sheets were damp with sweat. The soft tapestry drawn above gave her a moment of comfort. She sat up expecting every muscle to groan with pain, but there was none. She slid her legs over the side of the bed and dangled her feet to the floor. Slowly she stood, but still no pain. She walked over to the mirror expecting to see a bruised face. The reflection showed no damage. She slipped on her shoes, opened the door, and stepped out into the hall.

The inn bustled with dinner under way. The smell of smoked meats, garlic, and fresh baked bread filled the air. She shuffled down the stairs toward the parking lot, calculating her steps in case the pain was a delayed reaction.

Her mouth hung open when she saw her undamaged car. Her body relaxed. Her fingers tingled from returned sensation. "A dream! It was only a dream!" She hurried to her car and ran her hands along the driver's side door, whispering, "A dream… Thank God…only a dream."

Opening the door, she sat behind the wheel, replaying the dream in her mind. Her hands brushed the fabric of her seat until they fondled the softness of petals.

She twirled the daffodil in her hand. The words were nearly audible. She picked up her mini recorder and spoke:

From White to United

White paper stretched, stapled.
Dry colored squares, wet brushes,
On a vintage blanket opened on earth,
The visionary stares.
A damp brush symphony
Blends Payne's Grey with Ohio Sky.
Eyelash lace revealed by strokes of Ivory Black.
Hooker and Sap separate background hues.
A skilled sable twists intricate Umber branches
As watery greys blend for aged granite.
Soft shadows grace her cheeks.
The artist's head hangs low,
Mouth twisted, bitten lip, searching eyes
Drinking each detail with silent breath.
Tender touch, blending, swirling, with moisture lifted.
Watercolor, unforgiving timed art.

Goldie's eyes danced with the colored music.
Captured excitement, with held anticipation
Her smile lost in granite,
Seen only by the gifted,
Felt by all.
Warmed by a sense of watchfulness,
The artist's pink, flushed cheeks
Unite with Goldie's stare.
Spring's splendor bouquet graces
Her tiny welcoming hands
With a painted gift of daffodils.

She felt a strange sense of purpose when she entered the reception area. The woman at the desk interrupted her thoughts.

"Ms. DuVeau? Will you be joining us for dinner?"

"I would rather order room service. I have a lot of work to do."

She handed Suzie the menu. Suzie quickly decided on a salad and a glass of Cabernet. She was anxious to type her new poem.

When she opened the door of her room, Suzie was reminded of the charm and grace of the inn. It was a perfect place to draw inspiration. She laid the daffodil beside her computer. The color was vivid and its petals were flawless. She drew in a deep breath of its unique fragrance and began to type.

There was a knock on the door.

"Room service."

A vase of daffodils punctuated the presentation of her dinner. The waiter placed the antique tray on the fireside table.

"Would you need anything else, Ms. DuVeau?"

After a moment's pause, Suzie requested a second glass of wine. Quickly she added, "There really is no hurry. Bring it whenever it's convenient."

"I'll send it up with the fire steward."

Suzie smiled, enjoying the attention, "That would be wonderful."

"My pleasure." He tipped his head, grinned, and excused himself.

Suzie didn't realize how hungry she was until she looked at her salad. She picked up the wineglass, took a quick sniff of her bouquet, and devoured her dinner. She had the last piece of warm bread in her hand when there was a knock on the door.

The fire steward handed her the glass of wine. The brush of his fingers resonated on her skin.

"Thank you…."

"William." He added.

"William," she repeated.

She was taken by his appearance. His hair was dark and longer than she expected. She was drawn into the calm of his soft brown eyes. He was tall, lean, but toned.

She stepped aside and motioned for him to enter. She stood over him as he organized the kindling. His hair was damp and smelled of shampoo. Suzie knelt beside him. A spark made the kindling crack.

"I need to speak to David. My schedule has changed and I need to make arrangements to stay for another week. If he has this room reserved, I would gladly move." She chuckled. "Well maybe not gladly, but I will move."

"He's still here. I'll send him up."

"That would be great."

They stared at the fire for a few minutes. Suzie's thoughts moved with the flames that reflected in William's eyes.

He spoke first. "Are you enjoying your stay with us, Ms. DuVeau?"

"Please, call me Suzie…and yes, I am. This is the perfect place to draw inspiration and relax."

"Okay, Suzie it is. I have a question for you. If you would rather not answer, it is not a problem. It's really more to satisfy my curiosity."

"Sure, what's your question?"

"Who is the gentleman who brings you these daffodil bouquets?"

Suzie was stunned. She had no idea they were brought to her specifically. She turned and picked up the vase.

"You won't find a note. He never leaves one. He just asks us to give these to you each day."

Suzie's pulse quickened, "William, what does he look like?"

"Honestly, I have only seen him once, but he has caused quite a buzz around the inn. Everyone refers to him as your secret admirer."

"What does he look like?" Her voice was strained.

"I'm sorry. I didn't mean to upset you. He seems well mannered, quiet, reserved, and speaks with definite purpose."

"William, please," Suzie said almost through clenched teeth, "his looks?"

"Oh, he's tall, thin, longer dark hair I think. It is a bit difficult to say beyond that. He had on an old hat -- and a long black coat. I saw him yesterday when we had that late afternoon shower."

The room started to spin. The color left her cheeks and she stumbled to the edge of the bed, spilling her wine in the process. William knelt beside the bed and cupped her hand in his. She was trembling.

"I'm so sorry. I shouldn't have asked."

Suzie stared at the floor for a moment and tried to breathe. She felt overwhelmed but managed a smile.

"I'm fine. I just have no idea who this man is, or what he wants. I have seen him everywhere I have gone, even in my dreams..." Her voice faded.

William stood. "Do you want me to call the police?"

Suzie looked at him puzzled. "No."

She was silent for quite a while before she spoke. "I don't feel threatened. I sense no danger. I don't know how to explain it, but somehow I know he has something important to tell me." Her shoulders slumped. "Maybe it is about my deceased mother. She was from this area and perhaps he knew her. At any rate, the police won't be necessary." She placed her hand on his cheek. "I am grateful for your concern."

He took her hands and placed them inside of his. He caressed her fingertips.

"Have I caused you some level of discomfort?"

She covered his lips with her finger. "William…I'm fine."

Their eyes held each other. They stood close together. Suzie moved her fingers from his face and smiled. William was silent, but his eyes spoke volumes.

He lowered his head. "I'll send David up about your extended stay. I'm glad to hear that." With a quick smile, he was gone.

Once Suzie was alone, she thought about her secret admirer. She had only seen his face in her dreams. She wondered why the mystery and what he needed so desperately to tell her. She had a quick knock on the door and opened it to find David.

"Good evening, Ms. DuVeau. I understand we need to make extended reservations for your stay?"

"Yes. If this room is spoken for…."

David stopped her. "This room is available for as long as you will need it." He smiled. "Now, how long will that be?"

"At least another week. It may be ten days. I will know for certain in a few days. Is that okay?"

"That will be fine. I will make the necessary arrangements. Will there be anything else for tonight?"

"No, I believe that will take care of it. Thank you, David. You have been very helpful."

"My pleasure. What time would you like breakfast? It is supposed to be a beautiful spring day. I'm sure you will be off to an early start?"

"Actually, I anticipate working late this evening. Let's make breakfast for eight o'clock."

"Your normal table?"

Suzie smiled, "That would be great."

Alone in her room, she opened her computer and reread her poem. After a few changes, she felt it was good enough, for now. She saved it in a file she titled 'Goldie' and worked on the outline she had promised.

8

Madeline spent the better part of the morning finishing her errands from the day before. She rushed out of the Cheshire in such a hurry she forgot her responsibilities. When she arrived at the cemetery, the air was damp with mist. Before she removed the day-old flowers and replaced them with the potted one, the mist changed to heavy rain. She switched the flowers, apologized, and hopped back into her idling car.

Charlotte had left a large sum of money in a fund with The Flower Loft to ensure her gravesite would be graced daily with fresh flowers. Madeline felt a twinge of guilt when she brought a potted plant. She convinced herself it was impossible to bring fresh flowers every day. To her, a potted plant was more practical.

In the past, Charlotte correlated flowers with love. She made many remarks when she passed a gravesite unadorned with petal or leaf. She bantered, "How no one must have loved that person or there would be fresh flowers brought to the grave." Madeline knew how important it was to Charlotte. She was trying to create her own 'Goldie Bell legacy'. Many times the previous day's flowers were still crisp so Madeline brought them home with her and arranged them in a vase. She placed them on the dining room table despite Charlotte's specific orders to discard them daily. Again, this disobedience brought guilt. The flowers, however, brought life and finished grace to the dining room which otherwise was empty of living things, despite its beauty in furniture.

The dining room table, chairs, and sideboard were period Hepplewhite. The ebony inlay on the table edge and drawer fronts of the sideboard set apart the flame walnut burl with a rich style. The south wall had a game table that Charlotte's first husband, Grant, purchased as a birthday present while in Amsterdam. The table was inlaid with gold and silver cornucopias filled with harvest fruits. Its woods were rare and imported. Madeline had long forgotten their names.

On the top of the sideboard were two English walnut burl knife boxes. They were one of Charlotte's most prized possessions, not because of the value, but the story behind it. They were purchased on Charlotte's final trip to England. Acutely crippled with pain and a miserable person for it, she was determined to take this trip. Her doctor warned against it knowing how flippant Charlotte regarded her own health. He urged her to take Madeline, but in the end she won the battle. Charlotte and Kenneth Fischall left the following morning.

After a few days of antiquing in the Cotswolds, they stumbled upon an estate sale. The front stairs of the manor were long and steep. It took every ounce of Charlotte's strength to climb to the top. In her pride, she declined all offers of help, including Kenneth's. At the top she spotted the two knife boxes. Her husband, proud of her determination, couldn't deny her the satisfaction of calling the pair of boxes her own. He paid an exorbitant price of

2,100 pounds apiece, but seeing the joy it brought his wife, he would have paid more. So there they sat as a testament of strength with the other memories of Charlotte's world travels.

The only tragedy attached to the boxes was the loss of Kenneth three months after the trip. His poor heart could not take any more badgering from Charlotte. He died of a massive heart attack on August 9, 1989. She buried him in Hope Cemetery with an empty space between his grave and that of Grant Wilson Riley. That space was reserved for Charlotte, who completed the circle five years later.

Madeline never moved into the main house, although it was her right. Two weeks after Charlotte's death, she gathered enough courage to sleep in Charlotte's bed. When she crawled between the sheets, it was nearly midnight. She was tired from the day of cleaning but her mind was restless. She thought she heard Charlotte speak, cough, then pull the blanket from the bed. By three in the morning, Madeline moved into her own wing and slept. She never attempted that again.

The only change she made to the house was to add an open doorway from her sitting room to the kitchen in the main house. This allowed her accessibility without the need to go outside. Charlotte insisted Madeline have her privacy separate from her daily duties so when the wing was added no access was created. This ensured Charlotte of her own privacy.

In the beginning of this strange caretaker relationship, Madeline performed her duties between seven a.m. and six-thirty p.m. This allowed her to cover all meal times -- for preparation as well as clean up. On occasion when Charlotte's husband was out of town, Madeline's presence was required until Charlotte retired for the evening, which was around ten p.m.

Those particular days were difficult for Madeline, but she never mentioned this to her sister. Charlotte took good care of her financially, but lacked the emotional support. Those infamous words "After all, you were driving…" rang through Madeline's mind many times a day.

Madeline treasured the weekends. Her only requirement was Sunday dinner. On most Sundays, Grant or later, Kenneth took Charlotte and Madeline out for the afternoon meal. Both husbands insisted Madeline be a part of their daily routine - and they thought it only fair to return the favor when they dined outside of the home. Charlotte agreed, reluctantly, and permitted Madeline to accompany them.

Charlotte's health was somewhat better with Grant. The three enjoyed a picnic in the park after Sunday church service. When they were finished, Madeline gathered the basket and walked home while Grant and Charlotte stayed and fed the ducks on the pond. After the basket was emptied, Madeline had the rest of the day to herself. Even if Grant was out of town for the weekend, Charlotte allowed Madeline to enjoy the day, requiring nothing else.

Madeline adored both of Charlotte's husbands, but when Grant died of colon cancer, a piece of her died with him. He was soft-spoken with strong convictions. No matter how inconsiderate or harsh Charlotte was to him, he never lost patience or raised his voice. Instead, he softly brushed Charlotte's hair from her shoulder and kissed her cheek. "My darling Charlotte," he said. "Why can't I make you happy?"

Many times, Grant helped Madeline with the evening dishes while Charlotte rested in the parlor. He often reassured Madeline how much her sister loved her and appreciated her sacrifices. He was kind to say those things, but she wished she had heard it from her sister.

"She was incapable of showing many emotions, but that doesn't mean she didn't feel them," Madeline told herself as she drove from the wet cemetery.

When she arrived home, she noticed the flashing message light on the answering machine. She hit the play button.

"Ms. Crory, this is Jim Sutton from Sutton Monument. I know our arrangements were for tomorrow, but our driver is on his way with the replacement headstone for your sister. We finished it a day early and we need to make another delivery at Hope so we thought we could do them both today. I hope this isn't too inconvenient. He should be arriving between one and two. Would it be possible for you to meet him at Hope Cemetery to ensure safe and proper placement? Your signature will be required. Please call me to confirm. Thank you."

Madeline looked at her watch. It was 11:30 a.m. She dialed the number.

Jim answered, "Sutton Monument."

"Hello, Jim. This is Madeline Crory. I received your message. I will meet your driver at the cemetery."

"Thank you. I know I should have called you earlier, but to be honest it slipped my mind. It has been kind of hectic around here trying to fill the replacement orders for the headstones that were vandalized last month."

"That's not a problem. I'm glad it's finished early. It's just a shame the weather isn't cooperating."

"Oh, the rain has never stopped us before and it won't today either."

"Good for you. I'll meet your driver in about an hour or so."

"That will be great. I'll tell him to look for you. Thank you, Ms. Crory."

"You're welcome. Have a pleasant day."

"You do the same, ma'am."

Madeline grabbed her wet coat and purse. After making a quick stop for a few groceries, she drove back to the cemetery. The rain fell harder and the temperature had dropped eight degrees since morning.

As she waited for the delivery she noticed a woman wander from headstone to headstone. She was dressed in jeans, tennis shoes and a lightweight coat. Her jacket was soaked and she was without an umbrella. Madeline was about to get out of the car to see if she could help, but the delivery truck appeared over the knoll.

The driver got out of the truck and approached Madeline's car. "Ms. Crory?"

"That's me," Madeline said trying to sound cheerful. The cemetery magnified her emptiness and left her feeling melancholy.

"I have your sister's headstone here, but when the dockhands loaded me, they put it on the back. I'll have to place this one first." He made a motion to a statue of an angel with her hands wrapped around a heart. It read:

Angela Leigh Russell
Our Angel
Born April 10, 1999
Called Home May 3, 2003
Thank you Lord for the time we called her ours

Madeline watched as he carefully lowered the stone onto the pedestal, which had been poured a few days before. He jumped out of the truck, made a few adjustments, lowered it the last few inches, until he set it onto its final resting place.

A young man quickly scribbled his signature onto the proper papers. He placed his hands on the stone, bowed his head, and whispered a prayer. His wife stood beside him. Her hands wiped the rain mixed with tears from her cheeks. They both placed flowers below the angel. He helped his wife walk to their car. It was obvious that grief burdened their hearts. When the young man helped his wife into her seat, the wind whipped her long coat over her head and Madeline noticed the young woman was pregnant.

She turned her attention to the delivery truck. He backed into place and Madeline walked up to it. He lowered Charlotte's headstone in place with the same care that he had placed Angela's. Within a matter of minutes, he had made the proper adjustments and once again the beautiful urn with carved flowers rested above Charlotte.

Madeline sighed, "Thank you from me and my sister. Charlotte loved flowers and I know she will rest easier knowing they are back where they belong."

The driver walked up to her with his pen and paper. He stretched out his hand and said, "Just sign anywhere." He glanced at the headstone. "It's an awful thing to have something so sacred vandalized."

"Children these days don't have enough to keep themselves busy and out of trouble. How many did your company replace?"

"Twenty-three." His voice was loaded with pride, "And all were delivered ahead of schedule. We are all ready for a vacation after this month." He chuckled and Madeline joined in. It was nice to hear laughter for a change instead of tears in this place.

The sound of a horn interrupted their conversation. They both looked up in the direction of two cars at the top of the knoll. They watched a woman get out of her car and reach for something under Goldie Bell's statue.

Madeline said, "That poor woman is soaked through her clothes. She's not dressed warm enough for this weather. Not to mention without an umbrella."

"Looks like she found it now," he added as Suzie shook the umbrella and tossed it in her car.

Madeline then realized she had been watching Suzie. "I can't believe that was Suzie. She must be searching for Charlotte's grave. Without the marker, she never would have found it."

The driver looked at her puzzled, "Relative of yours?"

Madeline smiled at the question, "Yes, she is."

She signed for a job well done and hopped in her car. Her thoughts were focused on Suzie and for the first time in days, she knew exactly what to do next. She would wait for Suzie by Charlotte's urn. Her pulse quickened. She had much to share with Suzie. Sleep was a distant thought.

9

Suzie spent six and one half hours working on the outline. She had the basics completed, but felt something was missing. She finally closed her laptop at around 2:45 a.m. The inn had long quieted from a busy evening. The silence was eerie, but the warm glow of the fire accompanied by an occasional wood pop filled the room with warmth. She crawled into bed at three.

The last of the fire's flames danced their waltz on the ceiling. Their movement mesmerized her. She thought about the daffodils. The voice of her poem drifted in and out of thought…warmed by the sense of watchfulness…drinking each detail…soft shadows grace her cheeks…a damp brush symphony. She had long resolved to take her paint box to the cemetery tomorrow. The weather was supposed to cooperate. She wanted to give Goldie a gift -- one she knew would be very special. She drifted into pleasant dreams.

Surprised by the bright sun, she woke early. She felt refreshed despite her short night's rest. She dressed in layers and was anxious for breakfast when the knock came.

"Ms. DuVeau, are you ready for breakfast?"

"Yes, I am." Suzie opened the door with a fling.

The woman placed the last of the silverware on the table when a young man puffed up the stairs, "These were just delivered for you, Ms. DuVeau."

Suzie smiled at the fresh bouquet of daffodils encircled by narrow sprigs of forget-me-nots. "Aren't they beautiful!" she exclaimed. The pair waiting to spread the next rumor carefully calculated her reaction. She brought them to her nose and drew in the fragrance. She never enjoyed daffodils as much as she had in the past few days. Her face flushed as they stared. Their eyes recorded every detail.

She giggled out loud and said, "Please, thank him for me." She enjoyed this little game as much as they did. They excused themselves, raced down the flight of stairs, and vanished out of sight. She heard the murmur of other voices erupt in the distance. She laughed.

Her breakfast was delicious. The old fashioned pancakes were so thick she barely finished one. The warmed maple syrup was from a local gentleman who had made it the week prior, according to the label. The fresh squeezed orange juice was mixed with grapefruit as per Suzie's request. A carafe of hazelnut coffee made it complete.

Suzie finished her breakfast and tossed her paint box into the car. The morning was bright. She scrambled for her sunglasses. When she opened the case, a piece of paper fell out. Scribbled in her writing: Email outline to Paul. She needed a few more answers and it would be complete.

Madeline woke before the sun had shown its face. Her night's sleep was restless. She was as anxious as a child on Christmas Eve. She walked to the kitchen and made herself some tea. She hovered over her teacup, allowing the steam to awaken her senses. The permanent smile on her face was wide. She thought of Suzie. She admired her strength and independence and couldn't wait for the long overdue conversation. She poured herself a second cup and sat in the dining room to watch the sunrise.

The sun stretched a thin shade of rose across the eastern sky. Soon layers of lavender rested on their shoulders. Madeline watched as a bright ball of orange peered over the horizon. The clouds magnified its reflection.

Madeline rehearsed a conversation with Suzie. "How do I begin?" she asked. "Suzie doesn't know me. I can't assume she was looking for Charlotte's grave."

Her thoughts drifted to the idea of Suzie living in Salem. She loved this town. It was all she knew. A feeling of tenseness rose within her. She wondered if her plan to wait for Suzie in the cemetery was not a good one.

"What if she doesn't care about her mother? What if she doesn't want to know? What if my assumptions are incorrect?" Her voice trailed off to a whisper.

After a long silent battle, Madeline decided to go to the cemetery as planned. Her desire to see and talk to Suzie transcended all reason and the nagging sound of Charlotte saying, "We made a promise. We must keep it." She poured herself one more cup of tea and carried it with her to her bathroom.

She showered and dressed in record time. Grabbing her lukewarm tea and pouring it down the drain, she glanced at the Swiss wag-on-the-wall. "7:15 a.m. I should be there long before Suzie."

When Madeline arrived at the cemetery, she saw that she was alone for the moment. She parked in her normal spot at The Flower Loft and walked in the grass to bypass the closed gate. It was 7:22 a.m., over one half of an hour before the cemetery officially opened.

The sun was in full glory, promising a warm day. Madeline walked over to her sister's headstone. The monument company had duplicated the urn to perfection. She adjusted the potted plant that the wind blew over and whispered promises of fresh flowers after she spent time with Suzie. In her guilt, she imagined the groans of her sister's disapproval.

A silver Lincoln pulled beside her. An elderly gentleman hopped out of the car. He smiled at Madeline and tipped his hat.

"Good morning to you, young lady. What a fine mornin' it is too." His brogue was heavy and his Irish eyes sparkled as he spoke.

Madeline blushed at the words 'young lady' and replied, "It is a beautiful morning, young man." Her joke fell flat and she blushed.

He grinned. "Now, it's been a fair piece since I've heard those words. The name's Patrick McCelvy." He held out his hand to her.

"Madeline Crory." She nodded.

His eyes widened. "Did you say Crory?"

"Yes, Madeline Crory," she said hesitantly. The look on his face puzzled her. "Do you know the Crory family?"

"I used to know an Attie Crory in my younger years."

The sound of that name sent a flash of hot nerves down her back and her knees nearly buckled.

He reached to steady her. "Are you feeling faint, my dear?"

She searched her memory but came up with nothing. After a long pause, she said, "That was my nickname. I haven't heard it in years."

"You are Attie?"

"That was the nickname that my sister gave me when she was small. Since long before her death, we didn't use that nickname. She felt it improper to not use a person's full Christian name."

"Well, shock me silly," he yelled. "I was the intern who took care of you when you `ad your accident. Don't you remember me?" His face glowed with excitement waiting for her next response. He only saw a blank stare.

"I...I'm... sorry...no," she stammered. Madeline was very uncomfortable. How could she not remember being the patient of an attractive man with such a heavy accent?

"You don't remember me t'all?" Disappointment burned on his face and he hung his head. The pause was an eternity.

Finally, Madeline spoke, "My sister, Charlotte Crory, as you would have known her, explained my injuries many times to me. She described how I lost months at a time without a single memory. I slipped in and out of those 'dark times' as Charlotte called them, without notice. I'm sorry... I don't remember you," she sighed.

With that response, he managed a smile, "Aye, you knew me well." He faced her, reached for her hand, and kissed it. "How strange it is that I would `appen to run into you."

He felt guilty lying to her. The truth was he couldn't pack for Ohio fast enough once an old colleague sent him the article about the vandalism at the cemetery. There on the front page of The Salem News was Charlotte's headstone smashed to bits. The only thing recognizable was her name. Patrick admitted seeing her memorial lie on the ground in ruins brought a smile to his face. Now he found himself standing on the very spot photographed in the paper, holding the hand of his life's love.

Madeline made no attempt to pull back her hand. Although she had no clear memory of this man, she felt comfortable standing next to him. Her mind raced through the stories Charlotte relayed and still came up blank. Anger flickered in her eyes. She spoke a silent curse to Charlotte. Patrick reached for her other hand.

He smiled and said, "The years `ave been kind to you, Attie. I've thought about you often."

With her eyes filling with tears, she quickly turned from him. He placed his hands on her shoulders, pulled her back towards him, and lifted her face upward. He wiped the tears from her cheeks as he caressed them. His smile was wide and full of tenderness

"Attie," he whispered. She wept in his arms as he stroked her hair.

Suzie arrived at Hope Cemetery at nine o'clock. She spread her vintage blanket on the ground in front of Goldie Bell. The words from her own poem whispered on the breeze, called her name, and beckoned her to paint.

She noticed the flowers in Goldie's hands were the same gathering she received yesterday. At the base of the statue rested a bouquet of pink roses. They appeared fresh.

She arranged her brushes, water, and palette. She placed the stretched paper on her lap. The eastern sunlight cast her favorite shadow across Goldie's face. She was too busy sketching the outline to notice the flowers slip from Goldie's hands.

As she stood to rearrange them, she tripped on her blanket. She stopped herself just before her head hit the ground. She caught a glimpse of a pink gown skirt behind Goldie. Startled, she sat up. Her eyes were wide. Her heart quickened. She tiptoed behind the statue. No one was there. A wood thrush called from the distance.

A chill ran down her spine. Her hands went numb. She stood still, listening for any sound. Her heart thumped in her throat. A whispered voice came from behind her. "It's beginning to rain." When Suzie spun around, the rain touched her skin. She ran to the front of the statue and looked toward the sky. Not a cloud was in sight, but its mist remained on her face.

She glanced at her blanket. It was straightened! From the corner of her eye, she caught another glimpse of pink. A single pink rose lay in Goldie's hands. The daffodils and forget-me-nots joined the roses at the base of the statue.

As she stared at the ground, the bouquets grew to hundreds. The statue seemed to pull away as her vision widened. One by one, headstones disappeared. The colors faded to grey, all but the bouquets, which became more vibrant.

Bewitched, her heart pounded and her mouth went dry. The only sound heard was rushing wind and the song of the wood thrush. From the distance a woman glided toward her. The wind carried her closer.

She heard something behind her. She saw the man in the long black coat moving toward her. Panic gripped her. Unable to move or speak, she stood as a prisoner with lead for feet. They continued to advance. She felt trapped. She looked in the cemetery for help. She was alone.

The background darkened to charcoal. The flowers paled against the color of the woman's dress. Her hair was long and blonde. Its waves swirled as she walked. She carried a bouquet of pink roses. Her face was fixed on a target, but it was not Suzie.

Suzie turned to see the man stretch his black coat on the ground. He knelt before the approaching vision and reached up for her. Fresh daffodils rested before him.

The woman held out her hands to meet his. The roses fell from her hands - and their bodies were torn apart.

Suzie felt faint. Her knees buckled. She slid down the face of the memorial in slow motion. Her vision went black. Rain fell harder. She felt her body hit the ground. Her head pounded with hushed, whispered voices. They laughed, then cried, then faded.

10

When Madeline gained control of herself, she pulled away from Patrick.

"It's been a long time since my past has been a problem. Usually Charlotte was there to explain if I lost a detail, but this perplexes me. I've lost an entire person. How can this be?" She managed to smile through her confusion.

Patrick took her hands. "Time will explain much to you, my dear -- and it seems time is what I `ave a lot of these days."

"Do you live in town?"

"I do as of last week. I lived `ere during my internship. I accepted a position with an `ospital in Arizona. There wasn't much of an opportunity for me in this small town back then, and after you…" He stopped himself.

"After I…what?" Madeline asked more puzzled than before.

"'Tis nothing Attie. We `ave much time to discuss the past. What I'd like to know is what you `ave been doing? A lot `as `appened in forty years." He gave her a wink, "Now tell me what `as `appened to you since we last saw each other. You were seventeen and I was, oh let me see `ere… oh yes, I was twenty-five."

He paused at the look of panic on Madeline's face. The last thing he wanted was to make her feel uncomfortable. He spent his life wondering 'what ifs' and now with the opportunity standing before him, caution and patience were what he needed.

Patrick moved to Phoenix, Arizona in 1960. His life was busy as a young, aspiring doctor. He spent most of his time working, trying to drown who he missed the most, Attie. He filled the void any way he could. He found pleasure in the doctors' baseball team. The young vs. the old was great fun, but after the game when their wives joined them for dinner, the chair beside Patrick was always empty. That feeling overshadowed any fun on the diamond.

The person he felt most comfortable with was Isaac Tenbraughn. He was a fellow intern who followed Patrick to Phoenix. Isaac tried to play matchmaker, but after a year of failures, Isaac surrendered. "You don't want to be alone all your life, Patrick," he warned. Patrick couldn't imagine life without Attie. She was the only woman for him.

Time moved quickly, though, and before Patrick realized it, he was in Arizona two years. He was the best man in Isaac's wedding when he married Joanne, a nurse from the hospital. In two years Isaac and Joanne had their first baby. Eleven months after baby Elizabeth, came little Patrick, named of course for Isaac's best friend.

After five years alone in Phoenix, Patrick decided to make a trip back to Ohio to look for Attie. While driving across the country, he rehearsed his conversation with her. He needed to convince her to return with him to begin their life in Phoenix. When he arrived in Salem, his speech was prepared. As a safety net, he wrote his thoughts in a letter. He was pleased to see little had changed in the quaint historic town. The preservation of the old houses and buildings remained important to the people who lived there. He stopped at a pay phone and scanned the pages for Attie's name.

"Please," he spoke desperately, "don't be married."

His hands shook as he traced his fingers down the page. When he found her name, Madeline P. Crory, he held his breath, "Attie, sweet Attie." He jotted down her address, 851 South Lincoln Avenue, for it had changed since he lived here. "They sold their parents' house?" He was surprised because he knew how attached they felt to it. It was all they had left of their parents.

He counted the house numbers as he drove up the street, "639...715...803...817," he held his breath as he said, "851." His heart throbbed as he drove by. He found a place to turn around on the tenth block and drove past it again.

It was a large historic home, freshly painted in period colors, meticulously landscaped, and well cared for. There was a summer kitchen, attached to the house with an addition. It had its own front door and mailbox.

"Looks like an apartment...I wonder if...."

As soon as he spoke, the front door of the main house opened and two women appeared on the front porch, one walked with a walker and the other helped. A horn sounded behind him. Patrick was startled. He had stopped in the middle of the street. The two women looked up. Frazzled, Patrick moved down the street. The gentleman in the car behind him moved his hands wildly and blew his horn again. Patrick pulled over to the side and motioned for the car to go around him. As the man whizzed by, Patrick noticed that Attie tried to make her sister comfortable. Charlotte's eyes burned a hole through his soul. The old warning rang loud in his ears, "You must never see her again!"

He pulled into a drive on the third block to catch his breath. It was a beautiful summer day. People walked and worked in their gardens. It may have been his paranoia, but it seemed everyone recognized him and waved.

He could not shake the echoes of his last conversation with Charlotte. In the end, his desire to see Attie won over any promise he had made. He put his car in reverse, backed out of the drive, and continued on his original mission.

When he pulled into the drive on 851 South Lincoln Avenue, the women sat on the front porch. Charlotte waved a hand and Attie disappeared into the house. Patrick got out of the car and walked toward the front porch.

Cold and detached, Charlotte spoke, "Can I help you?"

For a moment Patrick thought he had been mistaken, but the fire in her eyes couldn't be missed.

"Charlotte. `ow are you?" His voice shook.

"What do you want?" she spewed.

"I came to see Attie."

"That's not possible." She crossed her arms.

"Charlotte, please, I've driven `ere from Phoenix. I `ave to see Attie."

Charlotte's evil laugh chilled him to the core. "She has no idea who you are," she sneered.

"Please, Charlotte."

Madeline returned with a glass of iced tea in her hand. When she opened the door, Patrick's eyes sparkled. She had grown into a beautiful woman. Her hair shone in the dappled sunlight. Her simple dress accentuated every curve. Patrick stepped toward her and Charlotte quickly stood up. Her move was so desperate that she knocked herself off balance and fell.

Madeline rushed to her. Charlotte reeled in exaggerated pain.

"Madeline…my medicine. Hurry!"

Madeline disappeared into the house.

Charlotte turned to Patrick and spoke from clenched teeth, "Leave, NOW! You are not welcome here. Leave!"

Patrick, stunned by the look in Charlotte's eyes yet determined to speak with Attie, tried to follow her into the house. Enraged, Charlotte lunged at his feet from the floor and tripped him as he walked.

She spit her venomous words, "I have the power to tell her what I wish, and of course she *will* believe me." Her voice was slow, deliberate, and hate-filled. "I told you to go. NOW!"

"But…I need to speak to Attie. I need to tell `er…."

"Tell her what? What a coward you are? How you showed her your feelings by leaving?" Charlotte's laugh was wicked. "Just go. Keep your promise -- or aren't you able to do that either?" Her eyes were unbearable. He knelt to reach for her arm to help her stand. She glared at him. Her eyes hollowed black.

Patrick hung his head in shame. His motive was pure. He wanted to see Attie and have the chance to explain. Charlotte's formidable power caught him unprepared.

He turned to go. As he took his first step off the porch, he remembered the letter he had written. He turned to Charlotte, still on the porch floor, and spoke in a soft voice, "If you `ave a change of `eart, Charlotte, please give this to Attie."

He tried to give Charlotte the envelope, but she wouldn't look at him.

"Charlotte, please." The silence was deafening. He heard Madeline approach. Ashamed and deflated, he placed the envelope at her side. She pushed it from the porch floor. It slid into the bushes. That was the last time he tried to contact Attie. Charlotte's words had crushed him.

Standing before Madeline now, his emotions were mixed. With the memory of his last meeting with Charlotte burned into his heart, he was torn between love and honor. He swallowed the lump in his throat.

"What brings you to the cemetery?"

"I came," Madeline began, "to check on Charlotte's flowers, and to see..." She stopped. Her cheeks blushed. It was difficult to admit that she came to find Suzie. She drew in a deep breath and lied, "see how the new headstone looked."

Her lie was easy to read, but Patrick didn't show it. He was afraid to push too far. He couldn't bear the thought of losing her. As Madeline explained the story of the vandalism, he memorized every move. It all came back to him like the rush of falling water. He smiled. They faced each other in silence.

Finally Madeline spoke, "I'm so sorry, but I must go. There is someone I was hoping to meet here."

Pain pierced Patrick's heart. By the tone in her voice, this person was important to her. He never considered that she might be in a relationship. "Whom?" he asked weakly.

"Suzie DuVeau," Madeline said proudly.

He was pleased to hear the sound of a woman's name. "Oh, well I best be on me way," he said chuckling. "I'd like to see you again, perhaps dinner? We can discuss old times."

The curve of her mouth fell to a frown. "I don't remember old times with you. I can't find your face anywhere in my memories," she blurted out with desperation. Her voice began to quiver. Patrick cupped her hands within his own. In her palm he placed a key.

"My dear Attie. It pains me to `ear you don't remember me, but maybe this will `elp. It's a letter I'd written long ago, locked away for safekeeping. I tried to give it to you once, but Charlotte stopped me. Said it would do more `arm than good. She was pretty...persuasive." He managed a nervous laugh. "You get the letter, and after you read it, if you want to talk about it, `ere's my number." He handed her a piece of paper with his name, address, and phone number. He kissed the palm of her hand, and said, "I'll be waitin' by the phone."

Madeline watched him walk away from her. She wanted to run after him, soothe his pain, but she was confused. Her mind was void of his sweet face. For some reason, he seemed distantly familiar. She watched his car disappear from sight. She stared at the key in her palm.

11

When Suzie sat up, the sky was clear, the wind was calm, and all was silent. Slowly, color returned to her sight. Everything appeared normal. The headstones sat in the correct positions. The man and the woman were gone. She turned to look at Goldie. She appeared aged, weathered from time, not as she had just appeared. Two bouquets were at her feet, daffodils with blue forget-me-nots and a nosegay of roses. In Goldie's hands was a single pink rose.

Suzie knew the differences between a dream and a vision. The strength of this message was overwhelming. It moved her from the past to the present in a moment. Her body felt stretched from the movement. She glanced around the cemetery. Her blanket was where she had placed it. Her paints were intact and ready for use. On the corner of her blanket was a daffodil.

She held on to Goldie's legs while she waited for the world to return to normal. She heard voices in the distance. She saw a couple facing each other holding hands. It touched her and she smiled.

It was then she saw a unfamiliar headstone. Suzie had been all over this cemetery many times.

"How did I miss that?"

Quickly, she gathered her blanket and paints. Tossing her things in the car, she looked back toward the woman. She was alone. Her head was lowered. Suzie realized that the woman was looking at something in her hand. She walked toward her.

Madeline recognized the bank's name on the key. It was an independent bank that had merged with a larger conglomerate. Her parents had an account there. Madeline remembered many trips to the 'bank on the corner'.

Madeline took in a deep breath of fresh air. She noticed a woman walking toward her. Her auburn hair swirled as she walked. She gasped when she realized it was Suzie.

Madeline held her breath until Suzie moved closer. The grace with which she walked reminded her of Charlotte long before the accident. At that moment, Madeline realized the enormity of what her childish inexperience had stolen from Charlotte. Between that revelation and Suzie approaching, Madeline began to weep.

Suzie spoke, "Is everything all right?"

Madeline was embarrassed at her weakness. She lowered her head and wiped her eyes. In a meek voice she offered, "Sometimes life brings us strange circumstances."

Suzie was drawn to this woman's eyes. She extended her hand. "I believe we have met?"

"Yes, at the café. My name is Madeline Crory. You signed my book on Friday."

"I remember you."

Madeline's heart jumped. Charlotte's warnings echoed in her ears. The silence hung like a heavy weight.

Finally, she offered, "Were you writing, Suzie?"

"No. I was painting or at least trying."

"What were you painting?"

"I started to paint Goldie Bell," she motioned toward the statue, "but, I had an…" Her voice dropped suddenly. Her mind replayed the experience. Feeling uncomfortable she added, "…interruption."

"I see," Madeline's tone begged for more.

"Maybe you can help me."

"I'll sure try," Madeline replied. "What can I do?"

"Well," Suzie began, "I have been to this cemetery several times looking for someone and I can't find her."

Madeline's voice inside her head screamed, 'I was right! She was looking for Charlotte!'

"I'm a bit confused, though," Suzie paused.

Madeline jumped at the chance to speak. "Confused about what?"

Suzie motioned toward Charlotte's headstone. "That." Suzie pointed, "That headstone was not here before."

"You are absolutely correct," Madeline stated calmly. "Last month, this cemetery suffered quite a loss. Forty some headstones were destroyed or vandalized beyond moderate repair. It was an act of utmost disrespect if you ask me. The police are still investigating the responsible parties. They stole a few cast iron planters too, although most of them have been recovered. Mostly teenagers were responsible, but not all of them have been charged." Madeline's excitement was difficult to contain as she continued, "I had that headstone replaced yesterday." She drew in a deep breath and studied Suzie's reaction. "It belongs to my sister, Charlotte Riley-Fischall. She has been gone ten years now."

Suzie was stunned. She couldn't believe her ears. Not only did she finally find her mother's headstone, but also the woman telling her the news was her aunt. She couldn't find the words. Her hands felt numb. Her feet felt frozen to the ground. A rush of cold nerves ran through her body leaving her limp and helpless. She heard this woman speak, but could not comprehend what she said. She had finally found her mother and oddly enough, her aunt.

She stared at the name on the headstone. Her mouth moved, but no voice was heard. Her mind shouted unanswered questions. Each one fought for attention drowning out the one prior. Why did you give me up? Who is my father? Why didn't you want me? What did I do wrong? How could you give up the very child you created? What did my father say? Didn't he want me either? Did you ever look into my eyes? Did you see me the day I was born? Did you think of me on my first birthday? How about love? Did you ever feel any love toward me? Why did you give me up? Did you think I was a bother? What could possibly have been going on in your life for you not to want me? Did I embarrass you? Did you ever see me? Why did you not try to contact me? Did you think I would just fade from your memory? Did pretending make the emptiness go away? Did I ever cross your mind? Did you ever consider my feelings, how I would feel or were you too wrapped up in yourself to think of me? Why…mother, why? How could you…?

Suzie held her hands over her ears and clenched her teeth. Her emotions rolled from pity to frustration to emptiness. She wanted answers. This dead woman owed her that!

No answers came, only screaming accusations from deep within her. She doubled over from pain.

Madeline felt helpless. She placed her hand on Suzie's shoulders, but she couldn't find any words. Tears blurred her vision.

Suzie fought to silence the questions. She thought finding her mother's grave would bring closure, but instead it brought feelings she had never explored. She moved her hands from her ears to her stomach. Suddenly, her hands plunged to the ground to stop her from toppling over. She covered her mouth and tried to stand. The nauseating feeling subsided and the questions dimmed. She fought to make peace with this woman. She was not the first child given up for adoption, nor the last. Life is not fair. No one ever promised that. She permitted herself to feel pity, but forced out the anger.

Suzie wiped her face. She looked at this kind woman who stood beside her and finally it all made sense - why this woman seemed familiar, her words at the book signing, and the warmth in her eyes.

She choked on her words. "I can't believe it! Did you say Charlotte Riley-Fischall?"

"Yes, Suzie, this is your mother's grave. You've found it at last." Madeline took her by the hand and walked her closer to the headstone.

The fact that Suzie stood before her mother's grave was surreal and overwhelming. She resisted the urge to pinch herself.

Cast in several colors, the headstone was a beautiful work of art. The urn's flowers looked like a Williamsburg print. The leaves were tinted a pale green. The flowers were various shades of pink, peach, and yellow. The urn had a band of ivy that trailed around its base. The letters written in Olde English script read:

Charlotte Riley-Fischall
Born February 13, 1941
Died April 9, 1994
May the flowers above,
Show her strength and beauty within.

Below the script two hands clasped a molded stone vase.

Puzzled, Suzie looked at Madeline. "Charlotte loved flowers. She knew the names, common and genus, of many flowers. She quoted them with great pride. Fewer things brought her as much joy." Madeline's words were automatic, as if she'd given this speech multiple times.

"She had a great love for nature," she continued. "The vase is for any passers-by who wish to share a memory with Charlotte."

She turned to Suzie. Tears swelled in her eyes. Emotion returned to her voice.

"For whatever series of events that have been set in motion that we should be here together on this day, it only seems fitting that you should place the first flowers on your mother's new headstone. Your place has been set." Madeline finished her speech with a snap.

Suzie spent a lot of time after her divorce in search of direction. She gained satisfaction and peace in painting as well as writing. She loved living in New England, but it never felt like 'home' to her. Hearing Madeline say that 'her place was set' had a calming effect. She felt a sense of purpose here and made a conscious decision to embrace this town.

"I'll need some flowers." She held open her empty hands.

"My dear," Madeline said with a smile, "The Flower Loft is at the southern entrance of the cemetery."

Suzie glanced toward the building, but her eyes settled on a large patch of daffodils at the top of the next knoll. "I have a better idea," she said with conviction. "Wait here, I'll be right back."

She watched Suzie walk to her car, and for a moment she panicked. Her heart screamed forty years of pent up emotions but her mind kept her silent. She opened the passenger side door and picked up a bottle of water.

Suzie walked toward a large patch of daffodils and picked a few. Bringing the flowers to her nose, she bent down to pick one more. Her hand reached out to steady herself on the headstone in front of her.

Madeline wished she had her camera. Suzie was kneeling in the midst of a large daffodil patch as she picked flowers for Charlotte. Suzie's movement froze. Her hands slid down the front of the cross. Her face landed in the patch of daffodils. Instinctively, Madeline ran towards her.

Suzie walked to the patch of flowers that encircled the cross. She remembered this headstone from a few days prior, but hadn't noticed the daffodils before. When she walked closer, she noticed petite volunteers of forget-me-nots bloomed in their midst.

"What a beautiful paint palette!" Suzie exclaimed. She admired the blend of color and leaf.

She picked four daffodils and arranged them in her hand. She brought them to her nose. "One more ought to do it." When she bent down to pick the last one, she lost her balance and leaned on the cross to steady her. The moment her fingers touched the cross, her surroundings changed.

The weather was damp and cold. The sky grew dark as many tombstones vanished from sight. In the distance she heard the same murmurings as before though now they were mixed with the laughter of a young girl. She found herself staring into the likeness fused on porcelain. It was oval in shape and showed the image of a handsome young man. He had wavy dark hair, a lean face, high cheekbones and determined dark eyes. Though in the picture he was not smiling, his eyes exuded happiness. Suzie looked closer and studied his face. She was certain this was he.

Her heart raced as if she finished a marathon. She felt her hands slide down the face of the cross, but before she hit the ground, gentle arms lifted her. When she opened her eyes, his face was clear.

It was the image on the headstone, the old porcelain photograph forever bound to granite. It was also the same face she saw in her dream, and again in the Wandering Cheshire. He smiled as he looked at her. She heard his voice, though his lips never parted.

"Suzie, I have been waiting for you." She closed her eyes in disbelief.

When Suzie opened her eyes, it was Madeline's face she saw. Her voice was tight with concern, "Suzie, are you okay?" She had grabbed the water bottle and gently patted the cool water on Suzie's face.

Suzie felt strange. Her movement was strained and unsteady. She felt narrowly stretched between two worlds. She rotated her head in small circles.

"I'm fine, Madeline. Really I am," she tried to convince her aunt as well as herself.

The grey world faded from view. Color returned to her surroundings. The sky glistened cerulean blue. The memorial garden at her feet popped with vibrant yellow and ice blue.

Suzie tried to shake the feeling of distance, but her ears held the remote murmuring. They spoke in hushed voices without audible words. A damp breeze blew across her face. Suzie pulled her collar to block its path. Her hands trembled. The lifeless daffodils tumbled from her hands.

Concern filled Madeline's eyes. "Suzie, you're trembling. Come to my house. I'll fix you a warm cup of tea."

Suzie smiled and said, "That sounds perfect."

Madeline stood and helped Suzie to her feet. They walked together toward Madeline's car.

"Do you live close?"

"Straight down this road."

"Then I will be fine. I'll follow you." Her voice was insistent.

Madeline felt as if Charlotte was standing before her so she lowered her head and said, "If you are sure you feel up to it."

"Truly, I'm fine." Suzie turned to Madeline and said, "I haven't put the flowers in Charlotte's...my mother's vase."

Before Madeline could speak, Suzie turned and marched toward the cross. Madeline watched her take a few steps, then decided to follow. She heard Suzie mumbling to herself but couldn't make out the words.

Suzie, filled with trepidation, approached the cross. Once again, she knelt and picked a few more flowers. She stared at the gentle image of the young man. The portrait was crushed. His mouth slid from view and was reduced to powder on the ground.

With the five daffodils arranged in her hand, she turned toward her mother's grave. With her first step the voices returned. A feminine voice calling 'Elam' entwined with the masculine reply, 'Rebecca' echoed in the wind.

Sadness filled the cemetery, moving Suzie to tears. The hushed expressions moved farther away from each other until they were gone. The only sound was the empty wind.

In the distance, Madeline motioned to Suzie. She stood before Charlotte's headstone. Suzie poured the water from her bottle into the stone vase and placed the bouquet in it. She turned to Madeline who was weeping.

Suzie moved to comfort her. Madeline's shoulders quivered. Suzie guessed it had been a while since Madeline permitted a release of these feelings.

After a deep breath Madeline admitted, "Suzie, I am so glad you are here." Her voice resonated desperation. "I have so much to share with you. I wanted to search for you for years, but Charlotte said we were bound by the promise we made to your adoptive parents. Bill and Rose were so kind. I secretly kept in contact with them. Charlotte never knew. She would have disapproved. I promised Bill, and Rose, that I would not make myself known to you. They knew you questioned your past, but felt it was up to you to make the first move."

Madeline sighed, "As the years passed, the desire became stronger. After Charlotte's death, I thought about you constantly. Even though we never officially met, I felt a deep connection."

Suzie understood. She felt it too, only it didn't make sense until now. Somehow it seemed fitting for this conversation to occur at Charlotte's gravesite.

Suzie took Madeline's hand and said, "When I met you at the café, I knew we were connected. It is difficult to explain, but I have a gift." Suzie's words were thick in her throat. She smiled. "Let's go have that tea. I'd like to hear more about you and my mother. Maybe see some pictures?"

Madeline's face lit, "Oh, I have many pictures. Some will be very special to you."

"Okay then, I'll follow you."

Excited and relieved, Suzie watched Madeline walk to her vehicle. When she climbed into her car to follow Madeline, she looked back toward the ivy cross. There he stood with his black coat tossed in the breeze. He held his hat in his hands. With his face revealed, his eyes held hers. Suzie heard his voice.

Suzie smiled. He nodded his head. Suzie turned to follow Madeline, to finally have her questions answered. She drove away from him. He stood. Still. Alone. Pleading for her return. In the wind, he called her name.

12

Patrick felt like a coward. Why did he leave Madeline? He tried to distinguish which feeling was stronger -- his love for Attie or his hatred for Charlotte. He imagined his wounds torn open as Charlotte filled them with salt. He was determined the dead would no longer dilute him.

His thoughts returned to the day he left the driveway on South Lincoln. It was the last time he saw Attie. His heart was burdened, but he kept his promise through his pain. At least, he held honor in that.

He remembered gathering the letter from the bushes and walking toward the car. He heard Attie rush out of the door to Charlotte's aid, but he never turned around. His throat was dry. Tears masked his eyes.

He got into his car, put the key in the ignition, and backed out of the drive. As he waited for traffic to clear, he watched Attie run to her sister. Charlotte glared at him until he pulled out. Attie never looked his way. Charlotte tossed her hands in the air as Attie helped her to a chair. He had no doubt that Charlotte was spinning a tale that Patrick could not disprove, especially from a distance.

He drove downtown and stopped at the first bank. He knew if he tried to mail the letter, Charlotte would intercept it. Her control over Attie was too thorough to let something slip through. If only he had mailed it prior to his visit, maybe it would have been undetected.

"Too late to think `bout that now. The damage is done. I must think `bout the next step," he said to himself as he closed the car door.

He pulled a large manila envelope from the back seat. Patting his front pocket for the letter, he walked into the bank. His vision was blurred.

One of the tellers greeted him cheerfully, "May I help you?"

"I need a safe deposit box," Patrick responded mechanically.

"Right this way, sir." She led him to another woman sitting behind a desk. "Debby, this gentleman would like a safe deposit box." She turned to Patrick and said, "She'll take care of that for you. Have a good day."

The woman motioned for him to have a seat. After gathering his information and checking identification, the transaction was complete. She led him to a small room to the left of the large safe.

After she put her key in, she turned to him, "Just place your key in here."

She turned both keys and pulled a long, metal box from its place. She turned to Patrick and asked, "Would you like some privacy?" Patrick nodded and she led him to a narrow room behind them, turned on the light, and left him alone with the long box sitting on a metal table. "I'll be waiting outside of the door. Take as long as you need," she stated automatically as she closed the door.

The fluorescent tubes hummed as Patrick stared into the empty box. He pulled the letter from his suit pocket and ran his hands over it as he placed it on the table. Slowly, he opened it and pulled the contents from within. It was full of photographs - pictures of Attie in the hospital, Patrick in his scrubs, along with pictures of them together. Some were taken in the hospital but the majority was from their daily walks.

One of the city's public parks was within walking distance of the hospital. Patrick and Attie had spent many hours there. They had long picnic lunches and even longer talks. Often Patrick massaged Attie's neck to relax the muscles from the morning's therapy. However, the thing Attie seemed to enjoy the most was pushing children on the swing set. Attie's love for children was obvious. It was in the park that Patrick confessed his feelings for her, and where Attie first spoke the words 'I love you'.

Patrick was overwhelmed with emotion as he savored the images in his hands. His eyes burned from the tears, but this time he let them come. Alone, in a strange place, he placed the photographs, one by one, in the bottom of the safe deposit box. He heard the whispers of 'Good bye' transform into an unbearable weight.

He placed the letter he had written on the top of the photographs. He moved one of the images to plain view. It was a picture of Attie sitting on a swing, her dress blowing in the wind. She was looking at Patrick, a loving smile on her face. Patrick remembered this day well.

He lifted the photograph from the box, caressed it with his fingers, and placed it in his front pocket. With tears dripping from his face, he removed a piece of paper from his suit. He began to write:

My dearest Attie,

Words cannot express the feelings I have for you. I have driven from Phoenix to see you, but Charlotte has prevented it. Contained in this box are some memories from the past I want to share with you. I wish I could be with you when you peruse them. Please call me if you would like to see me. I'll be waiting by the phone.

My love always,
Patrick

Patrick placed his business card inside the letter. He closed the lid of the box and carried it to the door. Debby was standing outside of the door just as she promised. She smiled but spoke not a word. His anguish must have been obvious. He placed the safe deposit box in its rightful place. As she handed his key to him, she opened her mouth to speak, but nothing came out. She nodded her head and they walked out in silence.

When Debby walked back to her desk, she gathered the papers to place in Patrick's file. She stared at the name Madeline Patricia Crory on the signature card. She penned the words 'verification signature to follow.' She placed the second key in his hand, as per his request. As his car left the parking lot, she silently wished him peace.

Patrick had little memory of the return drive to Phoenix. It was hard to imagine that just a few hours before he was filled with excitement and hope. He used his necktie as a handkerchief and by the time he arrived to Phoenix the colors had faded onto his white shirt.

He forced himself to return to normal. He saw his friend, Isaac, the following day. Isaac did not need to ask to know that Patrick's visit had not gone as planned.

It was Joanne, Isaac's wife, who pulled the story from Patrick a few weeks later. They invited Patrick for a barbeque, but before Patrick arrived Isaac was called to the hospital for an emergency. She listened to the sordid details of Patrick's trip. He pulled the photograph from his pocket and handed it to her. They sat in silence for thirty minutes. Later, Joanne sobbed as she replayed the tale to Isaac, who, knowing his friend, never mentioned it to him.

The next few years passed slowly. Patrick returned from work each evening, praying that the phone would ring. He threw himself into his patients' care. Many said he spent his life covering his pain by relieving others. His patients described him as the doctor with smiling eyes and strong faith, but Isaac and Joanne shared his pain as each day passed with the silent telephone.

13

As Madeline and Suzie pulled into the drive, Suzie gasped at the beauty of the historic house. The back hall opened into a butler's pantry. The room was modest in size, but not in beauty. Open hickory shelves loaded with cookbooks, a collection of herb choppers, mortise and pestles, butter molds, tobacco cutters, silver serving pieces, tea pots, cups and saucers covered the walls. The collection was better than an antique shop. Madeline grinned as she watched Suzie's eyes drink in every detail. It had been a while since she looked at this house through fresh eyes.

"Charlotte was a big antique collector. She had a difficult time getting out to the different shops, so the antique dealers would make house calls. She built a reputation with several dealers as having such exquisite taste that once she started on a particular collection, they practically fell over each other to bring their best for her to view." Madeline laughed at the memories. "And hopefully buy," she added through her laughter. "Come, let me take you through the rest of the house."

The butler's pantry led to a large kitchen. Madeline explained that Charlotte and Grant expanded the kitchen by incorporating it with the rear smoking room. They decided the room would be better served as a larger kitchen than for smoking meats.

The doorway on the north side of the kitchen led to a small receiving room. Suzie noticed one of her paintings that hung on the wall. A chill slithered down her spine. She stopped but Madeline had disappeared around the corner. She followed her to the dining room. Madeline shared all the stories this room had to offer. When Madeline turned around, she noticed Suzie's face.

"Oh, my goodness," she said, "I've forgotten to put on the tea!" She disappeared to the kitchen. Suzie returned to her 'Lunar Dream'.

Madeline stood beside her. "I bought your best of show that year in Rockport." Suzie's eyes begged for details. Madeline continued, "I just missed you. You had an emergency meeting."

"Yes, I remember. I had to meet my publisher," she said. "Claire told me about you. I missed you by a few minutes."

"I took one of those bus tours, and the driver sounded the horn for everyone to return."

"You paid extra for the painting." Suzie said in disbelief.

"Suzie, your parents and I kept in regular contact. I promised not to make myself known, but I must confess there were many times that I saw you from a distance, in a photograph, or your picture in the newspaper." Madeline lowered her head. "Your father sent them to me. He was a bit more receptive than your mother was. I guess I can't blame her for hesitating. After many years, though, your mother felt less threatened."

"Did they know Charlotte?"

"No. Charlotte had no idea I corresponded with them. Your father sent everything in his company's investment envelopes. I lied to Charlotte and told her I opened an account with his firm." Smiling from her cleverness to elude her suspicious sister, she added, "But it wasn't long before I actually did invest money with him. He guided me well."

"He is a great man. I'm sure you know then that Mom died of cancer two years ago."

"Yes, I'm sorry. I know it was rough for both of you."

"Dad's strong, but he needs a companion." Suzie said softly, "He deserves that."

"How about you, Suzie? Are you involved with anyone?"

Suzie laughed, "Heavens no. I don't have time. I guess I'm a little afraid," she admitted. "I don't want another bad experience."

"You'll do fine. Just keep yourself open to the possibilities." Madeline offered, "Now, come with me for some tea and photos."

The teakettle whistled as they walked into the kitchen. Madeline poured two cups and set the black tea in front of Suzie without asking how she liked it. Suzie guessed Madeline knew a lot more than she told.

They drank their tea and laughed at stories about Charlotte. Although Suzie felt that she was getting a better picture of her mother, the details were still fuzzy. After Madeline shared the tales of Grant, Kenneth, the accident, social committees, her gardens, and her obsession with fine antiques, Suzie grew quiet.

"Are you okay, Suzie?"

After a long pause, she answered, "Yes, I have so many questions."

"Then ask away. My life...our lives are open to you." Madeline sighed. "Do you have any idea how long I have wanted to hear you say those very words?"

"See, that's just it," Suzie said. "Why you and not my mother?"

The words cut deep and Madeline stiffened.

"I didn't mean that," Suzie said, seeing Madeline's discomfort. "Please hear me. It is an honor to have your aunt so concerned about you, to follow your life, to cry with you when you don't even know it, to know how you take your tea without asking..." Madeline blushed as Suzie continued, "I just don't understand why you cared so much, and my mother so little."

"Suzie, there is much about your mother you do not know. You were born when she was nineteen. She never spoke of your father. Adoption was the only answer. We were alone, our parents died in a private plane crash, and the only answer was to create distance. There were few people who knew of you. She was still hospitalized from the accident when you were born. The doctors were bound by doctor-patient privilege so her secret was safe." Madeline sighed, "I didn't even know of you. I never saw you. The only thing I saw was this." She picked an envelope from the box of photographs and carefully pulled the photograph from inside. She handed the worn photo to Suzie. "This was your hospital picture. I stole it. It was clipped to your information from the adoption agency. That is where I found your mother and father's name and address. No one knew I took the picture."

Suzie said, "Do you know who my father is?"

"No. Charlotte never spoke of him -- and I never asked. It was as if she didn't talk about it, she could convince herself it never happened."

"The adoption papers said 'father unknown'." They were both silent.

"Would you like more tea?" was all Madeline could think to ask.

Suzie shook her head no. "Charlotte…" she scoffed, "I have to quit calling her that. She was my mother, my birth mother -- and I'll never get the chance to meet her." Suzie's eyes filled with tears. She quickly wiped them away and turned to Madeline, "Are you hungry? I'm starving!"

Madeline jumped up from the table as if on autopilot. She opened the refrigerator and started to gather some vegetables.

Suzie laughed as she came up behind her, "I didn't mean for you to cook. Let's go to a restaurant."

"That sounds wonderful." Madeline relaxed her shoulders.

"Any suggestions? Someplace quiet, so we can talk."

"Hmm…" Madeline was running through all the local places in her mind.

Suzie blurted out, "How about The Spread Eagle Tavern in Hanoverton?"

"Oh, that sounds wonderful!"

"I'll call and tell them we're on our way." Madeline looked at her puzzled.

Suzie chuckled. "That's where I have been staying."

"Somehow that doesn't surprise me."

They made arrangements to meet at the inn in two hours. Suzie explained that she had worked late the night before and slept in a little so she hadn't showered yet. She wanted to feel refreshed so she could enjoy the evening with her aunt. Madeline agreed, although she was hesitant to let her go.

Madeline watched Suzie pull out of the drive. Suzie waved and blew her a kiss. She mouthed the words, "See you in a bit," and rushed down the street.

Madeline was eager to spend more time with Suzie. She drew a hot bath and as she undressed, she heard something fall to the floor. She gathered her clothes from a bundle. Alone on the floor was a brass key.

14

Patrick arrived at his home on Third Street without recalling the drive. Memories of years past consumed him. He had thought about Attie his entire adult life and remained hopeful she would remember him. Despite her reaction today, he was encouraged.

When Attie sustained her injuries, she had a long road to recovery. Her memory of current events vanished and she lived her life as if she was alone. Her relationship with her sister was non-existent. They suffered many horrible arguments.

Charlotte was paralyzed at the waist. The tree crushed her legs, hips, and pelvis. The damage to her right leg was more severe than the left, but neither had signs of movement or feeling. The doctors gave up hope long before Charlotte did. The severity of her pain altered her personality. The inability to control her sister made her hateful. The nursing staff struggled to keep her comfortable, but it was impossible to make her happy.

Attie, on the other hand, was carefree yet extremely emotional. Although she refused to visit her sister,

Charlotte's insistent pleading wore on the staff and they finally wheeled Charlotte to Madeline's room.

Attie screamed at the nurses to remove this evil woman. Only Patrick McCelvy could calm her. They formed a fast friendship. She trusted him. Madeline listened when he tried to explain her medical condition, and never questioned his judgment.

"I know you 'ave no memories of things past," he said to her, "but your memory will return."

He caressed her hands when he visited her bedside. The staff whispered about their relationship, but Patrick dismissed it as 'his job'.

After several months, her strength returned. She gave in to Patrick's insistence and visited her sister. Within a few minutes, they argued and Attie vowed not to lay eyes on that dreadful person again.

Charlotte blamed Attie and could not hide her hatred. She worried that her sister's memory would never return. She needed Attie to take care of her so she changed her personality overnight. The staff commented immediately about the transformation. Charlotte was surprised how quickly she fooled everyone and decided to use this new approach to achieve what she wanted.

The results for Charlotte were tri-fold. Her health improved dramatically. The doctors were willing to try alternative treatments. Once she developed a slight movement in her left leg, she gained strength - and her relationship with Attie changed drastically. Attie became her cheerleader and Charlotte regained the much-needed control. Although Attie's memory had not yet returned, she accepted Charlotte as her sister and did her best to improve the relationship. Finally, Charlotte began a relationship with a young man she met in the hospital while he visited his dying mother. His name was Grant Arthur Riley.

Grant and Charlotte were attracted to each other before words were ever spoken. He was the catalyst to Charlotte's changed attitude. He became her coach long before he convinced Attie to join the effort. Their relationship progressed rapidly. It wasn't long before Grant spent more time with Charlotte than with his mother.

Charlotte had perfected her 'sweet act' when Grant took her to visit his mother. Charlotte and Vera made fast friends.

Vera was a pleasant woman even in poor health. She was kind, thoughtful and barely weighed ninety pounds. She had taken good care of her son after becoming a war widow. The pair were inseparable until Grant met Charlotte. Unlike most women in that situation, Vera didn't mind. She was very vocal about her approval of Charlotte and felt peace in knowing her son would not be alone.

When Vera died, it was Charlotte's first outing from the hospital. The doctors advised against it, but through Patrick's insistence they permitted her leave. Patrick volunteered to take Charlotte and Attie to the funeral. Grant was eternally grateful.

The day was as normal as it could be with Charlotte in a wheel chair and Attie clinging to Patrick's arm. The four of them rode to the cemetery in the hearse. As they passed their parents' home, Attie said, "Charlotte, there's our house." The car fell silent and all held their breath.

Finally, Charlotte spoke, "Yes, Attie. That was Mom and Dad's house -- and now it's ours." For a fleeting moment, there was hope, but as quickly as the words were spoken, the dream faded. Attie's response was, "I don't live in that house."

A blanket of silence covered them. Patrick was the only one who remained hopeful. He knew how long it might take.

Charlotte's recovery moved forward quickly with Grant's constant presence. His encouragement, surrounded by love, was the perfect dose of medicine. Within two months of her final surgery, Charlotte took her first step. She spent many excruciating hours in therapy. Grant helped ease the cramps by massaging her legs, and singing softly to Charlotte. He had a beautiful tenor voice and she loved how it soothed her.

Charlotte complained constantly about the 'special treatment' her sister received with Patrick's supervised walks. The staff soon tired of her requests. After three months, the doctor's finally granted her a short leave. Their first outing happened in early May.

Grant spent much time preparing for this moment. Before Vera died, she coached Grant on the responsibilities of love. She had only been married four years herself before becoming widowed, but their relationship was strong. She felt she had a good basis to teach. Three days before she died Grant showed his mother the engagement ring. She was relieved that Grant had fallen in love and proud of the man he had become. She passed away in peace.

The day of their outing Charlotte was so anxious sleep eluded her. Even after the night nurse gave her a sedative, she woke alert and ready to go. The nurse helped her slip into a spring dress that she had delivered from home. It was a little loose from the weight she had lost, but she didn't care. She was looking forward to spending some time alone with Grant. She was dressed and waiting in her wheelchair by the door. Grant arrived at precisely 9:30 a.m.

He helped her into the car as Attie and Patrick watched from her room. Attie was as jittery as her sister. Charlotte waved to them as they pulled away from the hospital. Attie turned to Patrick in celebration and threw her arms around his neck. She kissed him on his cheek and twirled around the room. It was at that moment Patrick realized how deep his feelings were. He had fallen in love with her carefree attitude and uninhibited beauty.

Grant drove down the street as Charlotte chattered like a woman who was without a voice for a year. He laughed as she tried to make light of her flightiness, but it didn't matter.

He loved Charlotte and confessed to his mother that he was prepared to care for her the rest of his life. Vera approved of his nobleness. He pulled into the drive of a strange house. It was a beautiful historic home on South Lincoln Avenue. Charlotte questioned him as he helped her from the car. In silence, he led her up the front sidewalk, picked her up, and carried her into the house.

Charlotte was overwhelmed by the fragrance of flowers in the front receiving room. There were twelve vases placed around the room, each with its own unique bouquet of lilies, daffodils, hyacinths, iris, lilacs, and hellebores. The number twelve signified the number of months they were together. The room was void of furniture except for an antique marble top table and a parlor settee. She turned to Grant with tears. He motioned to the settee.

He dropped her hand and stepped to the edge of the settee. She moved her right foot and then her left. Her eyes were fixed on Grant. He stood with his hand outstretched.

The six steps that Charlotte took were symbolic in many ways. It showed Charlotte's determination, Grant's submission which allowed Charlotte to be her own person, and Charlotte's willingness to follow Grant's advice. Charlotte was committed to finish the walk as well as her charade.

When her fingers met Grant's, he said, "I am so proud of the woman you have become. You overcame monumental odds to be standing where you are today."

Charlotte laughed a nervous laugh as Grant continued his rehearsed speech.

"I have fallen in love with you, Charlotte. You make me the man I have always wanted to be. I know your level of recovery is uncertain, but it does not matter to me. I want to spend the rest of my life with you. I want to take care of you."

He knelt to one knee and pulled a small velvet box from his pocket. He looked deep into Charlotte's eyes. For a moment he thought he saw a glimpse of a veiled heart. He blinked and dismissed it as pain. He motioned for her to sit on the settee.

He continued, "Charlotte, will you marry me?"

Charlotte sat motionless. She suppressed the laughter of success and allowed only a thin smile to grace her lips.

She spoke softly, "My dear Grant, of course I will marry you."

Grant rushed to his feet and kissed her passionately. He placed the ring on her finger and smiled. Charlotte summoned tears to cover her flushed cheeks.

He stood and waved his hands in the air. "This, Charlotte, will be our home." Her mouth dropped open. "Walk with me. I will show you the rest."

Charlotte's first few steps were unsteady. She gripped Grant's arm tightly with both hands. He gently led her from room to room.

"Take your time, Charlotte. We have all day to see our new home."

They walked from the receiving room, down the hall to the library, dining room, kitchen, and butler's pantry. Grant picked her up and carried her outside where a wheel chair sat by the back door. He wheeled her around the back yard as Charlotte's excitement elevated. The garden had good basics but had been neglected for years. She asked Grant for a piece of paper and pencil to sketch a few ideas.

They sat in the sunshine and shared visions of the finished courtyard garden. Grant listened as Charlotte described her plan of action. He needed to keep her focused on the positive.

When Charlotte finished her last, "Oh, and let's do..." Grant asked her if she wanted to see the rest of the house. With new strength, Charlotte insisted she take the steps to the backdoor alone. Grant unwillingly agreed and watched nervously. He stayed within reach. She winced just a bit, but when she reached the top, she turned and smiled at Grant. Her face glowed with pride.

They walked inside to the front staircase where Grant insisted that he should carry her. She peered up the seventeen steps to the second floor. It looked like a daunting task so Charlotte quickly agreed.

"It doesn't look like the three steps from the back door," Charlotte laughed nervously as Grant carried her like a queen.

Grant gently placed her on her feet at the top of the stairs. She placed her hand on the curved cherry rail and followed its lead. She took his hand as they walked into the guest bedroom. The room was empty.

"It's the largest of the guest rooms." Grant swept his hands through the air. "Mother's bedroom suit is so large, I thought this would be the proper placement." He looked at Charlotte sheepishly, "That is, if you agree."

"That would be perfect. Vera would have loved this bright room. Let's paint it her favorite color."

"Yellow?" He crinkled his nose.

"Grant there are many shades of yellow." Charlotte mocked, "It doesn't have to be daffodil bright!"

They walked with their arms interlocked to the second, smaller guest bedroom. The room smelled of sawdust. Large holes were visible in the plaster.

"I had a contractor divide this area to accommodate an additional bathroom. It made this room a bit smaller, but I think the convenience of having its own bath was worth the sacrifice." Charlotte nodded in agreement.

They progressed down the hall. He showed her the main bathroom. It was in need of repair, but Grant quickly defended his intentions by saying the contractor was going to update the bath as well. They stopped in front of a Dutch door. Grant opened it slowly. It was his favorite room upstairs.

"And this room," Grant announced, "is the maid's quarters." He helped Charlotte walk down the two steps at the entrance.

"Here is the back staircase which comes down to the first floor between the kitchen and the butler's pantry."

Charlotte peered down the narrow flight of stairs. There was a beautiful stair runner running down the middle of the steps with polished brass carpet rods securing the runner. In the corner of each stair were brass dust shields.

"This room is beautiful!" exclaimed Charlotte. "Did you have this redone?"

"Yes," replied Grant. "This room was in horrible shape. The roof leaked for many years. Once that was fixed, the rest was cosmetic. I had the contractor add window seats under the twin windows and build the flanking bookshelves. I also had him build a surround for the staircase." He held his hand across the opening and grinned. "He is going to build a gate for here."

Charlotte looked at him puzzled, "Oh?"

"I thought we could use this room as the children's play room and I wanted it to be safe." He turned to Charlotte and held her hands to his chest and pulled her close to him. "Charlotte, you do want children, don't you?"

The words, "Of course," came quickly from Charlotte's mouth. She shuddered in spite of herself.

Charlotte hated children. She wished she had been an only child. She desired her parents' undivided attention.

Although it was never said, she knew her father favored Madeline. Charlotte held a deep resentment toward her for that. If her mother had a favorite, she had never shown it. As much as Charlotte hated to admit it, she admired her mother for that.

Charlotte carried much resentment and baggage from her past, the majority was self-inflicted, but it crippled her mentally. Compound that with her recent physical inabilities, and she was doomed except she had perfected the art of manipulation.

"Three would be the perfect number," Charlotte spoke with the sugared words dripping from her lips.

Grant took the bait. "That would be perfect."

He led her to the final room. He longed for her reaction for weeks. "Close your eyes."

"But...."

"Trust me, Charlotte."

He picked her up and carried her through the doorway of the master bedroom. She smelled the pungent fragrance of the flowers before she opened her eyes. She knew this was the master bedroom and she shuddered at the thought of the room's requirements.

Grant delicately lowered her until her feet touched the floor. "Open your eyes, Charlotte."

The room was decorated with a floral fabric, which matched the duvet cover. The bed was an antique mahogany four-poster bed. It was filled with throw pillows each complementing the decorator fabric. Two wing back chairs faced each other in one corner. In front of a fireplace was a chessboard ready for play. Vases of exotic flowers filled the room.

"Grant," Charlotte said as she turned toward him and took his hands in hers, "This is absolutely breath-taking. Your attention to detail has left me speechless."

She leaned into him and kissed him. He held her tight to him. His passion for her was obvious. Charlotte decided to take control of the situation. She took his hands and moved them down her body. She moaned as he caressed her. She kissed him with passion that was undiscovered until that moment.

Her hands fumbled with the buttons on his shirt. The look of longing on Grant's face was unmistakable. His eyes moved with fire. His hands hung limply at his sides. When she opened his shirt, she ran her fingers over his bare skin. She could feel his arousal and enjoyed the control. She took his hand and led him to the bed.

He positioned her on the rose petals that he had sprinkled on the duvet cover. His hands moved over her body. He felt the softness of her dress's fabric, the playfulness of each toe, the smoothness of her legs, the warmth of her breath, the desire of her tongue, and the invited touch of her breasts. He slowly moved his hands over her soft skin. Her hands met his. She helped him open the buttons on the front of her dress and encouraged him to touch her again. His eyes were transfixed as she leaned into him and unhooked her bra.

Grant caressed her bare skin. Their lips touched with passion and desire. He moved from the warmth of her lips to her neck and his desire could not be contained.

Her body rose to meet his as he entered her. She whimpered from excitement as his hands memorized every curve of her body. His lips and tongue were warm to the touch and continued to fuel the flame that burned within them.

They moved through the infant stages of making love and taught each other the pleasures of desire. There were no moments of awkwardness, only genuine desire for true satisfaction. He brought Charlotte through two climaxes before reaching his own. They collapsed in each other's arms and slept for nearly an hour.

Charlotte woke first. She was surprised by her contentment and pleased with her assurance of self. She was comfortable in nakedness. She played with his chest hair in hopes of waking him.

"Grant, we must be going," she spoke after a few minutes of unsuccessful toying.

He opened his eyes and smiled at her. He moved her hair from her face and kissed her shoulder. Slowly, he moved down to her body with sweet, passionate kisses. Charlotte surrendered herself to him again without a word. He stimulated her arousal with ease. She responded to his antics and gave in to pleasure, as did he. With their bodies still twitching from delight, they giggled at their indiscretion.

"Grant," Charlotte whispered, "we really must be going. We are an hour past due. The doctors will be worried."

"I don't want to lose this moment."

Charlotte smiled from her success, "My dear Grant, we will always have this moment." She softly kissed him and stood to redress.

Grant raised himself up on his elbow as he watched her button her dress. She bent to pick up his shirt from the floor. The pain was intense. She grabbed her thigh as her body crumpled to the floor.

Grant jumped from the bed. "Oh my God! Are you okay?"

Charlotte gritted her teeth from the pain. The only thought that raised her to her feet was pure hatred for her sister.

"This is all Madeline's fault!"

"Charlotte, we must accept what has been given to us without holding grudges."

"I can't. I hate her!" Her eyes mirrored black.

Grant reeled from her words. His body rejected her. He tore her arms from him.

She tried to gain control and sound convincing. Her thoughts screamed, 'If this plan is going to work…' With every ounce of energy, she smiled and touched Grant's cheek.

"You're right, Grant. It's the pain speaking."

He forced away the negative thoughts and tried to settle his spirit. He took a deep breath.

"Without your accident, we never would have met. Although I wish our circumstances were different, we have to be at peace with our situation."

"I'll just have to be more patient."

"And forgiving," he added.

Charlotte tried to cover her sneer. She repeated his words, "and forgiving." The laughter in her head was magnified through her eyes. She hid it all behind her face.

"Give yourself some time, Charlotte. Your recovery has just begun."

Little did he know how untrue those words were. The only person who truly understood was Charlotte.

15

Suzie burst through the door of the Lincoln Suite. She was excited to spend more time with her aunt. She replayed the conversation again. All of her questions would soon be answered.

She placed her hand under the water faucet. She tapped her foot on the floor waiting for the water to reach her desired temperature. A knock at the door interrupted her.

"Ms. DuVeau..." he stammered, "...Suzie, these just arrived for you."

When Suzie opened the door, William held a large bouquet of daffodils. His smile was wide.

"I wonder who these are from." Suzie toyed.

William handed her a note. "This came with it."

Suzie examined the note. There was no writing on the outside of the envelope.

Slowly she opened the aged paper. The handwriting was fluid and written in pen and ink. It read:

Before mid-day, the eleventh hour with Goldie Bell
Please.

There was something about the word Please that took her breath away. After they both read the note for the second time, Suzie sighed.

William spoke first, "You're not going, are you?"

"Of course." She answered quickly.

"Are you nervous?"

"No."

"Scared?"

"No."

"Worried?"

"No."

"Listening?"

"No," Suzie said laughing.

"Do you want company?"

"Yes." The response came without thought. The moment was awkward. Suzie struggled to regain control. She was in the presence of a man much younger than she, yet she was attracted to him. She hung her head from embarrassment.

"Thank you, William. That is very sweet of you, but I'll be fine." The look on his face made her feel uneasy. "I'll be fine."

When she closed the door, she carried the vase into the bathroom and placed the flowers on the small table. She moved the candle to the sink and lit it. She read the note again. She spoke out loud, "With Goldie Bell, what a strange word choice…With."

As she slid her body into the warm water, she couldn't take her eyes off the bouquet. She thought about the day's events in the cemetery, her vision, her feelings, his smile, the woman, the pink dress, the flowers, and the song of the wood thrush. Although she was confused about their meaning and what it had to do with her, she began to relax.

Her thoughts moved to Madeline. She was a sweet woman, short, petite, brown hair, much different from her birth mother. Her mother was tall and thin in her younger years, but from lack of exercise, had gained much weight over the latter part of her life. Her mother's hair was full, deep auburn with a bit of a wave, the same as Suzie's.

Suzie couldn't imagine Madeline's life. She sacrificed her own life to pay a debt she felt she owed her sister. Little did Suzie know how much Charlotte intimidated and manipulated her sister. Charlotte lived her life through Madeline. Those who knew the Crory sisters pitied Madeline although no one ever dared to mention it. Charlotte's power silenced them.

Her bath water cooled. Suzie grabbed her towel, dressed and walked out of the Lincoln Suite.

Her anticipation grew as she headed for the rathskeller to wait for Madeline's arrival. She bumped into William at the bottom of the first staircase. Her face flushed.

"Still planning a trip tomorrow?"

"Yes, I am." She noticed his tinderbox in his hand. "Are you going to make my fire?'

"I was, unless ..." He waited for her response.

"I'm meeting my aunt for dinner now. We will be a while so if you wouldn't mind maybe wait an hour or so before you come up." Her smile was irresistible.

"Not a problem," he said quickly. He gave her a wink.

Suzie dismissed the flirtatious gesture. She couldn't resist his smile…his lips…his…she jumped to speak, "William?"

He turned to look at her.

"Maybe it would be best if you came to my room last."

His grin spoke volumes and suddenly Suzie was embarrassed. She did her best to cover her thoughts. "I'm not sure how long we will be so...."

"I'll check with your server for the perfect timing." His eyes smiled.

"That would be great. Thank you." She turned to go.

William watched as she bounced down the lower flight of stairs. He waited until she was out of sight and turned to climb the stairs to her room. He pulled the small package and letter from his tinderbox and without hesitation, he opened her door.

Placing his tinderbox on the floor, he scanned the room for the bouquet. He had specific instructions and was well compensated to follow them. He found the vase in the bathroom and moved it to the desk. He placed the box and the letter beside it. He picked up his tinderbox and walked out of the door. The fireplace was still with yesterday's embers faded to grey.

Suzie waited anxiously for her aunt to arrive. She ordered a glass of cabernet from the bar and settled into a chair in the corner. She watched the bartender fill the orders while two waitresses chatted.

"Yes, he did," said the tall, blonde waitress.

"How do you know?" asked the redhead beside her.

"I saw him coming down the stairs. He said he would return later to start her fire."

Suzie listened disinterested, but the last comment caught her attention. She tried to appear inconspicuous as she slid her chair a bit closer to the girls.

"What was he doing?"

"I don't know. He mumbled something about a delivery to one of the rooms."

The redhead laughed, "Oh, please. We all know what he says about her."

Now Suzie was very interested. She knew they were talking about her and enjoyed the fact that they had no idea she was sitting next to them.

"Here you go, Sarah." The bartender slid her tray of drinks to the edge of the bar.

The red-haired girl took the tray and turned to the tall blonde and said, "I know he thinks a lot of her. They have nice conversations when he tends her fire. However, if you ask me, I think he is dreaming. She's got to be old enough to be his mother."

"Sarah, I think you're looking at this all wrong. I don't think he is interested in her. I think he simply enjoys talking to her. He said the man who brings her the flowers gives him the creeps."

"I know. I've seen him too. He's always wearing that old coat and hat. He looks like he bought it at an antique shop." She grinned and added, "He is cute, though. But there is something about his voice that...."

"Your tables are waiting, ladies," said the innkeeper. He turned to Suzie and said, "Ms. DuVeau, your aunt has arrived. I'll take you to her table." He shot a scornful look toward the girls, but they were already blushing.

Suzie smiled and said, "Thank you, David." The waitresses' eyes were wide from discovery.

When she arrived at the table, her aunt was waiting patiently, but the eager look on her face could not be mistaken. David asked Madeline if she wanted something from the bar.

"A glass of wine would be fine. Chardonnay, please."

"Coming right up."

Madeline turned to Suzie, "This place is so accommodating. Everyone seems excited to have you here. I even heard about your secret admirer." She raised an eyebrow, "I thought you said you weren't seeing anyone."

"I'm not!" Suzie said. "I have no idea who this guy is. He brings flowers, daffodils specifically. I've seen him at the cemetery, my art show, and here on the side lawn or thought I did...."

Madeline was concerned. "Suzie, is someone stalking you?"

"No, I don't think it is like that. I think he has something to tell me."

Suzie wanted to open up to her aunt. She wanted to tell her how confused she was, how she was feeling, and how very strange these past few days had been, but she was afraid her aunt would think her crazy. Many people in her past did not understand her gift. They dismissed it as odd, or living out in left field. Suzie decided to take this time to become more acquainted. She wanted to listen, not talk.

Madeline broke her train of thought, "Suzie, is everything alright?"

Suzie smiled at this concerned woman sitting with her and said, "Aunt Madeline, I'm fine. I'm just confused about my connection with this gentleman."

Madeline's heart leapt at the word 'Aunt'. She tried to cover her excitement by changing the subject. "You know, I noticed yesterday that Goldie was holding daffodils in her hands. They looked as if they had just been picked."

"I saw them too. They were just picked."

They directed their smiles at their waitress. She explained the dinner specials and placed Madeline's glass of wine before her. Suzie smiled at the red haired waitress.

"I'll check back with you in a minute to see if you have decided."

"That would be great." Suzie said, "Oh, and Sarah, I'll have another glass of Cabernet."

"My pleasure, Ms. DuVeau." Her cheeks were lit with color.

The pianist's hands moved effortlessly over the baby grand piano. The music mirrored the mood of the crowd. The song choice was light and fluid. It created a colorful backdrop for the evening's conversation.

"Madeline, what happened after the accident?"

"Those months are still unclear to me." Madeline's face became vacant. "Charlotte only shared a few memories of that period of my life. Her answers were brief."

Madeline felt crushed under a weight. Until now, she revealed only a pleasant view of her sister. She shared many memories with Suzie, good memories, and didn't feel the need to reveal Charlotte's hateful side. Suzie would eventually find that truth, but Madeline was determined not to be the means.

After a few minutes Madeline added, "Charlotte told me that we fought a lot. She said my personality changed. I guess I had no memory of our parents or her. This made her angry.

She held me responsible for the accident and it was my fault. I shouldn't have driven that night." Madeline looked away and brushed the tears from her cheeks.

She sighed. "This is not the time to discuss this. It is a sad, irreversible story. One in which I harbor much guilt. This night is to be spent getting better acquainted, not wallowing in the mire."

Suzie smiled at her diplomacy. "I didn't mean to upset you. I just don't understand. I feel you have left out a very important part of the story."

Madeline's face flushed from guilt and exposure. "You are absolutely right, Suzie. I have not told you the whole story because I don't have it either."

Suzie made no attempt to hide her disappointment. "How will we ever know? If mother didn't tell you anything about my father or about the first few months, how will we ever know?" Suzie's voice escalated. It drew the attention of those seated around them.

Madeline became nervous when she recognized a man and woman seated to their left. They were members of the local country club where Charlotte and Kenneth spent much time. Madeline hadn't noticed them until now. She tried to divert the subject. She spent all of her life living in the shadows and did not want to be in the spotlight, especially now in Suzie's company.

"Suzie, I know you are upset, but please, for the sake of Charlotte's privacy, keep your voice low." Suzie looked at her curiously. Her instincts were to glance around, but Madeline stopped her before she had the chance.

"You have to remember that this is a small town. Everyone loves gossip, and the juicier it is, the faster it spreads." Madeline smiled and made a motion to the couple from the country club with her eyes. "Don't look now, but there is a couple to my left who would love to have any morsel of gossip about Charlotte. We are not about to give it to them. Okay?"

Suzie waited long enough and glanced at the couple. The man spoke softly to his wife, but the woman continued to stare. She shook her head repeatedly. She made a motion to stand and her husband grabbed her hand. She shook her hand free and walked toward their table.

Suzie had just enough time to answer, "Okay," before the woman stood at their table.

"Why Madeline Crory, it is so nice to see you out of that big house."

"Hello, Betty. It is nice to see you. Are you and George enjoying your dinner?"

The woman made no attempt to answer Madeline. Her focus was Suzie. "My name is Betty Stillwell -- and you are?"

Suzie was amused at this woman's transparency. 'Town gossip,' she thought. She was aware of Madeline's concern, but she was confident in her approach. She had much practice with people like Betty when she entertained her ex-husband's clients.

Madeline held her breath as Suzie said, "My name is Patricia DuVeau." Suzie extended her hand. "Nice to meet you, Betty."

"How do you know Madeline?"

Madeline's face was white.

Suzie spoke with grace, "Madeline has been a fan for many years. She has purchased several of my paintings, as well as my book."

"Book!" Betty said abruptly, "You are an author?"

"Yes, and an artist."

Madeline took a breath.

Betty continued, "I couldn't help but overhear some of your conversation...."

Suzie cut her off. She had very little tolerance for this type of person. She toyed with Betty, "Well, my mother always said to only believe half of what you see and none of what you hear. Madeline is helping me with my next book." Suzie made a shooing motion with her hand. "Join your husband. He's finished his dinner without you."

Betty's body stiffened. She was still for a moment and then obediently turned to rejoin her husband. He spoke in a gruff voice. She snapped at him. His chair slid across the brick floor. He stood from the table and walked out of the room. Betty sat alone. She flagged the waitress and quickly followed him.

"That was brilliant!" Madeline exclaimed. "I'm sorry I had doubts."

"Do you think I would let her burn my aunt at the stake?" Suzie laughed, "I've had more than my share of people like that in my life. The older I get, the less tolerant I am. I just hope I wasn't too harsh."

"I don't think she will be butting in on another conversation for a while, or at least when she is with George." They both laughed.

Suzie picked up her glass, "To my dear aunt, may we have many wonderful evenings like this." Madeline picked up her wine glass and touched Suzie's.

Madeline spoke first, "It's getting late. I should be going." She paused. "When can I see you again?"

Suzie smiled at her timid aunt. "Tomorrow. I'll stop by your house in the afternoon."

"Great! What time?"

"Well, I have an appointment at eleven o'clock at the cemetery."

Madeline looked at her curiously. Suzie said, "I have quite a story to share with you, but it's too long to begin now."

"Oh?" Madeline begged.

"I promise I'll tell you tomorrow. Maybe I'll have more pieces of the puzzle by then." Suzie stood to leave.

Madeline followed. "Now you really have me curious."

"It has to do with the gentleman who brings the flowers. He requested a meeting tomorrow. Honestly, I can't wait to speak with him." She whispered, "He's been such a mystery."

They walked up the back staircase in silence. The hostess desk was empty. The evening's warmth still filled the cloakroom. Madeline found her wrap and threw it over her shoulders.

Madeline turned to Suzie. "Maybe he's interested in you."

"I don't think it's that. I think he has a message for me. One I haven't been ready to hear…until now."

"Now you're being a mystery."

"Tomorrow. I promise. I'll be there around four."

"That sounds great. Why don't you join me for dinner? I'll cook."

"I would love that."

Madeline gave Suzie a hug. "I'll see you tomorrow at four. We'll dine at 5:30, so if you're running late from your mysterious caller," she winked, "you'll have a little extra time."

Suzie watched her walk to her car. She admired this woman for her strength beneath the timid appearance. She tried to imagine her life as her mother's caretaker. She tried to imagine how they interacted.

"There's got to be more to the story," she said to herself.

Suzie wandered down the hall to the front staircase. She heard loud voices coming from the Barbara Bush room situated to the left of the staircase. Peering into the room, she saw Betty and George finishing their heated argument. She chuckled and walked up the stairs to her room.

When she opened the door, she was disappointed to find that her fire was not lit. She started to close her door when William came running up the staircase.

"I'm sorry. I'm running a little behind," he said.

Suzie shrugged, "That's okay. It happens sometimes."

He arranged the wood and opened his tinderbox. The fire sprung to life within a few strikes of the magnesium block. They watched the fire lick the sides of the logs. Sparks danced in the air like fireflies.

William secured the fire screen. "You're all set." He wondered if she noticed the secret delivery. "Enjoy the fire."

William hesitated at her door for a moment. He opened his mouth to speak but thought better of it. He walked through the doorway without another word. She watched him walk down the hall.

Suzie stared into the fire for a long time. She slid the wingback to the fire and placed her bare toes on the hearth. The warmth was intoxicating. She closed her eyes, leaned her head back, and recalled the day's events. She drifted into slumber without noticing the package or the letter.

Madeline smiled the entire drive home. When she pulled into her drive, the house was dark except for the two lamps on timers, one in Madeline's sitting room, and one in Charlotte's bedroom. For the first time Madeline viewed her home differently. It seemed happy. The lit windows sparkled. The streetlights cast a warm, inviting glow on the house. To Madeline it seemed full of life again.

Her evening with Suzie lifted her spirits. She felt rejuvenated, like a young child full of promise. She chuckled when she thought about the way Suzie orchestrated the scenario with Betty. She hated to admit it, but she took pleasure in watching Betty stumble. She was proud to call Suzie family, yet she was unsure how the community would accept her. The wagging tongues spent much time slinging mud on Charlotte's laundry.

She walked through the house. The photographs were strewn on the table. Madeline placed them back into the memory box. She took a few minutes to look at her favorites.

She held a photograph of her parents, smiled and uttered a quick prayer as she ran her fingertip over their faces. She laughed at the photo of her and Charlotte as small children. Madeline held a toad and Charlotte's nose was crinkled as she stood beside her. She picked up a picture of the family of four dressed in their Easter finest. She noticed it felt thick. She turned the picture over. Taped to the back was a small brown envelope.

Madeline found a brass key wrapped in a piece of paper. The words 'Forgive Me' were written in Charlotte's handwriting. She dropped the key.

"What is this? What have you done now?"

She stared at the key on the table. Her hand trembled as she made a fist around it and walked to her bedroom. She picked up the brass key that Patrick McCelvy had given her earlier.

She tried to make sense of it. She squeezed her eyes tight, afraid to compare the keys. In her mind, she knew they were the same. After a few minutes, she had enough courage to open her eyes and face the truth. She held the keys together to compare the teeth. It was as she expected. They were the same.

"Why, Charlotte? What is in here? What was so secret?" Madeline slammed her fist on her dresser.

16

When Suzie woke she was refreshed from a peaceful night's sleep. She glanced at her timepiece. It was 6:15 a.m. She hopped in the shower. She was ready by 6:55 a.m. She knew breakfast was at least an hour away so she decided to sneak downstairs for a cup of coffee. When she opened her door, the inn was still.

She walked down to the first floor, past the hostess desk, but saw no one. She walked toward the kitchen and peeked in the door. It was dark. She fumbled her way past the sous chef's stainless steel counter, and out the back door. She found no one. She checked her timepiece again: 7:10 a.m.

"Where is everyone?"

The inn was neatly organized after a busy evening. The table and chairs were arranged for breakfast.

Suzie felt peculiar but continued through the rooms. She walked to the top of the staircase and gazed into the darkness. Her feet carried her through the arched hall, past the table where Madeline and she had dinner. The sound of her heels echoed and seemed to hang thick in the air. She walked down the steps to Gideon Gavers' Rathskeller. She fingered the ivory keys on the baby grand. No notes could be heard.

She heard the shuffling of feet behind her. Quickly she spun around. She saw no one. A cold breeze blew across her face. She stared into the black tavern. She could see her breath. She felt eyes upon her.

Her feet pounded the stairs. She ran through the hall, up the back staircase. Her legs carried her faster through the dining room and past the upstairs bar. She took two steps at a time up the final staircase. Her body lunged at her door. It slammed behind her.

Safely inside her room, she began to feel more comfortable. The color came back to her cheeks and her breathing slowed to normal. She sat in the wingback and covered her body with a throw.

She shivered. The fire was reduced to glowing embers. She tossed another log onto the grate, with any luck it would catch.

Within minutes the flames scrambled up the log. Its flicker filled the room with warmth. She sank into the comfort of the chair. A small rap on her door startled her. She opened the door. It was David.

"Ms. DuVeau, sorry to bother you, but would you be requiring breakfast tomorrow morning?"

Suzie was confused by his question. "Tomorrow morning?"

"Yes. Would you like breakfast?"

"What about this morning?"

David gave her a look of uncertainty. He glanced at his watch. "It's eleven o'clock."

Suzie's eyes opened wide. "Eleven in the morning?"

David began to laugh. "No, eleven in the evening."

Slowly Suzie understood. She still wore the clothes from dinner with Madeline. She must have fallen asleep in the chair.

"I've got to stop eating so late." Her laughter was nervous. "I have the most vivid dreams on a full stomach." Her shoulders relaxed. "I would love breakfast tomorrow morning."

"What time would you prefer?"

"How about eight and coffee at seven?"

"I'll have it arranged." David smirked, "Sleep well."

She closed the door and shook her head in disbelief. She poked the log on the fire, tossed another one on the top and slipped into her pajamas. Just before her head hit the pillow, she noticed the flowers on her desk. She knew she had placed them in the bathroom but after the vivid dream nothing surprised her.

She walked over to the bouquet and picked up the small package wrapped in simple brown paper tied securely with a string. A letter written on old parchment paper was propped beside it. The writing was the same script as the one prior.

She loosened the string and unwrapped the package. She pulled an ornate gold pocket watch from its wrappings. A gold filigree key swung from a braided hair fob. The hair was blonde. The time read eleven o'clock.

The watch didn't appear to be working. Suzie used the tiny key to wind the timepiece. The hands didn't move. She held it to her ear. It was silent. Curious, she opened the letter:

Bring this with you.
The eleventh hour with Goldie Bell.

She looked at the watch again and stroked the hair. It was long, and skillfully crafted. She had been around antiques enough to know the significance of hair art. She wondered why this memorial was given to her. She laid her head onto the pillow and watched the flame's reflection above her bed.

Madeline woke with a start. She wondered if she had been dreaming, but the twin keys lying on her bedside table screamed the truth. It was hard to suppress the anger. She looked at her alarm clock. It was 4:22 a.m.

She rolled to the opposite side of her bed. She tried to think of pleasant thoughts so she could return to sleep. After forty-five minutes she gave up and got out of bed. She wrapped herself in her robe and walked to the kitchen. She placed her teakettle on the stove and sat at the table.

She placed Patrick's telephone number beside the brass keys. The kettle whistled. She poured a large cup of tea. She glanced at the antique wag-on-the-wall clock for the third time.

"Four hours until the bank opens. It'll seem an eternity."

Patrick didn't sleep. It was difficult to wait. He wanted to talk to Attie. He left her yesterday morning literally holding the key to many of her questions. How could she not have rushed from the cemetery to the bank? Guilt flashed through his body.

"What if I scared her off?"

He paced the floor for hours. With first light, he went for a walk. He thought fresh air would ease his anxiety. He tossed his overcoat over his shoulders, grabbed his hat and walked out of the door.

The morning air was cool and crisp. The sky showed promise of another beautiful spring day. He tried to shake the nagging feeling of insecurity by diverting his thoughts. He thought about the spontaneity of his decision to move as he walked down Third Street onto Highland Avenue. He contacted a local realtor from Arizona. The realtor sent him information on several different homes that were for sale. Patrick purchased the Third Street home sight unseen.

It was a quaint home on the northeast side of town. It was a quiet neighborhood filled with young families. Originally it was a dead end street. However this past year, in an effort to relieve some congestion on the main street, it became a secondary road for through traffic. Patrick saw this as a great resale point. His view differed from those who have lived on Third Street their entire lives.

Patrick lived in the house barely a week. He met the moving company on his first day and within seventy-two hours most of the work was done. Only a few unpacked boxes remained in the corner of the dining room.

Patrick lived a modest life. He loved to travel. He spent time in third world countries teaching and training the local doctors to be self-sufficient. He struggled most with the children's suffering. Many were malnourished and endured ailments caused by poor diets. He tried to make a difference in their lives. As a result many children and their parents thanked him with a gift of their handcrafted wares. Patrick displayed them proudly in his home. Some were skillfully made, others were crude, but he loved each one as he did the individuals who gave them.

One of the pieces, which he held dear, was a pair of thin clothes pins carved from bone. A young child, Janiell, whom he had treated for a food-borne illness, offered Patrick the pins. It was a difficult and long recovery for this five-year-old, but in the end, Janiell pulled through. He carved animals and flowers on the pins as he recovered.

Patrick cried when Janiell opened his small hands with the gift.

He had expensive, exotic furniture to match his sentimental gifts, much as a necessity rather than a personal desire. Isaac's wife, Joanne was an interior decorator. She tried to fill Patrick's loneliness with things. She meant well, but Patrick was unmoved.

Patrick's walk had done little to take his mind off of Attie. He hoped they would grow old together. He wanted to spend his last breath making up for precious time lost. Releasing the hatred he felt for Charlotte was more difficult, but he knew she was not the only one to blame. He had been a coward, and maybe for that reason alone, Attie wanted nothing to do with him.

Near eight o'clock, he undressed and turned on the shower. The hot water did not relieve his tension. He never heard the telephone ring.

17

Madeline sat at the table. Her hands were wrapped around her cup for warmth, but she rarely took a sip. After pouring three cups of cold tea down the drain, she gave up and moved into the parlor. She held the two brass keys in one hand, the telephone in the other.

She paced around the parlor. She sat on the Victorian settee. It didn't take long before she was re-straightening the books on the marble table in front of her. She arranged them several different ways until she caught herself. She stood and walked out of the room.

She glanced at the clock. It was 6:30 a.m. She decided to pass the time by taking a long bath. She placed the telephone beside the keys and slipped into the water.

The effects of the warm water relaxed her somewhat. Her thoughts were focused on the contents of the box. She knew her life would never be the same.

When Madeline dressed it was close to eight o'clock. She waited long enough. She thought it was a respectable time to make a morning phone call. She picked up the telephone and dialed Patrick's number.

Her heart raced as she rehearsed her conversation. With the third ring she felt her disappointment rising. After the sixth, she hung up.

She snatched her purse and walked out of the door. She had over an hour to waste before the bank opened. She walked eight blocks on South Lincoln Avenue until she came to State Street. She glanced at her watch and decided to stop at the café for her fourth cup of tea.

"Good morning Madeline," Kathy said cheerfully.

"Hello, Kathy."

"Out for a morning walk?"

"Yes. It's a beautiful morning."

"What can I get for you?"

"I'll have a Chai with a splash of apple syrup."

"Coming right up."

Madeline waited patiently for her tea. She checked her watch. The bank would open in twenty minutes. She finished her tea and took her cup to the counter.

"Have you seen Patricia DuVeau's show at the Wandering Cheshire, Kathy?"

"No, I haven't. I've heard wonderful things, though. Have you seen it?"

"Yes, I have. She is very talented. I have several of her paintings that I have collected over the years. I enjoy the feeling they give me."

"Art is a personal thing, isn't it?"

"Yes, it is. You'll have to make time to see her show before it is gone."

"I will."

"Have a great day, Kathy."

"You do the same."

Madeline walked out of the café feeling good knowing she helped to promote her niece's success. She wasn't sure about having a great day. She walked the last five blocks to the bank. The hanging brass clock chimed nine times. Madeline took a deep breath and walked into the lobby.

She was greeted immediately, "Can I help you?"

"Yes," Madeline spoke timidly, "I need to open this safe deposit box." She handed the women the key.

"103. Okay come with me please."

Madeline followed the woman to a room in the back. She worked her fingers quickly through the filing system. When she pulled the card from the file, she frowned. "Are you...?"

"Madeline P. Crory," Madeline answered though she didn't like the look on the woman's face.

The woman turned the card over and made a noise of disgust. "I'm sorry. There seems to be an error here."

Madeline held her breath and thought, 'Oh please. I have come this far. What possibly could be wrong? What did Charlotte do now?'

The look of bewilderment on Madeline's face stirred the woman's curiosity. "Your signature doesn't appear on the card."

"I just found out about the existence of this box yesterday..." her voice slid to a whisper, "...from two different people."

"It seems the box was secured by a Patrick McCelvy in July of 1965." Her tone was strictly business. "You were named as the second person, but your signature has never been captured." The woman looked suspiciously at Madeline. "May I see some identification?"

"Sure," Madeline spoke without hesitation and fumbled for her driver's license. "This should be sufficient."

"Would you please sign this paper for signature verification?" She slid the activity card to Madeline.

Only one signature appeared on the card. Patrick signed it the day he secured it. She smiled at his signature, quite legible for a doctor. She signed her name.

The teller compared the signature to her driver's license. "I'm sorry for the confusion. The woman that opened this box for Mr. McCelvy is no longer working here and hasn't for quite some time. She was supposed to contact you for your signature in 1965 but obviously didn't. She was a nice person, but not very efficient." She managed a thin smile.

"One more signature...." She handed the signature card to Madeline and pointed to the proper space. She held the previously attached note. After Madeline signed the card, she crumpled the 'signature to follow' and threw it in the trashcan.

"Ready?"

Madeline nodded.

"Follow me."

Madeline breathed a sigh of relief as she entered the room. The woman placed her key in box number 103 and pointed to the keyhole beside it. Madeline slid her key into the slot. Her hands were trembling. The teller turned both keys and pulled the long metal box from its position.

"Would you like some privacy?"

Madeline nodded. The woman carried the box into the back room and placed it on the table in the center. The fluorescent tube flickered from little use.

"I'll be outside of the door if you need anything."

"Thank you," were the only words Madeline could manage.

She stared at the closed box. She walked slowly over to the table and placed her hands on the lid. Her hands were moist and tremulous. Slowly she opened it.

Folded on the top was a piece of paper. The handwriting was Patrick's. She recognized it from the signature card.

My dearest Attie,

Words cannot express the feelings I have for you. I have driven here from Phoenix to see you, but Charlotte has prevented it. Contained in this box are some memories from the past I want to share with you. I wish I could be with you when you peruse them. Please call me if you would like to see me. I'll be waiting by the phone.

My love always,
Patrick

Madeline read the letter three times. She squeezed his business card in her hands. Her instincts called for Charlotte. Her confusion switched to anger. She knew this letter would fill the void but as much as she anticipated that it also petrified her.

She folded the letter and set it off to the side. Her eyes fell onto her own photograph. She was swinging a little girl in a park. Tears filled her eyes. Madeline couldn't recall the memory or having the picture taken. Her stomach wrenched as she looked at the back. Written in Patrick's handwriting were the words: October 2, 1959.

"Nearly six months after the accident! That can't be right. Patrick must be mistaken. I had my memory back by then." Madeline's voice echoed in the tiny room.

Immediately, there was a knock on the door. "Is everything all right?"

"Yes. I'm sorry." Madeline walked to the door and opened it. "I may be a little longer than I had anticipated."

"That's okay. Take as long as you need."

Madeline smiled and closed the door behind her. She walked over to the table and looked at the next picture. It was a photograph of Charlotte in her hospital bed with Grant standing next to her. Madeline sat at the foot of the bed. She smiled at the camera. She looked at the back for a date. June 29, 1959 was written in Patrick's handwriting.

Madeline's confusion grew with each photograph. Although she felt she didn't own these pictures, she decided to take them home to familiar surroundings. She opened her purse and placed everything inside. She double-checked the empty box and closed the lid.

When she started to walk toward the door, she saw something float to the floor. On the floor lay a photograph with the backside facing her. In Charlotte's handwriting were the words June '59. She knelt down and picked up the photograph. When she looked at the picture, the room suddenly felt hot. She gasped and dropped the box.

Quickly she said, "Everything's okay. I just tripped. I'm coming out."

She picked up the photograph and rushed toward the door. The woman looked concerned. Madeline was dizzy, confused, and nauseated.

"Did you hurt yourself?"

Madeline shook her head and gave her the empty box. She rushed toward the door. Her feet felt as if she were walking on a treadmill that was moving in the opposite direction. Her eyes were focused on the glass door.

The teller called to her. "There is no need to hurry. You can be in there as long as you need."

The faster she walked, the farther away it seemed. Her body felt weak and limp. Her head floated. Her vision narrowed. Finally, she placed her hand on the brass door handle.

The teller saw Madeline's key on the floor. "Wait!" she yelled, "…your key." She held it in the air.

Madeline opened the door. A cool, welcoming breeze greeted her skin. She felt her feet stumble toward home. She took long, deep breaths.

She had no memory of the walk home. When she entered the front door, she nearly collapsed. She scratched at the hives on her neck.

She sat at her kitchen table and emptied the contents of her purse. She needed to be alone. She tried to piece it together.

She found the photograph that fell on the bank's floor. She stared at the date on the back. She trembled as she turned it over. It was a photograph of Patrick kissing her. She smiled at how young and handsome he was. His eyes were filled with tenderness. She was overwhelmed with sadness.

As Madeline looked through all the photographs, she placed them on the table in front of her. She arranged them in order by date. According to the dates on the back, she suffered two significant setbacks. Charlotte never mentioned this and she was confused. Patrick wrote all of the dates but one.

She rose from the table, gathered paper and a pencil, and started a list of questions. Her sister deliberately lied to her. She needed to know why.

She returned to the table and caressed the final piece of the box's puzzle, a letter. She opened the papers to reveal Patrick's fluent writing.

My dearest Attie,

It is July 1965. I have been in Phoenix for five years. My life has not been the same without you. I have decided to make a trip back to Salem in hope to convince you to return with me. I vowed to Charlotte not to contact you again, but my heart is empty. I can no longer honor that promise. I will try to explain my reasons for leaving as I did, as well as offer an explanation for your life. I know Charlotte kept many things from you. Please do not judge me harshly.

Enclosed you will find many photographs of your life. I have arranged and numbered each one for your clearer understanding. I will attempt to take you through your lost

time in the hospital and through our relationship. Walk with me, Attie, through our life together.

Madeline picked up one of the photographs in front of her. On the back, in the bottom right hand corner was the number 6. She picked up the photo beside it. On the bottom was the number 8. She searched until she found number 7. Realizing she had a few of the pictures out of the proper order, she flipped them over and arranged them by numerical order.

She rose from the table and put her teakettle on the stove. From across the room, Madeline was in awe as her own life unfolded before her. She vowed not to permit Charlotte to control her life anymore - not today, not ever.

The teakettle whistled. She bruised a few mint leaves she had picked earlier. She placed the wilted stems in her favorite Meakin teapot and poured the hot water over them. She returned to the table with her teapot, cup, a box of tissues, and the telephone.

Madeline started at the beginning.

Patrick's thoughts held only Attie. He needed to shake the nervous feeling in his stomach and thought food would do it. He rehearsed his speech from many years ago as he drove downtown. He decided that after breakfast he would visit Attie. He knew the move was bold, but he spent his entire life guilt-ridden with unfulfilled desires. He couldn't bear the thought of being without Attie another day.

He was about to settle into the driver's seat when he noticed a woman trip out of the bank. It was Attie. Her face was flooded with despair. It was apparent from her reaction that his dreams would not become a reality. He cradled his face in his hands and wept.

Suzie's joints ached from a restless night's sleep. The fire embers were dark and silent. She glanced over to the flowers. Crumpled brown paper was tossed on the floor.

She walked over to the table and held the watch in her hands. It was still. The time was eternally stuck on eleven o'clock. She brought it to her ear again. It was silent. She placed the pocket watch beside her purse. She felt eleven o'clock would never come.

She filled her time with her laptop. She thought about Goldie Bell's tragic story. Her thoughts drifted to her vision of the man and the woman, daffodils and pink roses, of life and death, shadows and sun...

On the Edge of Death

for Goldie Bell Taylor, born Aug 22, 1884, died Sept 8, 1886, who rests in Hope Cemetery

I Waking Hours

Pink roses smother her name
Etched in mind and granite.
She waits for the waning moon,
Lives on the edge of shadows.

Her eyes feel all intruders.
Their gathered cloaks drawn tight
Against her cool stare,
Collars pulled by the breeze.

Her comfort tires from the cold marble chair,
Spent flowers fall from her hands.
A tiny face carved from a father's love,
Dressed in eyelash lace.

A century of visitors, all adrift,
Chisel soft features from death.
Her feet lost to childish pranks.
The crumpled pieces gather cold,
And listen for their call.

II Dusk

Clouds settle to a thin white line
Covering the shame of her feet.
Moist air thickens the breeze;
Wanderers swallowed from sight.

Darkened minutes slide through time,
Lamps lit to create a screen
Silhouettes glide through the mist
And gather on shadows.

Layered vision fools the mind.
Life has lost all reason.
Pine trees grow arms, and walk above stones,
Their movement strobe and scattered.

Maize squares of distant houses
Beckon the lost to roam
Close to safety, warmth, laughter,
Forgotten from another time.

III Witching Hour

"Midnight to one, time for fun,"
Whispers in the wind.
A thrush startled to flight
From their cold breath and longing fingers.

Goldie slides from her hardened chair.
Her feet eager to dance on the earth,
Run through the smokescreen of death,
Skip past an age forgotten,

And fall drunk into Daddy's laughter.
The sweet smell of elderberries
Linger on their skin.
Memories shade the shadow.

Viscous steam encircles the black pot,
Hot bubbles burst and spit
Erase the elderberry memories
As rust sours thick on her lips.

IV Dawn

Crisp, pink morning light
Stretches from its slumber,
As clouds blanket the earth.
The night spirits tossed by the breeze
Are placed behind their shadow.

With the granite stage set, places etched,
The sunlit world remains unchanged.
A rose nosegay softens Goldie's hands
As she's pulled from longing moments.

Her delicate body folded in lace,
Soft ribbons entwine blonde curls.
The farm sold for enchanted marble;
Daddy's heart carved in stone.

When she was finished, she slid her chair from the desk. There was a quiet rap on the door.

"Coffee, Ms. DuVeau."

Suzie opened the door, "Thank you."

"Sorry it's a bit late. We are running behind this morning."

"Honestly, I hadn't noticed," Suzie confessed.

"Your breakfast will be ready in about twenty minutes."

That will be great. Thank you."

Suzie closed the door and carried her coffee tray to the desk. She poured herself a cup as she read through what she had just written. After a few minor changes, she saved the file.

After her second cup of coffee she sat at the table in the hall. A cool morning breeze stretched through the open window. She glanced at her timepiece. It was nearly eight o'clock.

When her breakfast arrived, she devoured it. She didn't realize how hungry she was.

"Would you like more coffee?" the young waitress asked.

"How about a cup to go?"

"Coming right up."

Suzie went back into her room and gathered her paint box, brushes, blanket, and recorder. When she came back to her room for the second trip, a foam cup was placed on her desk. She grabbed her purse, coffee, and the pocket watch.

The drive to the cemetery was quiet. She didn't turn on the radio or her cell phone. The silence gave her opportunity to process the past few days. She whispered a prayer of thanks for bringing her aunt into her life.

When Suzie neared Salem, her usual route was detoured due to an accident and she drove through a neighborhood that was new to her. The homes were from the sixties, smaller and closer together. The lawns were well maintained and she smiled at all the pots of annuals that were planted.

"I guess they are hoping for an early spring too."

The detour brought her to the end of the street. There were no signs to tell her which way to turn. She glanced in her rearview mirror and no one was behind her. When she looked straight ahead, she noticed a quaint little house before her. It was Dutch with a long slanted roof. It had her favorite dark green shingles. Her eyes traced each window frame until they rested on an attic window. In it sat a jack-o-lantern. She laughed to herself and made a right hand turn.

The indirect route brought her through the north entrance of the cemetery. She passed Goldie Bell almost immediately. She was disappointed at the sight of her empty hands. She drove down to the chapel parking area and parked. She was alone. It was 9:30 a.m.

She carried her paint supplies to Goldie Bell. She painted the sky a clear cerulean blue. The grass was a blend of Sap green with Hooker's light and dark. Goldie's face took shape with varied intensities of Payne's grey and the natural white of the paper. Her brush strokes were fine. She commanded her sable rigger and favorite number 4 brush to obey every move. Her skillful hands moved over the paper.

Goldie's hands were still empty. The void was too oppressive. She decided it was her responsibility to fill them.

She walked to the memorial garden at the ivy cross. It held the promise of many unpicked daffodils waiting to become a part of something wonderful. The sun caressed the flowers as they competed for attention. Suzie picked a handful. She caressed the image of the young man forever secreted within the porcelain portrait.

She carried the gift to Goldie. Her steps felt strange as if they led to a pre-destined place. When Suzie arrived at the statue, she lifted the flowers.

In an instant her world changed. The sky grew dark and silent. The colors faded to grey. Only the bouquet held color. Headstones disappeared. Goldie's face softened. Her sweet features returned to their newly carved luster.

The wind swirled around the headstone and picked up leaves and small debris. It tossed them into the air like confetti. She heard the haunting giggle of a child. Goldie's feet swung with excitement. When she leaned forward to receive the bouquet, she nearly fell from her century old marble perch. The laughter continued louder, more pronounced -- magnified by those unseen who gathered to witness the event.

Suzie felt a part of all that was happening yet detached. The laughter persisted within and around her. She no longer trusted her eyes to reveal the truth. She felt bewitched -- a member of the present and the past.

She hesitated to give the flowers to Goldie. The young child's eyes flashed full of life. Her small voice was joined by others and soon was overtaken by hushed, whispered laughing tones. Their words indiscernible, yet Suzie understood. She tried to shake her head clear. Their laughter grew louder until it drowned out all others.

Suzie moved her hands over her ears to muffle the sound. The un-offered bouquet tumbled to the ground. All fell silent. Slowly, she heard whispers of her name behind her. She turned to face a young man.

She heard his voice, soft and gentle, though his lips never moved. She felt a slight vibration. She pulled the pocket watch from her pocket. The hands leapt from idleness. It was eleven o'clock.

"I knew you would come."

19

Patrick took a few minutes to collect his composure. His hopes were crushed. He spent so much time and effort he didn't want to give up. He was convinced it was the right thing, but his confidence was shaken from Attie's response at the bank.

He drove back to Third Street and pulled into the garage. He picked up the cordless telephone, just in case.

Madeline stared at the writing. There was something lonely about with the way 'My dearest Attie' was penned. After a few minutes, she gathered strength and started to read.

We met in the hospital after your accident, although, that part I'm sure you know by now. You had no memory of your life before the accident. You knew nothing of your parents, of their accident, or of Charlotte as your sister. The doctors diagnosed you with an Arteriovenous

Malformation (AVM), a tangle of thin-walled blood vessels, which have a large blood flow situation. Many times this congenital condition remains undiscovered until it causes seizures, ruptures, or is found through an accident. Yours was the latter.

After the accident, you went through an extensive series of tests. This process took several weeks. During an angiogram a small cluster of abnormally formed blood vessels in the brain was found. Small deposits of calcium were present in the AVM. This could cause the brain to become more irritated, resulting in periodic seizures. At the time only one tangle was located. We were mistaken.

In the beginning, you wanted nothing to do with Charlotte. You said many horrible things about her to her face and to the staff. Many were true, although Charlotte resented you for your candor and inability to be manipulated by her. At this point, the doctors began to treat you for a dual or split personality. You were put through many horrible psychological tests that left you feeling very insecure. This was done, in my opinion, because you had no memory of the things of which Charlotte accused. Many, which I am ashamed to say, were mere fabrications and distortions of the truth so Charlotte could move the doctors' opinions in the direction she thought they should go.

I know my judgment of your sister seems harsh, and please forgive me for it, but I have consulted many different people in the medical and psychological field to root my opinion in fact rather than emotion.

Initially, my relationship with you was purely medical. I was an intern and eager for some personal experience to blend with my text book learning. It's not every day a case like yours and Charlotte's comes along in a small rural town. It didn't take long before I felt an emotional attachment to you. I was warned by an associate about your age, but it didn't matter to me. I was drawn into your world by your love and zest for life, and your attraction to me was just as obvious.

I do not need to tell you, however, that your sister did not approve. When you were allowed certain privileges, Charlotte was indignant. She loathed the idea of your freedom to leave the hospital, especially since you were able to walk. Her deep animosity caused us many problems.

Charlotte underwent many surgeries and was still bedridden. Your physical health had returned more rapidly than your sister's and Charlotte's resentment could not be hidden. Many of the staff was terrified of her. Much of that changed, however, when she met Grant. Her disposition softened and she actually was pleasant to be around.

When Grant's mother, Vera, passed away, her funeral was Charlotte's first authorized leave from the hospital. I assumed full responsibility for that trip, although I am certain she was not aware of that. It was that day, when the hearse passed your parents' old house, that you showed the first sign of your memory returning. It was a fleeting moment, though, and a large disappointment to Charlotte. She had a difficult time controlling the 'new Madeline' so the return of your memory and hopefully your old personality was exciting for her.

I had spent much time in research on this subject that I felt encouraged by the window of light you had seen. At that point we spent more time together.

I received special approval from your doctor to take you on many outings. Charlotte was kept in the dark about many of our excursions because she created chaos for us both. I have to admit, my motives were mostly selfish because I had fallen in love with you and I wanted to be sure that the woman I loved, was the true woman I called Attie.

In many of the medical journals of that day, it warned of split personality traits and the consequences the return of the memory would cause. I had myself convinced, however, that what we felt for each other would span that valley and remain true through that discovery period. I forgot to factor in Charlotte.

Her control and manipulation of others became painfully known to me. Unfortunately, being aware did not make me immune. And, yes, I fell prey to her desires. I became the mouthpiece of many things she wanted your ears to hear, many without my conscious knowledge. Her stronghold was woven like a poisonous spider's web. Many of her prey were unaware they were a pawn until it was too late.

When I confronted Charlotte about her level of control, her guttural laughter was frightening. She dismissed me with a sweep of her hand. It was then my approach took a different turn.

Although it would be difficult to explain, I convinced the doctors to admit you to the psychological ward. I knew it would not be permissible for you to visit Charlotte or for her to visit you. I felt I would be able to move your memory forward and we could begin our lives together.

You hated that ward and rightly so. My guilt for having you admitted was strong, but I convinced myself it was for your own good. You needed to be independent of Charlotte and so did I.

I spent as much time as I could with you. You cried when I left. I heard you sob as I left your room. I brought you ice cream and we laughed as though we had succeeded in committing an illegal act. I can still envision how your eyes danced when you laughed.

I cherished that time together. You asked to be held. I cradled you in my arms for hours. You loved to have your hair brushed. Believe me, it was my pleasure. Your feet ached from inactivity and you asked me to massage them. We talked about your day, the flowers I picked for you, the color of my whiskers, and how quickly they grew.

We spent much time in close quarters. Your laugh was infectious. Your playfulness filled me with desire, though our lips never touched. Until one day I could not withhold my passion.

You asked me to look at a tiny dark spot that appeared on your cheek. You acted concerned. I gathered my wits and moved close. Your eyes never left mine. You held me in a tight stare until my eyes met yours. The look in your eyes left me with no doubt of your feelings although no words were spoken. I tried to maintain my medical composure, but the gentle stroke of your hand to my face overcame my professionalism. You moved into me and I kissed you. The sensual moisture resonated long on my lips. I knew at that moment you were the one for me.

Those months we spent together without Charlotte's influence were a dream. Our bond grew closer and our feelings stronger. When the doctors placed you back into a basic care floor, your appearance was normal, all but your memory.

We were, once again, granted leave from the hospital grounds. It was during this time most of the photographs were taken. We spent time at the park, by your insistence. You loved to play on the swing set with the children. They fought over who would be first. The line of giggling children quickly formed. Before I could blink, you had four children side by side on the swings laughing hysterically as you fought to keep them in motion.

There were many days the playground was empty of little voices and our laughs were the only ones heard. We enjoyed a picnic lunch on a blanket spread under the large oak tree, just outside the perimeter of the merry-go-round circle. We would speak of our future together, of our days of swinging our own children. It was on one of those days which we first spoke the words 'I love you'.

It is difficult to explain the depth of our love when your memory of this time is lost. Within six-weeks the doctors released you. Your health was strong, but your memory had only shown a few signs of returning. Those signs were so remote from each other, with no clear reason for the enlightenment, that it could not be said if your memory would ever return. You seemed to enjoy your new self and your confidence was solid, according to those who knew you prior.

The day you were released from the hospital, I took you to your parents' home. I contacted your groundskeeper and housemaid to reinstate them full time and briefed them on your condition. They were anxious when you entered the door, but you met them with grace and dignity to their relief.

After the evening meal you dismissed both of them to enjoy their own lives for the evening hours. This was an apparent change from their normal routine, but you quickly admitted things would be different. They were shocked, yet grateful for the change, and although it was never spoken, thankful to have you home.

As I was preparing to leave that evening, you gently took my hand and asked me to guide you through the second floor. I remember how embarrassed and insensitive I felt when you mentioned that you did not know which bedroom was yours. At that moment, I understood your confidence was only a façade and you buried your insecurities. I was ashamed for being blind.

We looked at all three bedrooms. One obviously had belonged to your parents. The other two were a bit more similar. We dug through the clothes drawers and closets and determined by the size of the clothes which bedroom was yours.

I held back the tears when you gently ran your hands through your clothes, sporadically stopping at a piece and holding it up to yourself. At times the crinkled look of disapproval was comical. But when you found a piece that you liked, the way you caressed it brought a hard lump to my throat. I chastised myself for not thinking to bring you there sooner. The thought of leaving you alone in that house the first time you had seen it, made me nauseated.

Your hands stopped at a beautiful pink dress. It was a summer dress, yet it was long in length, nearly to your ankles. You held it close to you. When you slipped your head through the hanger and let the dress fall down in front of you, you giggled and asked if I would wait until you tried it on. As you spun around watching the dress flow around you in gentle chiffon waves, I could not hold myself back from touching you. We kissed with unparalleled passion and I quickly dismissed myself to give you time to undress.

Standing in the hall, I had a difficult time controlling my desire for you. I forced my mind to wander to other things, but I kept coming back to the softness of your skin and moisture of your lips. When you came out of your bedroom and stood before me, I realized you were no longer a young girl of seventeen, but a beautiful young woman whom I wanted to grow old with.

The soft pink dress hugged every curve. You pinned your hair up leaving a few thin wisps to fall softly across your face. I moved closer and brushed the hair from your eyes. We longed without words before you begged me to stay with you. I wrestled between honor and desire before I conceded.

We talked into the narrow hours of the morning. I slept on the sofa. I didn't come prepared for an overnight stay so I decided to leave prior to your waking. I didn't want your housemaid to know nor did I want to arrive at the hospital in the same clothes.

As I entered your bedroom to kiss you goodbye, I was surprised to see you were awake. Your eyes were rimmed in red. Although you lied and said you hadn't been crying, I held you. As I caressed your shoulders, you leaned into me and kissed me. Our passion and desire for each other became so strong that neither of us could stop. We made love as the sun showed its first light.

I felt a twinge of guilt as I left that morning, but you insisted on secrecy. As I drove down the main street toward my apartment, I passed your housemaid. I watched in my rear view mirror as she turned down your street. I laughed out loud. I stayed many nights since that day. You insisted we share your bed. I gladly accepted.

We kept your move home a secret from Charlotte as long as we were able. Charlotte had become very involved with Grant and focused her attention to his manipulation. She was enraged when she discovered she had been deceived, but when their engagement was announced, Charlotte's disposition improved. You withdrew.

Your health seemed to take an immediate turn for the worse. You became weaker by the day. Finally, you were re-admitted. There was a time we thought we were going to lose you. I couldn't bear the thought. I consulted the staff on your immediate issues, but it was through my discovery that you were diagnosed with a nosocomial infection. It was little known then. You slipped into a coma for over three weeks.

Madeline nearly dropped the letter. Her confusion grew as she read. She felt she was reading tales of another person's life. The length of time Patrick described as was much longer than Charlotte explained. According to her sister, Madeline was only hospitalized a few months. According to Patrick's letter it was nearly eight months and counting.

Her hands trembled. She reread the last few paragraphs for better comprehension. She understood much of her life was secreted, though she didn't know why. She picked up the letter again.

During your comatose state, you began to mumble. This amazed the doctors and we watched you closely. You had a nurse at your side constantly. The staff was very attentive to your needs.

When I sat with you, I permitted the nurse to leave. It was then I noticed your ramblings had significance. Your words were garbled, but most were decipherable.

You spoke to your parents as if they were standing before you. You spoke to Charlotte. You knew she was your sister. At times you argued with her, others you laughed. You spoke to your dog, Giza. You spoke of intimate thoughts. I began to take notes.

Most days your inner voice was quiet, but on the days when you chattered, the staff found me quickly. I sat for hours with my notebook. As long as my schedule permitted it, I was at your side.

I coined this time as your 'awakening'. These vivid memories began with the sudden opening of your eyes. It was only a reflex and your vision to the present was still veiled. It was a major breakthrough in discovery, both medically and personally. My only regret was in the final process.

You were in this state for twenty-two days. The twenty-third day began as the others. I was busy with my rounds when a nurse shouted that you were convulsing. When I entered your room, two doctors and three nurses were with you. Your mouth was open and your breathing came in short bursts. Your body shuddered. The staff administered Phenobarbital.

It was clear through your words that you were reliving the accident. You begged to drive. You shared your conversation with Charlotte. Through your screams, we heard the word deer. Your breathing became erratic until it slowed then stopped. The room burst into panic. I was pushed against the back wall as they wheeled in the machines. As the order to clear was called, your eyes flew open. The staff held their breath as you gasped for air.

Your first words were, "Where am I?"

I moved from the back of the room and took your hand, "Attie, welcome back." My smile was wide and full of hope.

The words you shouted cut deeply, "Who are you?" Your eyes were cold and full of fright. You pulled your hand away from mine and tried to pull yourself from the bed. Panic set in. You clawed at the tubes. The only name you screamed was, "Charlotte!" My dreams were shattered.

For the next two weeks, you refused to see me. You screamed if I entered the room. If I touched you, you sobbed. All I wanted was to explain who I was, what we meant to each other, our experiences, the love we shared and the memories we made. Your eyes were distant. You held no memory of me, of us. Something had snapped and you returned as you once were. The doctors decided it was time for me to turn my research over to another. "For Madeline's well being," they explained. My heart was broken.

In all my research I never thought it would end like this. I reluctantly agreed with the doctors and placed your care in another intern, William Plythe. The staff nicknamed him Buddy. His was the only name you sought but Charlotte's.

During that time, I was contacted by a hospital in Phoenix, Arizona. I applied for a position several months prior and completed the first group of interviews. The candidates were narrowed to four. I was one.

My heart was torn to shards. I felt isolated. I sought Charlotte for advice. She taunted me and accused me of sabotaging your recovery. She convinced me to return to Phoenix and pursue the position.

When I returned from the interviews, it was clear that I had a strong chance of securing that position. I tried to discuss it with you, but your cry for distance was apparent. You were finished with me. The staff escorted me from your room. I was warned to keep my distance. Charlotte warned of a restraining order. I thought it only a threat.

Many times I wandered past your room only to find Buddy with you. Once, I found him combing your hair and my resentment could not be contained. Buddy and I suffered heated words. Your screams were heard over our argument. They ended in a whimper. We were both thrown from your room. I felt ashamed and responsible. My self-punishment was enough, but when Grant wheeled Charlotte toward me, I knew the harassment had just begun.

Your setback lasted two weeks. I was prohibited to see you, as was Buddy. I was pleased with the latter. Your relationship had been growing with him and it broke my heart. Knowing the love we shared and made, I couldn't bear the thought of not being together. I accepted the position in Phoenix and left the following week.

The day before I left, Charlotte had me served with a restraining order. Many times I thought to reason with her, but she had broken my spirit. I knew she held me responsible so I left without a word to your sister.

The evening of my departure, I slipped undetected into your room. You were asleep. You were so beautiful, so peaceful. I had watched you sleep so many times in my arms it was difficult to leave you there. I was mesmerized by the moon's shadow as they played across the gentle curves of your face.

As I knelt to kiss you goodbye, tears fell from my cheeks to yours and in a moment to this day I am unsure, I thought you looked at me, and then quickly closed your eyes. After our lips touched for the last time, you were sound asleep. I held on to the hope in those last few moments, you felt my love for you, and with that feeling of deep contentment, you drifted off to dream of us. I have held on to that thought for the past five years. It was the only way I could walk out that door.

I kept in contact with an associate on your progress. You were released from the hospital three weeks after your last collapse. Although your memory still moved erratically, according to the doctors, your recovery was sure. This seemed certain except for a short five-day admission four months after you had been released. I understood from Grant, this final hospital stay was when your memory fully returned. I inquired several times, but my associate moved to another hospital. No one else would release information to me.

I'm sorry to tell you this piece of the puzzle remains unclear. According to my research, a trauma would cause the full return of your memory. Perhaps that is why you were hospitalized the last time. Of this, I am unsure.

Not a day has passed without thoughts of you. I won't bore you with the details of my career except to say it has been the only feeling of contentment that has sustained me. However, I have grown restless.

I decided to take my first vacation in five years and return to Salem. My hope is you will return with me to Phoenix. The reason for this letter is to explain all I can in case I am not permitted to see you. I am nervous as I write this letter, Attie, and unsure of your reaction. I hope I have not caused you pain.

I trust much of what I'm saying is a mystery. I know it will contradict much of what Charlotte has told you, but I swear to you, it is the truth. I love you, Attie, with all of my being. I can't imagine life without you. Please return with me to Phoenix.

All my love
Patrick

Madeline placed the letter on her lap. She picked up a photograph. It was a picture of Patrick in his scrubs with

Madeline seated at the edge of her sister's bed. Charlotte sat upright while Grant stood beside with his hand on her shoulder. Her eyes stared at Patrick. He was so young, very different from the man in the cemetery. She held the photograph and the letter to her chest and cried.

20

He held out his hand for her. His hand was cool. Her grey and white world soon changed to vibrant colors."I knew you would come. I have much to share, but little time." They no longer stood before Goldie Bell in Hope Cemetery but in a private garden.

Suzie's eyes bounced from the purple and white cleomes through the pink hollyhocks past the tall spikes of amethyst liatris. She watched the heads of the shasta daisies sway to a tune her ears could not hear. It tossed the sweet peas until they joined the waltz. The air was heavy with fragrance. The heads of the autumn sedum started to form. Their clusters were small and tight. She thought it must be late June.

The sound of his voice broke the spell, "My name is Elam Wade Barsan. I am aged twenty-six. It is the year 1865."

Suzie felt weak. Her head felt light. She swayed until she lost her balance. Elam caught her in his arms before she fell. His cool hand calmed her.

"What do you want with me?" Suzie asked weakly.

"All in due time. You must come."

When Suzie sat up, she was on a dusty wooden bench. She scanned the buildings that surrounded them. "This is Salem!" she exclaimed.

Elam looked at her puzzled, "Of course. Where else did you expect?"

Suzie watched as people rode by in their horse and buggies. She watched a group gather at the entrance of Broadway Street where a large watering trough for the horses was placed. The people laughed and passed the time making small talk as their horses lapped the cool water. Two women in wool brocade dresses walked past them while fanning themselves with feathered fans.

"This is just like watching a movie!" she said to Elam. The return look was a puzzled one. "Never mind. What are we doing here?"

Elam chastised her, "The more you talk, the longer it will take. Please watch and listen as I share the reason for our meeting."

Suzie watched Elam closely as he replayed the story.

This was where I first saw her. She was fair, beautiful, and walking in the street unaccompanied. Dusk had settled and it was not a fitting time for a young lady to be out alone. I approached her and offered my help.

She never spoke to me that day, but her eyes were filled with tears. She handed me a metal rod and she placed in my hand two notes:

For the one who cares,

My father is ill. He has an important errand to tend. I do not know the specifics. He asked me to give this to the first man who offers assistance. Your presence is required at ten o'clock sharp this evening. Bring with you this rod to signify your intentions.

God speed,
Rebecca

I was puzzled by the mystery surrounding this woman. I only recently arrived in town and felt compelled to help her. At ten o'clock that evening I arrived at the address given to me in the second note.

With her rod in hand, I slid from my horse and slip-tied him to a nearby tree. I approached the house slowly, for from a distance shouting could be heard coming from inside. I peered into the window and was horrified by what I witnessed.

Standing along the wall were four slaves, badly beaten and bound. Lying on the floor in front of them was a white man with his face buried in a pool of his own blood. A large group of men were holding iron rods and waving them erratically. I stepped backward from the window in a feeble attempt to slip away unnoticed and tripped over a stack of metal rods placed just outside the side funeral door. The sound of toppling metal was difficult to muffle and in a matter of seconds, the door flew open and out of the house poured several men all armed with the same metal rods. I dropped mine and ran toward Jasper.

Through a kind act from God, he had freed himself from the tree. I whistled as I approached him. He trotted toward me, I jumped onto his back, and he carried me away to safety.

When I arrived at the barn where I had been staying, my horse was covered in froth. His gait was more rapid than I had ever experienced. For that I was eternally grateful. I gave him food and water and gently brushed him to settle his nerves. I nestled myself in the soft haymow, but sleep eluded me.

I felt restless, uneasy. It is a difficult feeling to explain, but I felt hunted. After only a few minutes, I rose, saddled Jasper, and rode into the darkness under the cover of night.

The air was cool and the rush of wind invigorated me. Even my horse eased from tension as we moved farther away. We slept under a large oak tree in the midst of gravestones. The night air seemed restless, eager to finish its business.

In the early morning, heavy fog blanketed the damp earth. Jasper stood in the near distance grazing on the moist grass. My bones were stiff from my night's bedding of tree roots and hardened ground, but as I stood and stretched, it was then I saw her again.

She was dressed in a summer housemaid's dress. Her hat was pulled close to her ears, and she had a white bed jacket thrown about her shoulders. Her golden hair lay innocently on her shoulders, shining in the early light.

I crouched to my knees, but too late, for she had spied me. I held my breath as she moved closer. Her demeanor confused me, for she appeared to be saddened.

She studied my eyes before any words were spoken. I felt her thoughts reach my core. She calmed my apprehension with a whisper.

"Thank you for coming."

My mind was bewitched and confused. We had no prearrangement to meet at the cemetery. I opened my mouth to reply, but she quickly covered my lips with her fingers. She hushed my thoughts and gently kissed my cheek. I stood frozen with wonder as she whispered, "They are looking for you. Follow these instructions and you will find help. If you need me, place some flowers here and I will come. Listen for my coming on the wind." In my hands she placed another note.

In the distance I heard the song of the wood thrush. Quickly, its song was drowned by the sound of many galloping horses. I was their destination. I whistled to Jasper. Rebecca motioned for me to go and mouthed the words 'God speed. Hurry'. I jumped on my horse and headed in the opposite direction of the approaching fury.

When I turned to catch another glimpse of Rebecca, she had vanished.

Suzie watched intently as Elam spoke of his tale. She had many questions, but she dare not ask. His tone was soft and calming, but his story disturbed her. As he spoke of his plight, Suzie watched the story unfold in movie-like fashion. She saw his horse, the rods, the cemetery, and Rebecca's face as it disappeared into the thick vapor.

Elam stood quickly. His eyes stared into the distance. He placed his fingers to his lips and whistled. Jasper appeared, throwing his head with wild anticipation. Elam leapt onto his back and disappeared into the approaching fog.

She heard the sound of the galloping horses. The fog danced with hidden images, creating a veil for the unseen. Their hooves pounded the earth. They paled to the echo of their angry snorts. Their movement was swift. Suzie felt the vibration move through her. She could feel their moist breath on her skin. She knew they were upon her, but her vision was obscured.

Slowly she stood. She extended her hands and moved in blind fashion. Her feet moved forward to steady her stance. Immediately her world changed. The veil was lifted. She faced the statue of Goldie Bell, whose hands held Suzie's daffodils.

In the distance, she saw a lone rider on a black horse. The horse reared, whinnied, and pawed the air with its front legs. The rider remained steady on its back. With a toss of his head and mane glistening in the sunlight, the horse moved from her. The rider's coat swirled around his hips as they disappeared.

Suzie held her breath. His coat faded into a black mourning flag tossed by the breeze. She noted the condition of Goldie Bell. With the weathered features on her innocent face, it was clear Suzie had returned to the present time. She looked toward the place where Elam disappeared. The flag waved from beside a distant headstone.

She pulled the pocket watch from her pocket. The minute hand remained in a fixed position. The bezel read 11:09 a.m. She witnessed an evening and morning of Elam's life, yet she was held for only nine minutes...in this century.

She stared at the watch. Its hands were still. Time froze until more of the tale could be told. Suzie was determined to be patient and wait for Elam to continue when it was right for him.

She rearranged the bouquet in Goldie's hands. She waited for her world to change. Nothing happened. She walked toward Elam's headstone, a cross, encircled with carved ivy. In the center was a porcelain oval of his face. His eyes burned with fire. The likeness was seared into her mind.

She gently stroked the image. "I'll be here when you need me. Just place flowers in Goldie Bell's hands and I will know."

Goldie Bell's innocence waited. She seemed to call for Suzie to return. Suzie settled on the blanket she had spread before the statue. She continued to paint the likeness that consumed her thoughts.

21

After Patrick's emotions were permitted to run their course, he couldn't wait for Attie. He drew a deep breath and dialed Madeline's number. His heart pounded in his ears.

Madeline was startled by the sound of the telephone ringing. She wiped the tears from her eyes and answered, "Hello?"

"Attie?" Patrick's voice was strained.

"Yes." Madeline's reply was automatic. The pause was an eternity.

Finally, Patrick spoke, "Attie, are you able to see me after what you `ave read?"

Madeline was stunned by the question. How did he know she had just finished the letter? Her hesitation was easily read.

Patrick broke the silence with, "I was downtown for breakfast. I saw you leave the bank." He hesitated before he continued, "It was obvious that I `ave upset you. Attie, I never meant...."

Madeline interjected, "Patrick, after reading your letter, I'm confused. Practically all of its contents are new to me. I'm still trying to absorb it. There is so much I don't understand…"Her voice trailed off to mumbles.

"May I see you?"

"I'm not sure."

Those were not the words Patrick wanted to hear. "Attie, please. I `ave lost so much time with you, my whole life. I know it appears very selfish and forward, but I've got to see you. Please."

Madeline's head spun, but she wanted to see him. The man she met at the cemetery charmed her, and she needed to blend him with this man who penned the letter.

After a long pause she said, "Come over in an hour."

Patrick was elated with the invitation, "In an `our. I'll be there." Madeline hung up without saying goodbye.

Patrick rushed throughout the interior of his home looking for his old notebook. He placed it in several different locations and couldn't remember where he last saw it. Within ten minutes he managed to locate the aged notebook and ransack his house simultaneously. Armed with his necessities, he ran out of the door.

He stopped into the Downtown Café for his cappuccino and a cup of tea for Attie. He ordered her old favorite and wondered if it was still her preference. He whistled as he left.

He felt the nervousness rise to an uncomfortable level as he pulled into Madeline's drive. His spirits were high, yet he held himself somewhat guarded. He nearly tripped over the top step of the front entrance.

When he reached the front door, he raised his hand to knock, but Madeline quickly opened the door. Patrick made the motion of knocking on the opened door. In their apprehension, they burst into laughter.

"Please, come in," Madeline said automatically. Patrick smiled and tipped his head. He was having a difficult time containing his excitement.

He held up the cup of tea, "Still drink it black?"

Madeline smiled. "Yes, I do."

The pair faced each other and sipped on their drinks. Their eyes never strayed. They stood motionless, silent, and waited for the other to speak first.

Patrick stepped forward and took Madeline's hand. He brought her hand to his lips and kissed her palm. The simple, yet sensual act made Madeline blush. Her eyes were as he remembered.

Madeline spoke first, "Did you ever marry?"

"No," Patrick stammered."I buried myself in my patients' care, `ere and abroad. The days were filled with many friends, but the nights..." he hesitated, "they were...lonely."

His answer unnerved her. She wished she had asked another question first.

Patrick sensed her discomfort. He quickly added, "I've `ad a good life, Attie. Don't feel responsible for my sadness. `Twas my own doin'."

Madeline managed a thin smile She motioned to the kitchen table. As Patrick walked closer, he noticed all the photographs and of course, the letter. His face flushed from memories rather than embarrassment. He took a chair and slid it beside Madeline. He laughed out loud as he picked up a photograph.

"Now, I remember this day."

It was a picture of Madeline sitting by her hospital window staring outside. She was seated in a wheelchair. "This was one of the first photographs I took of you. When the camera flashed, you didn't flinch. I don't know if you even knew I `ad taken this picture."

Madeline watched as he caressed the photograph with his fingers. His smile was wide. Madeline asked, "What are you thinking, Patrick?"

"I'm thinking,"he looked deep into Madeline's eyes, "that I am so `appy to be sitting `ere with you. It's been a long time coming, this wish of mine." They stared at each other without speaking. Patrick broke the silence. "I know you `ave a lot of questions, so since I'm `ere, ask away."

Madeline took a deep breath, closed her eyes and whispered, "How long were we..." she sighed, "intimate?"

This question took Patrick by surprise. He didn't expect it to come so soon in the conversation. He answered, "Four months."

"Four months before my memory returned?"

"As I explained in the letter, we spent four months sharing ourselves before the change in your memory."

"How long was I in the hospital initially?"

"The accident `appened in the first part of April. You were in intensive care for three weeks. You regained consciousness but did not speak for over a month." Patrick picked up the photograph he had discussed earlier, "That's when I took this picture. I `ad the nursing staff place you in front of the window so your mind would stay active until you were able to speak."

"I was unable to speak?" Madeline asked in disbelief.

"No, I didn't mean you weren't able to speak, I meant you were unwilling."

"Go on."

Patrick opened his notebook. Madeline was surprised at the detail and even more that he kept it at all. She understood how much he cared for her. She wanted to be angry with her sister for stealing this happiness from her, but she would not allow those thoughts to surface. She would deal with that emotion later.

Patrick thumbed through a few pages. "On the twenty-ninth of May you spoke your first words. You told a nurse that you were thirsty. She practically knocked me over with the news. I got to you as quickly as possible. When I entered the room, you were carrying on a conversation as if nothing `ad `appened. The news traveled quickly through the `ospital and Charlotte requested to see you immediately. She was recovering from surgery so I wheeled you to her. I witnessed firsthand `ow belligerent you were. You insisted Charlotte was not your sister. The look of dismay on Charlotte's face was almost comical, yet one couldn't `elp but feel compassion."

"Your letter stated that I said horrible things about my sister?"

"Yes, Attie, that's true. It took several months before you came to terms with your relationship with Charlotte. You refused to `ave anything to do with `er for weeks after that first visit. It was only through the growing trust in our relationship that you agreed to try once more." Patrick laughed, "Charlotte actually thanked me. I think that was the only time those words passed `er lips."

"Charlotte had a terrific mean streak."

Patrick laughed at Madeline's confession."You don't need to explain it to me. I saw much of it first `and." The hard lines on Patrick's face softened. "Attie, Charlotte `as stolen much from both of us. Let's not allow that to continue."

"My thoughts exactly." Madeline sighed with relief. "Tell me, why didn't I finish high school?"

"You don't know?" Patrick replied stunned.

Madeline hung her head and muttered, "Charlotte never answered me. She said it didn't matter and that it wouldn't change anything." She sighed. "She didn't speak much of the past. It disturbed her somehow."

Patrick looked at her through squinted eyes. He couldn't imagine living her life. He took a deep breath and answered her question. "You were tutored while you were `ospitalized as long as you were physically able. During one of your setbacks, the tutor was asked to discontinue coming until your mind was ready. After your initial release, the tutor came to the `ouse. You were scheduled to take your final exams the week you…" Patrick's eyes filled with tears, "…collapsed."

"My collapse with you and Buddy?"

"No, the one before that. When you came back into the `ospital."

Madeline felt agitated, 'How many set backs or collapses did I have?"

"All together from beginning to end, four."

"Four?" Madeline's voice was tense. She pushed her chair back and stood abruptly. She paced in front of the kitchen sink.

"This is so frustrating! I have a man in my kitchen that I don't remember, whom I have been intimate with, which I don't remember, telling me a story, that I have never heard before." Her voice escalated in volume and pitch as she continued, "I feel like this is a bad third-rate film and I am the unprepared star actress without a script!" Her face was red from anxiety.

Patrick jumped up to rush toward her, but Madeline held out her hand to stop his advancement.

"Attie, I know this is `ard to understand."

"Know! How do you know? In a matter of a week, my whole life has changed and I feel as if it is spinning out of control!" Her eyes filled with tears that quickly dropped to her cheeks. Patrick felt helpless as Madeline held him at bay. She dropped her hand and head and took a deep breath. When she looked at Patrick, he was wiping tears from his own eyes.

"Please, Attie let me comfort you."

Those words were what Madeline needed to hear. She opened her arms to receive him. Patrick stepped forward and held her until her sobbing slowed to whimpers. He gently lifted her face and kissed both of her tear-stained cheeks.

"You are so beautiful. I `ave missed you, Attie."

Madeline could not find the proper words for her reply. His eyes were so gentle and full of sincerity. She was torn between emotions. She gathered her strength to continue and led him back to the table.

She picked up a photograph and handed it to Patrick and said, "Tell me about this day."

Patrick looked at a photograph of Madeline pushing children on a swing. He laughed and said, "You loved children -- and they loved you. They actually fought over being first. They never tired of your affection. There were many times I believed the children `elped your `ealing, both physically and mentally." He tapped on the photograph. "This was one of those days."

"It was a warm day in late autumn. When we arrived at the playground, it was empty. The children were still in school. We planned our outings many times around the school schedule." Patrick's eyes drifted to restore the memories. He chuckled, "Oh, `ow I loved to watch you play with the children."

"One by one, the children walked `ome from school. They stopped at the playground. They recognized you from a distance and ran for their `ug. On this particular day, one of the little boys was escorted by `is older brother. I didn't recognize this young man, but `e knew you. `e stood removed, unwilling to join the fun. You coaxed him. Finally, you walked over to `im, knelt beside `im, and called `im by `is first name, Charlie, I believe it was."

Patrick grinned as he continued. "Only I noticed that you called `im by `is first name without being introduced. I asked `is little brother `ow they knew you and `e replied they used to live a few doors down from you. I kept this information to myself until our walk back to the `ospital. I remember the conversation well:

"Jack's older brother was cute."

"Yes, but he sure didn't want to join us. Did he?"

"What did you say to convince `im to come play?"

"I told him it would be alright. His mother would want him to play and have a good time."

"`is mother?"

"Yes, she passed away a little over a year ago. Poor Charlie has been so quiet and introverted since."

"`ow do you know them?"

"They live on my street, just three doors down from us."

"Us?"

"Yes, Mom, Dad, Charlotte and I."

"That was it. After you mentioned Charlotte's name, your memory was gone. When I probed further, you became agitated and swore that we did not `ave that conversation." Patrick flipped through several pages of notes in his notebook and added, "I made some very interesting notes about those bright spots." He frantically thumbed through pages, moving forward and back again. He sighed, "I know they're in `ere…" as he flipped through the pages one more time, " … but I can't seem to find them."

He glanced at Madeline. She was smiling. "What is so funny?" he questioned.

"You were trying to fix me, weren't you?"

Patrick smiled, "Yes, I guess I was. I desperately wanted to know the old Attie because I `ad fallen in love with the new one."

Madeline was pleased with this gentle Irish man sitting before her. At times when she listened to him speak, she heard distant humming and hushed songs. It was a peculiar sensation. She didn't know what to make of it, but her experience was the same when she met Patrick in the cemetery. It seemed to be the strongest when he held her.

Madeline listened as Patrick spun tales of their long walks and late night talks. She loved to watch him laugh. She was mesmerized by his gentle touch. He explained each photograph. His recollection of the details amazed her.

22

Suzie labored over every detail of Goldie's face. With each stroke of the red sable, she blended the colors and added fine lines. The movement felt guided from the unseen. When she washed the last bit of pigment from her brushes, she smiled at the end result.

"When a painting is spun from inspiration, the final result is haunting," she whispered.

She collected her painting, damp brushes and the blanket and walked to her car. She placed her precious cargo into the back seat. She glanced at her timepiece which dangled from a gold bar pin. It was 3:30 p.m.

She drove to her aunt's house.

Patrick pulled the final photograph from his pocket. He whispered, "This picture I saved for last. I kept it for myself the day I placed all the others into the safe deposit box. I took this photograph the afternoon after our first time together." He handed the photograph to Madeline.

When she looked at the picture she gasped. She was seated on a swing. Her dress curled around her legs as she moved. After looking through all these photographs, this was the only one that held something familiar.

"I know this dress. This is the one you described in your letter." She looked back at the photograph. "I still have it. Every time I gathered clothing to give to charity, I could not part with it. I never knew why…" She looked at Patrick with her tears dripping from her lashes, "…until now."

She threw her arms around his neck. "I don't know where to go from here. I'm intimidated in your presence when you know more about me than I do. The woman that you described is a part of me, yet somehow removed. It will take me a while to feel comfortable with those aspects. Can you understand?"

"Not only do I understand, but I encourage you to explore and try to remember. If it never comes back to you, it doesn't matter. Most important is the fact that after all these years, we are still `ere. We `ave been brought together again, and this time, I'm not leaving."

There was something in his voice that calmed her. She took a deep breath and stared into his eyes. At that moment, she decided to allow herself this relationship no matter how careless it appeared to others. She was at peace with her decision and felt her body and mind relax. She mentally knocked down the last few rows of the brick wall that kept her guarded for so many years. Her face was lit with excitement.

Patrick placed his hand under Madeline's chin and lifted her face. He kissed her forehead. "I am so blessed to be with you again."

Madeline smiled, "I just wish I had known. I wish Charlotte had told me the whole truth. I just don't understand why she...."

Patrick cut her off. "Attie, Charlotte `as caused us much lost time, I'll grant you that, but I'm at fault too. We must move beyond the blaming stage. I want us to think of this as a new beginning. We `ave been given a second chance, something most people are never granted. We must make the best of it. Looking back is not the way to do it."

"But..." Madeline interjected.

Again, Patrick stopped her, "No buts. We `ave the rest of our lives for you to ask me any question you wish. They need not all be answered today."

Madeline remembered Patrick's notebook. She dropped her eyes. "May I ask you something?"

"Anything, Attie."

"Your notebook...could I read it?" As Patrick hesitated she added, "I think it would help to fill in more blanks. Maybe I would have some questions answered without having to bother you."

Patrick knew she would ask. He knew it would help her. It may even jar a memory or two, but it was too risky. He needed more time. There was one thing that remained unspoken. He was unsure how to refuse her. It was a chance he was unwilling to take.

"Madeline," Patrick began. "I don't know where to begin." He cleared his throat and tried again. "There is one thing I `ave to...."

There was a knock on the door.

"Oh my goodness," Madeline jumped. "That's Suzie."

When Madeline opened the door, she looked as if she had been crying.

"Are you okay?" Suzie asked.

I'm fine. Actually I'm great!" She wiped the moisture from her eyes. "Come in, Suzie. I have a surprise for you."

"Oh?"

"There is someone here I want you to meet."

Patrick stood as she approached. "Patrick, this is Suzie DuVeau." She turned to Suzie, "And Suzie, this is Patrick McCelvy."

Patrick held his hand out to Suzie and took her hand in his, "Nice to meet you, Suzie."

Suzie smiled, "It's nice to meet you."

Patrick and Suzie faced each other while Madeline explained, "Suzie, Patrick was an intern who took care of me in the hospital. He shared some photographs he took before he moved to Phoenix. We have been reminiscing all afternoon." Madeline looked at Patrick and smiled.

She turned to Suzie and said, "Patrick, this is Charlotte's daughter, Patricia. Her adoptive father gave her the nickname Suzie. Her birth name was given to her after my middle name."

Madeline was not sure whose mouth fell open the widest. It was the first time Suzie made the correlation to the P. in Madeline's name as Patricia, and the first time Patrick heard that Charlotte had a daughter.

The room fell silent.

Madeline burst into laughter, "Today is the day for revealed secrets. My, how you two look!" Her laughter was infectious.

They spent the next hour discussing the photographs, Charlotte, the dress, Phoenix, art, and Suzie's adoptive parents. Nothing was mentioned of Patrick and Madeline's former relationship, and Patrick's notebook was forgotten, for the moment.

When the dinner of roasted chicken, mashed potatoes and gravy, broccoli and spring greens was placed on the dining room table, Madeline called them to eat. She enjoyed preparing dinner this evening and refused help from either of them. She responded by telling them it was the perfect opportunity to become better acquainted.

They retired to the library after dinner. Madeline excused herself to prepare coffee and tea. She hadn't given herself enough time to make a 'proper dessert', so she scooped ice cream into three dishes. She crushed a few walnuts and heated chocolate syrup. She finished it by adding whipped cream and a cherry. She walked to her herb garden and pinched off a few mint leaves. She nestled them beside the cherry in the peaks of the whipped cream. She carried her creation into the cozy room.

For the first time she recalled, her heart felt content. Patrick and Suzie were flanked in the leather-buttoned wingbacks. They shared stories of their lives. Madeline stood in the threshold of the door and listened to their conversation.

Suzie explained her life in New England, but what Madeline heard next made her pause. "My father always told me I had a birthmark the same as my mother's." Suzie laughed, "But for the life of me, I have no idea where it is. I have searched my body over and found nothing." She paused for a second and snickered, "Once I even asked my ex-husband to search my scalp. It was the only place I could not see." The two of them laughed together.

"Suzie, sometimes birth distinctions are not so obvious. They are not necessarily a discoloration of the skin. I was not Charlotte's doctor, though, so I can't `elp you with your mystery."

The truth was, neither could Madeline. She entered the library with her tray of caloric sins and placed them on the coffee table.

"Umm, that looks good enough to eat," Suzie mused.

The evening was filled with conversations of years past. Madeline found herself listening more than talking. Her mind wandered several times from the present conversation to the exchange around the kitchen table. It was during those daydream moments the soft humming was heard. When she tried to focus on the voice, it stopped. When her mind rejoined their conversation, it was when Patrick was speaking.

23

Suzie arrived late. She entered her room without a glance to her surroundings. By the look of the smoldering fire William was there some time ago. She slipped into bed without trying to revive it. She closed her eyes and fell asleep immediately. Propped against the new vase of daffodils was an unnoticed note.

Suzie woke at 5:30 a.m. She showered quickly and dressed in layers. Suzie wanted to arrive at the cemetery early to continue her encounter with Elam.

She drove north on route nine to Salem. The number of daffodils that appeared overnight overwhelmed her. She wondered if she had overlooked them or if they emerged as a reminder. Her thoughts returned to Elam.

When she arrived at the cemetery, she was filled with anticipation. A thick fog hovered two feet from the earth and covered nearly ten feet in height. Her heart raced. It reminded her of the end of the tale yesterday.

She parked her car in front of the locked gate and walked to Goldie Bell. The flowers in her hands were the ones Suzie had placed. She stumbled with direction in the blanket of vapor, but she found her way to Elam's cross. To her surprise the daffodils were gone. Her heart sank.

In her mind she retraced the order of events when the visions came. One by one, she exhausted them all. The fog lifted and in a matter of minutes the sun burst through the veil. It warmed the ground with its strength.

The sound of a lawn tractor stole her thoughts. It was followed by a weed trimmer that spun with erratic acceleration. She noted that Wednesday was maintenance day. The consistent hum of the motors lulled the world to a sleepless state void of motion.

She looked toward her mother's grave and to her delight spotted Madeline as she replaced the flowers in the stone vase with a fresh bouquet. Madeline's hands and body language screamed of anger. When Suzie walked within hearing distance, Madeline was shouting.

"Why didn't you tell me, Charlotte? Were you afraid I would have left you? You knew how responsible I felt for the accident. You knew the way to control was through guilt! And even in your death, I am overcome with a sense of duty. You robbed me of a life with Patrick."

Suzie held her breath as Madeline continued, "Why, Charlotte, why? It was an accident. I didn't wreck on purpose. I prayed daily for your complete healing. Don't you think I felt guilty each time I walked past you? I gave up my life to help you with yours. I'm sixty-one years old and have never felt love. You stole that from me to satisfy your own selfish desires. You had two husbands. They adored you and you repaid them with hateful bitterness."

Madeline fell to the ground in tears. Suzie's instincts were to run and comfort her, but as she moved toward Madeline, she heard, "And now that I have found Suzie..." Suzie slid silently behind a large obelisk.

Madeline screamed, "You continue to control me! I am afraid to tell her the truth about her mother for fear she will leave. I can't bear the thought of losing her now. I have spent years living in the shadow of her life, and now I find comfort in sharing face to face. We are beginning a wonderful relationship, but in the back of my mind I hear your words of disgust. I know you disapprove, but I am here to tell you, I have gathered new strength. For the first time in my life, I am comfortable with who I am. I am spending time with Patrick, and he is helping me explore the world you kept from me. I resent you for that, but I am taking away your power."

Madeline threw her shoulders back in defiance. "Today is the last day I will bring you flowers. I will ensure The Flower Loft brings a fresh bouquet to you weekly, but it will not be me. Perhaps in the future when I have found it in my heart to forgive you, I will return. Until then, you must suffer alone."

Madeline turned from Charlotte's headstone and walked toward her car. She left the cemetery without a backward glance.

Suzie watched her car until it disappeared, then she walked up to her mother's grave. "Mother, what have you done?"

She felt sorry for Madeline, yet she was confused by her words. Madeline and Patrick painted a bright picture of Charlotte. Obviously the story was more shrouded.

She returned to Goldie Bell and to her thoughts of Elam. She replayed her action when he appeared, what she did, touched, and heard. Disgusted she was unable to call him, she walked back to her car. She drove in the opposite direction. She needed to see Patrick.

Alone in the Lincoln Suite sat a bouquet of daffodils. The note attached read:

Goldie Bell
Before mid-day, nine minutes past the eleventh hour

Patrick's night sleep had been restless. He enjoyed the evening with Madeline and Suzie, but the request for the notebook burdened his mind. He sipped his morning coffee and read his words of many years ago.

Feb 12, 1960

We woke early this morning. We made love at the break of dawn as we did our first time together. Attie is so beautiful in the early light. We made plans to meet at the park for lunch. New snow had fallen the night before leaving the earth to cast visions of thousands of prisms across the fresh crystalline powder. Attie waved from the window as she always did, her body barely covered.

I waited at the park for fifteen minutes, but Attie did not come. I drove to her house and found her lying on the floor. When I ran to her, she smiled weakly at me. She said she remembered feeling dizzy and slowly her world faded from color to black. I was concerned. I insisted she return with me to the hospital, but she refused. Attie convinced me it was because she had not eaten. I was unsure.

Feb 19, 1960

The day began as most others. The snow mixed with freezing rain and the drive to the hospital was treacherous.

Attie phoned to insure my safe arrival. She mentioned she was still tired and hadn't slept well the night before. I encouraged her to slide back under the covers and dream of me. I would look in on her later.

The hospital was hectic due to the weather. Lunch slipped by without a thought. I was reminded my stomach was empty from its loud rumblings around three o'clock. I was surprised how quickly the day had passed and thought it strange that I had not received a message from Attie. I tried to reach her by telephone, but she didn't answer.

I became more concerned with each passing moment. Until I could break away from the hospital, she consumed my thoughts. I drove to her house. When I entered, all remained as it was. I called out to Attie. There was no response. I ran up the staircase taking three steps at a time. When I entered her bedroom, Attie was lying on the bed.

As I rushed to her side, she rolled over and smiled at me. I was relieved to see she was fine, but when I told her she had slept the day away, she didn't believe me. Her skin felt cool and clammy, but she insisted she was not going to the hospital.

I watched her as she slept into the night. In the morning she awoke refreshed and all seemed to return to normal.

Feb 23, 1960

I stayed with Attie a bit longer this morning. She had a nightmare last night about the accident, but when she woke her memory of the dream was erased. I tried to jar her memory, but she became agitated. I let it pass.

Feb 26, 1960

The sun was bright this morning as I woke. I slipped out of bed quietly, careful not to disturb Attie. Her sleep patterns were erratic. I didn't want to wake her. I watched her sleep peacefully before I placed a note on my pillow and left for the hospital.

The air was cold, but crisp and I thought it was going to be a good day. I couldn't have been more wrong.

The hospital was calm until eleven o'clock. A flushed intern hurried to find me. The look on his face only meant one thing: Attie. I followed him to the emergency room. Attie was unconscious and her vital signs were weak. Her mouth was moving though no sound came from her lips. The doctors shuffled me from the room, and to my surprise I was escorted to the break room.

What seemed like hours was only a few minutes. A nurse summoned me to join the physician in his office. The news he shared with me left me speechless. I remember asking him if he was sure. He assured me there was no mistake. Attie was pregnant.

Feb 27, 1960

I entered Attie's room to a faint smile. She sat by the window and stared outside. I enveloped her in my arms. We cried together.

March 1, 1960

Our news was shared with Charlotte. The reception was not favorable. Since Attie was a minor released to her sister's care, Charlotte's decision was swift and final. The procedure was set for the following week.

March 3, 1960

Attie showed signs of depression. She refused to eat, spent her day staring out the window. Sleep eludes her. Charlotte refused to reason.

March 4, 1960

Attie grew weaker. The hospital staff administered fluids and food intravenously. Attie removed the tubes twice today. The strain between Charlotte and me grew stronger.

March 6, 1960

Tomorrow our baby will be no more. Charlotte had me removed from Attie's room. I was warned not to return.

March 7, 1960

Attie never woke this morning. Her vitals were weak. Her blood work showed signs of infection. The doctor cancelled the procedure.

March 10, 1960

After many days of uncertainty, Attie was diagnosed with a Nosocomial infection, a condition which can only occur within the hospital. Though Attie had not regained consciousness, her body was in turmoil. Her eyes flashed open. Her words aren't audible. Her movement was violent. I am helpless.

March 18, 1960

A second AVM was found. Many tests and procedures were reworked and rechecked for any other oversights. To our relief, no additional abnormalities were found. Attie's condition remains the same.

Patrick thumbed through many pages of detailed daily notes. It highlighted type and quantity of medication, her mumbled words, and crossed references. This was the only part of the notebook that appeared disheveled. He made many notes in the margin that underlined his discoveries. The pages were littered with red, black and blue pen scribbled over each other when a theory was thwarted. He made little mention of his feelings or his trip to Arizona. Most of the fourteen pages were devoted to Attie as she wrestled with the past.

He smiled as he read some of Attie's recollections. She mentioned things that surprised Patrick. He felt he discovered a very different person. She spoke incessantly of the oppression from Charlotte. She had conversations with her sister. After many, 'and one more thing…' of her imaginary badgering, the emotion that won was guilt. Attie's love for her sister was shrouded by deep remorse, and Charlotte used that to her advantage as much as possible.

The strained relationship between Patrick and Charlotte soon turned to pure hatred. After twenty-two days of 'the awakening', Patrick understood the sick power Charlotte held over her sister. He long resolved to take Attie to Phoenix when she was able, far from her sister's claws.

His eyes fell on a painful memory.

March 29, 1960

After twenty-two days, Attie woke today. I was the enemy.

Patrick dropped the book in his lap. He knew this story well. He knew how it ended, and the pain he felt today, over forty years later, was as violent as the day he first experienced it. He flipped through the pages one more time.

May 1, 1960

I was greeted by a police officer as I entered Attie's floor today. My going away present from Charlotte was a restraining order. As I left the floor, Attie was transported on a gurney. I turned to follow, but was muscled by an officer. I was informed Attie was having minor surgery. Nothing else needed to be said. I knew Charlotte had finally won.

May 2, 1960

I slipped into Attie's room to say goodbye. The room was dimly lit by the moon. I was overwhelmed with sadness as I knelt to kiss her goodbye. Though I am unsure, I thought her eyes opened and her lips parted to receive my kiss, but when I moved from her warm breath, she was still from sleep. I left for Phoenix.

That was the final entry in the book. He closed the book and stared at the cover. After a long time in thought, Patrick decided before he would surrender the book to Attie. He had to explain the final puzzle piece. He knew it would be a difficult task.

He gathered his coat and hat and walked toward the door. The weight of the notebook felt like a barbell. When he opened his front door, Suzie was running up the sidewalk.

24

Suzie admired the Dutch style home and mused that it looked like a home that Patrick would buy. When she got out of her car, a bee flew towards her. She fanned the air, but it landed on her eyebrow and stung her. She ran toward the front door.

"My, my, what's the `urry?"

She looked at Patrick from her swollen eye. "I've been stung."

Patrick shuffled her into the house and gently placed her in a chair. "I'll fetch my bag."

He disappeared into the next room. Suzie felt her eyelid swell thick. She was nervous, yet she felt comfortable in Patrick's care.

He rounded the corner with his black satchel in his hands, "Any allergies?"

Suzie shook her head no. He unwrapped a syringe and pulled a glass bottle from the bottom of the bag. He tapped on the side of the bottle and plunged the needle into the liquid.

After extracting the correct amount, he turned to Suzie, "This is going to sting like..." he chuckled, "...never mind."

He squeezed Suzie's arm and flicked the ruched skin with his finger. Without hesitation, he administered the shot of Solumedrol and covered the pin dot with an alcohol-soaked cotton ball.

"You should notice the effects soon. Your swelling will release and the burn will be replaced by an itch." He rolled back on his heels, "I never could figure out which is worse, the burn or the itch." His hearty Irish belly laugh was infectious. Suzie joined him.

After a few minutes Suzie asked, "Do you have a mirror?"

"Yes, I do." Patrick responded. "Somewhere `round here." He disappeared around the same corner as before and returned with a silver hand mirror.

As he extended the mirror to her, he said, "It was my mother's."

Suzie took the embellished mirror and ran her hand over the back of its well-crafted case. It was molded with tiny winged angels slightly obscured by surrounding clouds. The angels weren't the typical cherubs with the protruding bellies, but graceful women dressed in flowing fabric twirled around their hidden bodies. The quality of the silver was very high.

Suzie looked at Patrick with an astonished look on her face. "This is the most beautiful mirror I have ever seen." She ran her hands over the design again and added, "But I'm afraid to see what is looking back at me." She chuckled nervously.

Her eye was swollen less than it felt, but she looked somewhat monstrous. "Now that's a sight!" She looked at her reflection in the mirror. "I like the back of it better."

Patrick smiled gently at her, "You're just as beautiful as ever."

"Hardly," came the word out of Suzie's mouth, "but thanks anyway."

"Would you like a cup of coffee?" Patrick asked. Suzie hesitated, but he added, "I need to look at your eye once the swelling has gone down a bit." He stood and walked toward the kitchen without waiting for a response. "I'll put on a fresh pot."

Suzie did not want to argue. She felt uncomfortable with her face swollen, but she didn't want to go. She wanted to find out the answers to her questions about her mother. She hoped Patrick would know.

She heard him coming from the clang of the dishes. She waited for the right opportunity. Patrick carried a tray of coffee cups and two pieces of coffee cake. Suzie noticed there was no sugar or cream on the tray.

Patrick interrupted her thoughts, "You take your coffee black, right?"

Suzie smiled at his observance. "Yes. Thank you."

Patrick looked at her knowingly, "So tell me what brings you `ere."

Suzie fidgeted in her chair. "It's difficult to ask."

"What's on your mind?"

"I just came from the cemetery. I saw Madeline there, though she did not see me. She brought flowers to my mother's grave." Suzie sighed. She felt she had witnessed one of the most intimate conversations of a person's life, and was about to share it with another. She winced from discovery.

Patrick probed further. "Was Attie angry with `er sister?"

"Yes," Suzie said hopefully. "Then you know?"

"Yes, I do but...."

"But what? You both painted a rosy picture of my mother. I had no idea there was a deep conflict."

"Suzie, you must understand that Attie surrendered `er entire life, in all aspects, to care for your mother. Though Attie did it willingly, mostly through guilt, Charlotte would `ave it no other way." Patrick crumpled his face in thought, "Charlotte was a very persuasive woman. She always got what she wanted."

"At anyone's expense?" Suzie asked timidly.

"Unfortunately." He hesitated. "Yes."

They sat in silence and stared at each other. It was obvious that Patrick was not willing to volunteer any information. She thought back to the conversation she overheard.

"Madeline said that if I found out the truth about my mother that I may leave."

Patrick was startled by this comment, and it showed on his face. "She told you this?"

"Not exactly. She told my mother."

"Suzie, please `ear what I am about to tell you and try to understand."

Patrick rubbed his head with his hands. "Their story is a long and sad tale. I am not sure if it is my place to tell it."

Suzie waited for him to continue. She picked up her coffee cup and took a long drink. When she realized he revealed all he intended, her eyes flashed with anger.

She stood quickly. Her vision narrowed. She held out her hand for the placement of the chair. Patrick gently placed her in the chair and pushed her head between her knees.

"`old that position. I'll be right back." He returned with two damp towels. He placed one on Suzie's forehead, the other on the back of her neck. "Feeling better?"

"Yes."

"Let me `ave a look at your eye."

Suzie sat in the chair. He pulled his instruments from his medical bag. She thought he looked confused or concerned.

"Is everything okay?" Suzie asked in response to the look.

Patrick didn't answer. He was lost in thought as he stared into her eye.

"Patrick? Is it okay?" with a bit more force in her voice.

Finally, he responded, "Yes, my dear. It is fine." He chuckled nervously. "'Tis still a bit swollen though." The moment grew uneasy.

Finally, Suzie spoke, "Are you going to explain?"

"I think the three of us should discuss it together. I don't want to be the one that tells you without Attie."

"So that's it?" The sound of disgust was laced through Suzie's words, but Patrick was determined to hold his silence. He felt he had already caused Attie much duress and still had a bit more to reveal. His thoughts drifted to the notebook and the daunting task of sharing it with Attie.

Patrick placed all of his medical instruments back into his bag. He rose without a word and disappeared again. Suzie picked up the mirror and looked at her reflection. She laughed at what she saw.

Patrick poured another cup of coffee for each of them. He sat in the chair across from Suzie and stared at her.

Suzie spoke first, "So do you think we should call Madeline?" Patrick did not respond. Again Suzie asked the same question. Patrick smiled. His eyes were moist with tears.

"Patrick?"

"Oh dear, I'm fine. I just `ad a pleasant thought."

Suzie waited for him to continue, but he sat quietly.

"Are you going to share it with me, or are you going to keep me in suspense?"

Patrick sat unmoved by the accusatory tone in Suzie's voice. He decided before he flooded her with information, he must do some research. He diverted the conversation.

Finally, he laughed, "Suzie, my dear, why are you so defensive? I told you I `ad a pleasant thought. A memory from long ago."

He relaxed into his chair, closed his eyes, and clasped his hands in front of him. "Attie loved to swing. We spent much time at the park. When there were no children for Attie to swing, I swung her." He took a deep breath. "I can still smell `er shampoo as `er `air flirted with the wind and brushed my face. Oh, and `er perfume smelled of fresh picked roses." He opened his eyes and smiled at Suzie, "Something brought that to mind."

Suzie hoped for more information from Patrick. She slapped her hands on her knees and stood slowly.

"I think I'm going to see Madeline. Would you care to ride with me?"

"I `ave an errand that I must run. I'll meet you there, say in an `our?"

"That would be great."

Patrick walked Suzie to the front door, "Are you sure you want to drive?"

Suzie laughed, "I've looked worse than this before. I'll be fine."

"Are you sure?"

"Yes. Thank you. I'll see you over there."

"I'll give Attie a quick call to prepare her."

"Thanks."

Patrick dialed Madeline's number. Suzie watched as the hushed conversation took place. She could barely hear Patrick as he spoke. Within a minute, he hung up the receiver.

"All set."

"Okay. I'll see you there in an hour or so."

"It's a date," Patrick said with a skip in his voice.

She walked down the sidewalk to her car. Patrick watched her every move. He could hardly contain his anticipation. He grabbed his coat and hat and walked over to the tray of coffee cups. He gathered up both cups in his hands, placed them into a bag, and walked out of the door.

Suzie was determined to get answers to her questions. She felt frustrated. It was a week of highs and lows. She was overwhelmed, like a chef without time to sample each creation.

Her mind drifted to Elam. His tales were intriguing and filled with suspense, but she couldn't see their connection to her. What was the significance of all the connectors - the daffodils, the pink roses, the wood thrush, Goldie Bell, and the gold pocket watch?

Before her thoughts drifted further into the obscure, she pulled into her aunt's drive. She admired the majesty of the house as she walked up the front porch steps.

"Come in, Suzie," Madeline said as she opened the front door. Suzie greeted her with a hug and kiss.

Madeline gasped, "Oh, my! What happened to your face?"

"I had a fight with a bee." Suzie said automatically, but added with humor, "Guess who won?"

Madeline wasted no time. "I understand you have a few questions for me."

Surprised by her aunt's directness, she said, "I didn't mean to spy. I just happened to be there."

"Spy?"

"Yes, at the cemetery earlier."

"Oh?"

"I...I saw you from a distance," Suzie's words were thick in her mouth. "You looked...upset." She shifted her weight from one leg to the other, then back again. She stared at the floor. "I started to walk toward you and I heard you say my…" She sighed again. "I heard my name, and so I hid." She hung her head from shame, "I didn't mean to spy. I thought you would be upset if you saw me, but when you mentioned my name and that I may leave if I…."

"If you found out the truth," Madeline finished her sentence. She smiled at Suzie and added, "Come and sit with me. We have much to discuss."

Without waiting for a response, Madeline walked into the front parlor. A tea table with a fresh pot of tea and three teacups waited to be shared. Madeline motioned for Suzie to have a seat. She handed Suzie an ice pack wrapped in a towel.

Madeline faced Suzie, "Patrick told me on the telephone you witnessed my conversation at the cemetery." She grinned. "He also explained that you deserved to know the truth." She sighed as if a mountain range had been removed from her shoulders. "We owe you that."

"Why are you so angry with my mother?"

"I know Patrick wanted me to wait until he arrived but…."

Suzie sat in silence as Madeline explained her strained relationship with her sister. She wove a tale that was easy to follow but difficult to hear. As much as Suzie wanted to believe in the goodness of her mother, she was appalled at Charlotte's manipulation. Madeline walked her through the accident, the months in the hospital, and how her sister deceived her about her relationship with Patrick.

Suzie listened as Madeline's voice escalated and fell with each word. She watched Madeline cry from sadness and flush from frustration. It was easy to become enveloped in her aunt's emotions. Suzie felt she was reliving the story. It was difficult to imagine her mother was so evil, manipulating, and consumed with hate-fueled jealousy.

Each time Madeline stopped to take a breath, Suzie held hers until finally the story exhausted itself. Madeline crumpled like a discarded rag in her chair. It was taxing to reveal Charlotte's shortcomings.

Madeline shook her head, "You know, Suzie, it's unnerving. Even as I explain, I feel the cheek slap from my sister. I know Charlotte disapproves. Not only does she hate me for telling you, she despises that I am sitting here with you." Madeline shook her head in disbelief. "If I concentrate hard enough, I swear I can actually hear her chiding me."

"Then don't listen."

Madeline was shocked at Suzie's response. "What?"

"Don't listen. If there is one thing I have learned from all my counseling is the fact that people will continue to have power over you as long as you give them permission. My ex was a master at this. Although I think he could have learned a few things from Charlotte!" Suzie chuckled. "I used to think he was the worst. Now I know why God never gave me the desire to look for my mother until she was dead."

They both laughed. It felt good to release some of that pent up emotion. Madeline looked at her watch. They had been sharing stories for nearly three hours. She was surprised at the time.

"Where in the world is Patrick? It's a good thing we didn't wait for him."

"He said his errand was only going to take him an hour. I wonder where he could be. I hope he's okay."

"I'm sure he is fine. I would know here if he wasn't." Madeline brought both of her hands to her heart.

"You are taken with him, aren't you?"

"Yes, I am. It's the strangest feeling I have ever known. He has the memories of our prior relationship. I only have pictures and a letter." Madeline sighed.

"And a long letter it was." Patrick said as he walked into the parlor.

"I didn't hear you come in," Madeline said startled. She stood with intentions to pour him a cup of tea.

Patrick walked over to Madeline and placed his hand firmly on her shoulder. Madeline eased back into her chair. Patrick kissed her forehead. "Stay seated. I can fill my own cup." His eyes smiled at Madeline and her face blushed from excitement.

Patrick walked over to the tea table and filled the last teacup. "Sorry my errand took a bit longer than I thought. I assume I `ave missed much?"

"Your assumption is correct," Suzie stated matter of fact. She added with anticipation, "You were saying…."

"I returned five years later with `opes Attie would return to Phoenix with me. I found both of them on the front porch. Attie `ad just opened the door with a pitcher of iced tea when our eyes met."

He smiled with his eyes closed as he continued, "I can still smell `er perfume. The fragrance was heady and swirled around `er like delicate waves of pink petals as they floated on the warm afternoon breeze." Patrick opened his eyes and looked at Madeline, "She was so beautiful."

Suzie enjoyed the admiration. She watched Madeline's face blush from the compliment. She knew it was something she wasn't used to from her mother. Thoughts of Charlotte fueled a burn deep within her. The swing of emotions showed in her facial expressions. She couldn't escape the stares from Madeline and Patrick.

"What?" Suzie asked somewhat irritated.

Patrick spoke first, "I know what you're feeling. Believe me when I say, you are not alone." He reached out for Madeline's hand and held it within his own. "We `ave experienced full doses of Charlotte's poison. It's the kind of control that spans all energies. You must be careful to not allow it to consume you. Charlotte `ad some good qualities and we `ave shared some of them with you. If you choose to dwell on past feelings, do so on those."

Suzie blurted from desperation, "But she has done so much harm to you both! She robbed you of a life together away from her." Suzie's eyes flooded with tears, "How can you dismiss that?"

"Dismiss?" Madeline asked. "No, it must be forgiven. No one knew my sister better than I, not even Grant or Kenneth. I knew how she squeezed, melted, and molded me to be what she desired. I would be lying to you if I told you it didn't bother me. Daily I resented her control, but yet I tolerated it. I could have left anytime, but I was weak. Truth be told, I needed to be needed. I made Charlotte my life because I chose it to be so."

Patrick and Suzie sat in silence as Madeline revealed thoughts she had never uttered before. Those thoughts were difficult to admit, yet freeing to hear them spoken. When she finished, the room fell silent.

Without a word, Patrick pulled his notebook from his coat. He placed it on his lap and opened it to the pages he had read earlier. He also had things he needed to say.

25

Elam waited for Suzie. It was 11:09 a.m. He had given specific time instructions and she wasn't there. He rested at the base of Goldie Bell and fell fast asleep.

He spent the evening and into the early morning hours on Jasper's back as he was chased by a band of angry riders. It seemed they knew his every move and anticipated each change in direction. By the first light of daybreak, he finally found peace from the pounding hooves. He knew his time was drawing near, but he had much to accomplish.

His thoughts drifted to a distant place, one he hadn't been able to visit for a while. It was there she joined him. He heard the call of the wood thrush and was stirred by the softness of a woman's hand as it caressed his unshaven face. His ears were filled with her playful laughter.

When he opened his eyes, he saw Rebecca. She was enveloped in layers of soft pink satin, which opened itself to imported lace at the bodice. The French lace gathered at her neckline released itself leaving a hint of coverage. A sheer veil covered her face.

She softly spoke to him, "The time quickly approaches."

"Not soon enough. I tire of this continuous madness."

"Noon is but a few minutes away. We must be patient."

"Patience eludes me, yet comes knocking when not desired."

Rebecca laughed and stroked Elam's face. She moved her hands over his eyes, down the bridge of his nose and across his lips. She moved her fingertips to her lips, kissed them and shared the moist gesture with Elam. He held her hand in his and kissed each finger as his eyes smiled at her.

She spoke softly, "Do not tease me. I cannot linger."

"Please, just a moment longer. It has been too long."

"Noon. We will meet at noon. I should go before bad luck finds us and serves its purpose."

"I'll not breathe 'til then," Elam spoke in whispers.

Rebecca closed his eyes with her fingertips still damp from his warm kisses. She kissed his cheek and placed a note in the palm of his hand. The wood thrush sang from a bending tree. When he opened his eyes, she was gone.

His timepiece read 11:18 a.m.

The Spread Eagle Tavern was alive with the lunch crowd. Elam slipped by a small crowd in the parking lot without being noticed by any of the afternoon's guests, save one. A little girl held her mother's hand and anxiously waited to set off to their next destination. She waved to Elam as he slid past her. He smiled and waved to the little girl. Her mother never looked his way.

When he entered the inn, he was hidden behind the large bouquet of daffodils he held in his hands. The receptionist smiled as he approached the desk.

"Hello again," she snickered.

"Would you please deliver these as well as this?" Elam asked as he presented another fresh gathering of daffodils and a note.

The paper was the same aged parchment paper, but the writing was noticeably different. Instead of the normal scrolling script it appeared hurried, somewhat erratic. She glanced back at Elam. He patiently waited for a response.

"I'll be sure she receives them, sir."

"Thank you. You are most kind."

As he walked out of the door, she thought he seemed sad. He walked as if he carried a heavy burden and the light had left his eyes. She felt compelled to call out to him, but decided against it. Whatever weight this man carried was not her business. She whispered, "Goodbye," as he disappeared from her sight.

The little girl in the parking lot noticed him again as the inn's door closed behind him. She danced impatiently on her toes. Her mother continued a conversation with her friend. She stopped prancing when Elam held out a single daffodil to her. She ran to his side and thanked him for the flower. He watched as she skipped back to her mother. Her mother chided her for running away.

"Where did you pick that?"

"I didn't pick it. He gave it to me," she said pointing her finger in Elam's direction.

Her mother looked directly at Elam but never saw him. She turned to her friend and said, "Emma has such a vivid imagination. I hope it doesn't get her into trouble when she starts school." They both laughed.

Elam watched as their car left the parking lot. He waited for the van to pass him before he left. The little girl waved as they drove away.

"Whom are you waving to, sweetie?"

"The nice man who gave me this flower." She lifted up her prized daffodil.

"What man?"

"The one right over there, mommy."

"Where?"

"There," she said while pointing her finger at Elam.

Her mother looked where Emma was pointing and saw nothing.

26

Patrick sat with the brown leather notebook on his lap. It was well worn from daily use and bore the signs of its age. He waited for the right opportunity to present it to Madeline.It was opened to a tear-stained page. Suzie noticed his silence. His mood retreated from his normal gaiety.

"Aunt Madeline, you were wrong to think I would leave if I found out the truth about my mother. Since my adoptive mother passed away, I am thrilled to find a relative that I can spend time with." She smiled as she continued, "You are so kind. I will cherish the time we have to become better acquainted." Suzie turned to Patrick, "And somehow I know that where my aunt is, you will be also. I look forward to many years of conversations."

"Years?" Madeline asked.

"Yes, years. You don't think I will just disappear and never visit again, do you?"

"Well, I would certainly hope not," Madeline added.

Patrick sat in silence. Suzie was aware that he wanted to discuss something with Madeline in private. The look on his face was unmistakable.

"Listen you two. I really must go. I have a myriad of phone calls and a date with my lap top."

"Must you leave so soon?" Madeline said with a slight whine.

"Soon? We've been talking for nearly five hours."

Madeline glanced at her watch, "Oh my. I guess we have."

Suzie turned to Patrick and gave a quick wink. "I have a few errands to run first, but would you two like to join me for dinner at the inn?"

"We would love that," Madeline answered with excitement.

Patrick was hesitant but decided his conversation could wait. He closed the notebook.

He responded, "That would be great."

"What time should we join you, Suzie?"

"How about seven? Is that too late?"

Patrick answered first, "Seven would be great. Should we call for reservations?"

"No, I'll take care of that. The staff has been wonderful. I'm sure they will find room for us."

She walked over to Patrick and kissed his cheek, then gave Madeline a hug and said, "I'll see you at 7:00 sharp."

Madeline stood and made a motion to walk her to the door. Suzie placed her hand on her aunt's arm, "I'll show myself out. Thank you again. It was a good afternoon." She blew them a kiss as she rounded the corner.

Madeline waited for the sound of the closing door. "Was it me, or did that seem abrupt?"

"I think she is a very wise girl," Patrick said while clutching the notebook in his hands. "Come sit with me, Attie. I `ave something for you to read."

Madeline noticed the notebook and felt her heart moan. The look on Patrick's face was grave.

"Patrick, you seem so solemn."

"Attie, what is written will be difficult for you to read. There is no easy way to share this, but once you know the whole story, I believe you will understand many of Charlotte's motives." He sighed and patted the settee beside him, "Come sit with me. I do not want you to read these words alone."

Madeline sat close beside Patrick as he guided her eyes through his own words he had written so many years ago. He held her hand. She mouthed his words out loud. Her breathing was erratic as she read through the notebook she had begged to see.

When she read the entry from May 1, 1960, she collapsed in Patrick's arms. He tried to calm her, but her wailing could not be harnessed. Patrick knew she was releasing many years of pent up frustration and anger. He listened calmly as she screamed at her sister.

Madeline jumped up from the settee and ran into the parlor. It only took a minute before Patrick heard the crash. Madeline had taken the three photographs of her sister, which were specifically placed on the mantelpiece, and threw them onto the floor. She ground her foot into the image of her sister. The smug smile on Charlotte's lips had been permanently torn from the rest of her face. Chards of glass lay on the floor like tiny needles amidst shimmering diamond dust. Madeline's hands were bleeding.

Patrick helped her to the kitchen and washed the blood from her hands. She was consumed with rage. She didn't remember crushing the images first in her hands. Madeline slumped to the floor. Patrick held her close and rocked her gently as they sat together on the kitchen floor. Madeline's hands were wrapped in a towel. Her sobs drowned out the sound of the water rushing from the faucet.

Patrick didn't stop Madeline from sounding her feelings. He knew it would be a starting point of healing. Charlotte had spent many years squeezing Madeline into the mold of a perfect servant, and he knew how much Madeline needed to release the negative feelings she harbored. She tried to put up a brave front, but he knew her better. The path to wellness had just begun.

When Madeline exhaled and her body fell limp, he spoke. "I know that was `orrible for you. I promise you, Attie, I will be `ere to `elp." He smiled at her tear stained face.

"I can't believe..." Madeline's voice began to quiver, "that Charlotte killed my baby." Her words were barely discernable, "our baby, Patrick...ours."

Her sobs suddenly stopped. Her eyes flew open wide. She looked at Patrick. Her feeling of despair changed to hope. Tears pooled in her eyes, "I remember," she looked confused, "I remember the operating room."

Patrick opened his mouth, but no sound was heard. He held his breath as Madeline continued.

"I remember the stiff white sheet, the hum of machines, and the pungent smell of disinfectant. The doctor hovered close to my face and told me to count to ten and all would be fine when I woke." Madeline's eyes looked distant as she continued, "But I was restless. My mind fought the anesthetic. My arms were strapped down. My legs were in the air. I fought to stay awake. I was nauseated. The room spun and everyone moved in slow motion. Their voices were muffled and their faces were close to mine. I felt hands on my legs. I tried to kick but couldn't."

Madeline stared at the wall and tried to shake the memories from her mind. Patrick sat mesmerized by her words.

"What else do you see, Attie?"

"Nothing." She held her head in her hands. "But…I can't forget the smell. It haunts my dreams. I never knew what it was…until now…."

She ran her hands over her face in a scrubbing motion. She pinched her nose with her fingers. She started fanning the air in front of her face violently.

She screamed, "Make it go away, Patrick. Make it go away!"

He reached for her hands to calm them, but she would not allow it. The erratic movement opened her fresh wounds and blood began to splatter from her cuts. She stood and bounced around the room. "Make it stop. No crying. No more crying. Make it go away." Her body rocked back and forth. "…Shhh, be good girl. It will be okay…count to ten…" Her eyes were blank.

Patrick realized what he had done. He had made a grave error and he did not anticipate this reaction. He chastised himself for allowing his emotions to cloud his professional judgment. He grabbed Madeline with force and held her hands to her sides while he wrapped his arms around her. He picked her up and carried her to the bedroom.

When he laid Madeline on her bed, her body was limp and her breath came in whimpers. Patrick was panicked and sickened by the trauma he had caused Madeline, but he had seen this many times before.

He ran to the kitchen and dampened a towel. Blood littered the kitchen floor and counter top. He brought the wet towel and placed it on Madeline's head. He spoke softly as he positioned her body on her left side. He snuggled behind her pressing his body against hers. He recalled her happy childhood memories, he had memorized. He talked of picnics, cotton candy, and an elephant that soaked her father at the zoo, carousel rides, the swings at the park, and of her puppy, Giza.

Slowly Madeline responded. She turned to face Patrick. He held his breath and hoped to be recognized. His fears were calmed as she spoke.

"That was so real. Do you think that was an actual memory?"

Patrick was so relieved, he began to weep. Madeline watched his emotion with curiosity and was overwhelmed with passion. She kissed him and caressed his face. Patrick kissed her fingertips and smiled at her. She was still beautiful to him.

She swallowed the lump in her throat and whispered, "Patrick, I love you."

Patrick pulled her close and buried his head in her shoulders, "I `ave never stopped loving you." He gently brushed the hair from her eyes. "There `as never been another woman for me, Attie. I `ave loved you for over forty years." His voice began to shake. He fought the tears that fell from his eyes. "You are my world."

They kissed with passion unleashed from depths unknown. Not an awkward moment passed between them. Patrick moved over her body with skill spun from memories of much pleasure.

Madeline watched as he unfastened the buttons on her blouse. Her skin tingled with the touch of his fingers. He slid her blouse from her shoulders and kissed every part of her body that he exposed. His hands moved across the front of her breasts and she gasped with excitement. He pulled her to him and kissed her again. After whisperings of assurance from Madeline, he continued.

With Madeline's help, he removed her skirt and bra. He caressed her naked body as she moaned with approval. When he touched her, she had glimpses of sensual moments flash from her memory. Her mind and body enjoyed the pleasure he brought her.

Patrick brought Madeline to her first climax before he entered her. The arousal of his sensual touch was enough to satisfy her, but when he continued to tantalize her, she easily surrendered. The pleasure she felt when he moved into her was erotic. Their bodies moved with familiar motions brought from the past into the present.

With spent energies, they slid into each other's arms. Their bodies damp with pleasure clung to each other. Madeline refused to drift into sleep. As much as she enjoyed the moment, she was aware of the time.

She stroked Patrick's face to awaken him. His smile was a welcomed sight. Madeline convinced herself that she wasn't dreaming.

"That was very sensual. I love you, Patrick."

"And I love you."

"I hate to lose this moment, but we must meet Suzie for dinner."

"Yes, it will be a most enjoyable evening, watching the flicker of candlelight dance shadows across your beautiful face."

Madeline giggled and tapped him on his bare chest, "Come on. Let's go, Mr. Romantic."

"I `ave long dreamed of this moment."

She kissed him and slid from her bed. "I'm going to take a quick shower."

"Can I watch?"

He chased her into the bathroom with returned youth. As she stood with her hand under the falling water waiting for its warmth, Patrick came up to her and held her close. He kissed the back of her neck and shoulders. He stepped into the shower with her and made love to her again.

As Suzie drove to the inn, she processed all the information from the conversation. It was difficult to absorb what Madeline and Patrick shared about her mother. She still had questions. Some things didn't make sense.

Her thoughts drifted to Elam. Suddenly, she felt restless. She wondered why he didn't come to her today. He seemed anxious the day before and had left in a fury. She didn't understand what was happening to her, but she convinced herself to be patient and allow it to be revealed as planned.

When she pulled into the parking lot, the inn was quiet. The time was 3:15 p.m. The lunch crowd had long gone and the dinner crowd had yet to arrive. The same woman was at the receptionist's desk.

"Good afternoon, Ms. DuVeau."

"Hello."

"Will you be joining us for dinner?"

"Yes, I will."

"Table for one?"

"Actually, I'll need a table for three. Seven o'clock?"

She looked through her dinner reservation book, "Would the Taft Room be satisfactory?"

"That would be great."

"See you at seven."

"Thank you." Suzie turned to go to her room.

"Ms. DuVeau?"

Suzie stopped and looked at the woman, "Yes?"

"I...I know it's none of my business, but..." she stammered, "but a gentleman was here earlier with a bouquet of flowers. He's been here many times. I saw him yesterday too. He asked me to be sure you received the flowers and a note he had written."

"When was he here?" Suzie asked.

"Around one o'clock, I think. We were very busy. The lunch crowd was heavy today."

"Did he say anything else?"

"No, not really. He seemed sad or burdened somehow." The woman smiled thinly, "He told me I was most kind."

Suzie could tell the woman was taken by his demeanor. "He's a kind man," she added.

"He seems…" the woman paused in search for the proper words, "old fashioned."

Suzie smiled, "Yes, he is."

With nothing else said, Suzie walked to her room. When she opened the door, two large bouquets of daffodils greeted her. The bouquets were identical in color and quantity, with only one difference: one had a cabbage rose in the center. It was pink. When she bent to take in their fragrance, she saw the notes. The paper was the same, but the writing was different.

One note said:

Goldie Bell
Before mid-day, nine minutes past the eleventh hour

The other read:

Please join me at the memorial for Goldie Bell Taylor.
Nearing noon, the eighteenth minute of the eleventh hour.

Suzie was confused. Why the time difference? Who wrote the second note? What is the significance of the pink rose? She walked into the bathroom. She fingered the flowers that filled the vase in the bathroom. They were just as fresh as the day they were brought to her. Her eyes saw the kindness of Elam's face, the calmness of his voice and the haunting way she heard him when his lips never moved. She slid her body into the warm soapy water.

27

Suzie woke with a start. She shivered from the coolness of the water. Quickly she washed, stood, and wrapped a towel around her. She rushed to her timepiece. It was 4:10 p.m. She calmed her racing heart.

She dressed for dinner and sat at the desk. Her skin, still moist from her bath, left her chilled. She was about to search for William when there was a knock at her door.

"Suzie? It's William."

Suzie opened the door with a smile. Her hair was wet on her shoulders. "I can't believe it. I was just going to call for you."

"Do you need a little warmth?" he asked as he opened his tinderbox.

"Yes, I do. I can't get warm."

Suzie watched his skill as he created a blaze in a matter of minutes. They exchanged conversation about the past few days. William noticed the painting of Goldie Bell propped in the corner.

He pointed to it, "Did you paint that?"

Suzie laughed at his enthusiasm, "Yes."

"That's great!"

"You are most kind."

As soon as those words left her mouth, she realized the significance. They were Elam's words. His voice rang in her ears. They stared at each other.

William spoke first, "Is that from the cemetery?"

"Yes. This is Goldie Bell Taylor." She held the painting of Goldie in her hands and brought it closer to William. "She died as a young child in the eighteen hundreds. Her father had this memorial commissioned by an artist in Italy." Her fingers tapped the painting. "She's made of Italian marble. It was very expensive back then. Her father, Jacob, wanted to preserve her memory." Suzie looked long at the painting. She spoke in a hushed voice, "Her passing broke his heart."

William pointed to the vases placed around the room. "Has he been there too?"

"At times. Not always."

"Is he a ghost?" William asked with his eyes wide with wonder.

"Not exactly, more like a wandering spirit. He's trapped here for some reason."

"What does he want from you?"

"That, I don't know. But I think I am beginning to understand."

Patrick dressed before Madeline. He left her sitting at her vanity and went to the kitchen. He cleaned and disinfected the areas where her blood spattered earlier. He gathered the teapot and cups from the front parlor and washed all but Attie's cup. He placed it in a plastic bag and slid it into his coat pocket. Madeline came into the kitchen just as he finished. She knew he had cleaned up the blood but made no mention of it.

"Are you ready?"

"Yes. I'm famished."

"So am I."

"Have you ever been to the Spread Eagle Tavern before?"

"No, this will be my first visit."

"Good. I'm looking forward to sharing it with you."

Patrick grabbed her and pulled her close. "I'm looking forward to sharing the rest of my life with you." He kissed her. Madeline smiled.

The drive to the inn was filled with conversation though no mention of Charlotte or the notebook ever occurred. They both enjoyed the happiness of the moment and neither wanted to spoil it.

When Patrick drove into the parking lot, he pulled close to the door. He quickly got out, walked around the car to Madeline's door and opened it.

"Go on in and warm yourself by the fire. I'll join you after I `ave parked the car."

Madeline toyed, "If you have never been here, how did you know there was a fireplace?"

Patrick brought his finger to his nose, "I can smell it."

Madeline watched him as he returned to the car to park. She was not used to this kind of attention, but she enjoyed it. She turned when she heard Suzie's voice.

"Well, you two seem to be enjoying yourselves."

Madeline blushed from discovery. She whispered to Suzie, "I feel like a giddy school girl."

When Patrick joined them, they were laughing. He stopped and looked down at himself, "What do I `ave something on me?"

"Come on. Let's eat. I'm starving," Suzie laughed.

Gaiety filled their evening. Their dinner was excellent as always and left them feeling fulfilled.

"Save room for dessert?" the waitress asked. They looked at each other, each waiting for the next to speak.

Patrick spoke first, "What do you `ave?"

The waitress excused herself and soon returned with a tray filled with temptation. "Tonight we have warm apple pie a la mode, chocolate hazelnut torte, mixed berry cobbler, a trio of truffles - raspberry, chocolate, and cherry almond, triple layer cake blended with semi-sweet, dark, and milk chocolate, and of course our own crème brulee topped with fresh berries." She pointed to each selection as she tempted them with her descriptions. By the time she finished speaking, each of them found room for something.

Patrick extended his hand to Madeline and Suzie, "Ladies?"

"I'll have the torte," Madeline said.

Suzie added, "I'll have the cobbler.

Patrick smiled at their enthusiasm and said, "And I'll `ave the crème brulee."

"Any coffee?"

Patrick spoke for the table, "Two decafs and a tea."

"I'll be right back with your drinks."

She returned with a tray, two cups of coffee, a china teapot and teacup. Once the painted tole tray was cleared, she lifted the lid. Individual packets of English, flavored, herb, and citrus teas filled the box.

Madeline selected a tangerine lemongrass blend and placed it in her china teapot. The waitress presented her with a tea cozy embroidered with the Inn's logo to cover the pot as it steeped. The presentation added to the warmth of the evening's conversation.

When they had finished dessert, they excused themselves from the table carrying their cups. They stood in the doorway of the rathskeller and listened to the pianist.

His movement over the keyboard fell like a rhythmic waterfall.

Without a word, they moved into three empty chairs. Madeline's hair brushed the top on her shoulders and Patrick twirled her hair in his fingers, keeping time as the music played. The motion was so automatic that neither of them was conscious of it. Suzie watched with interest. They seemed so familiar. It warmed Suzie as the pianist created memories.

28

When Suzie woke, it was early. Her night's rest was peaceful and sound. She knew nothing from the moment her head rested on her pillow until the light of daybreak scattered thin across the sky.

She stretched her limbs and walked to the window. The sky showed soft pink clouds trimmed in a subtle shade of lavender. She glanced at her painting of Goldie Bell. It was the same sky she had painted.

Her eyes wandered to the vases of daffodils. She was curious about the two different time frames, each nine minutes apart. The difference in the handwriting stirred her curiosity and time would soon tell if her suspicions were true.

She walked to the desk and bent to smell the flowers. She fingered the ruffled edges of the rose. The bud opened to reveal a multitude of petals held within. Suzie lifted the aged paper to read:

Please join me at the memorial for Goldie Bell Taylor. Nearing noon, the eighteenth minute of the eleventh hour.

"Time draws near," Suzie whispered.

She walked into the bathroom and drew a hot bath. She added a splash of the bubble bath that she packed on a whim. She sat naked on the edge of the bathtub with her toe just barely below the water's surface. When the temperature was comfortable, she slipped into the water. She allowed the bubbles to nearly touch her nose before she turned off the water.

Suzie lay still in the hot water. She thought about Elam's story. She was apprehensive to meet him today. She finally understood that she could not call to him. It must fit into his time frame. She was curious about what she missed.

When her water changed from hot, to warm, to tepid, she was ready to begin her day. She had answered many questions in her mind this morning and before she lost these thoughts, she wanted to type them into her computer. She wrapped a towel around her body and another over her hair.

She typed feverishly. The words came in paragraphs rather than sentences. After a while, she pulled the towel from her head, tossed her hair free and continued to type. She was so involved, the knock on the door barely registered. She grabbed her timepiece. It read 7:45 a.m.

"I'll be right there," she said somewhat rushed. She ran to the bathroom and wrapped a terry cloth robe around her. When she opened the door, she was out of breath.

"Sorry," she said, "I was engrossed in my laptop."

"Where shall I place this?" the young woman asked as she held the tray filled with Suzie's breakfast.

"Just place it on the table out front."

The young girl looked at her alarmed because of her present attire, "You want me to put it out there?" she asked.

"Yes, please."

The young girl arranged the table with Suzie's food while Suzie dressed. When she had finished, Suzie was standing behind her.

"That was quick."

"It doesn't take me long," Suzie said while tossing her hair with her right hand. In her left was her laptop. "This looks delicious."

Suzie ate her breakfast as she continued to type. It didn't take her long to finish. The early morning was extremely productive. She scanned the information she entered, made a few corrections, and closed her laptop. She finished her project and her breakfast simultaneously.

The morning sky was filled with clouds, which rolled in from places unknown. The front line was clear and precise and left nothing to the imagination. Rain was definite today.

The wind gained strength. The trees were tossed like rag dolls. Their new leaf buds shed their thin layer of protection. They appeared as clumps of downy feathers tied to the end of each branch. Between this and the graceful movement of the tree limbs, the coming storm seemed bewitched.

Suzie pulled into Hope Cemetery at ten o'clock. She knew she was early. It was her choice. She found a parking place and watched the clouds as they lowered from the weight of their rain. Within minutes her windshield was littered with dampened debris. She struggled with her rain poncho. Dressed for the inclement weather, she walked toward Goldie Bell.

The visible world seemed anxious as if it held its breath. Suddenly, the wind stopped. The trees swayed until they settled into their normal stance. Several branches littered the landscape. Their desperate fingers clung to the gravestones which they imprisoned beneath their weight. The sky grew dark. It appeared as a force poised to capture its prey. Suzie shuddered from the sense of watchfulness that surrounded her.

Her steps pounded the earth. It quaked beneath her feet as she walked past Elam's carved cross. Whispered voices surrounded her. Their words were undecipherable, but their intent was clear. They were as anxious as Suzie, but their reason for being so, was very different.

Her throat was dry. Every step was labored and tense, heavier than the last. By the time Suzie's fingers touched the base of Goldie Bell, she crumpled to the ground exhausted.

Her breath came in panicked bursts. It grew more difficult to breathe. She sensed the clouds move closer to her body. They blanketed her in a veil. She heard the horses. They advanced at an incredible rate of speed. Within seconds they were upon her. Their hot breath singed her skin. She sat in silence, unmoved by their presence.

From the opposite direction a single horse approached. Its gallop was swift and sure. The feeling of hope slowly replaced dread. She knew it was Elam. He was coming for her.

Jasper whinnied as he drew near. She saw a faint outline of a lone rider surrounded by black. He rode furiously toward its destination. The rider extended his outstretched arm to Suzie. She grabbed his hand. He swung her to the back of the horse. Jasper never stopped moving.

With a swift kick the horse turned and headed from whence it came. Suzie held tight to Elam as they rode through the fog-laden cemetery. Not a word was spoken during their flight. To Suzie's surprise the other horses and their riders did not follow. Their presence was felt, but the sounds of their anger were still.

They rode for what seemed like hours until with a great leap forward, Jasper jumped over a deep ravine. When they landed on the opposite side, the world was colorful again. They were at the edge of a forest. A large field lay before them with sunlight so bright it pierced her eyes. Suzie covered her face with her hands.

Elam touched her hands gently and pulled them from her face. At the top of the hill a woman motioned for Suzie to join her. Suzie pointed to herself in question. Elam nodded his head to signal yes. He helped her slide from Jasper. The horse nudged his shoulder. Elam stroked Jasper's mane and jumped skillfully onto his back. The band of riders could again be heard. They were fast approaching. With a short burst of energy, Jasper, with Elam on his bare back, disappeared into the thick fog of the forest. The feeling of doom covered them.

Suzie tried to shout, but her voice was stolen from her. She spun around desperately to plead with the woman for help. She was gone. Suzie was alone, in an unknown place, without a voice. A burst of wind whipped her hair and forced her to the ground. Her world went black.

Suzie woke to a soft touch on her arm. A woman stood over her smiling. Suzie's head felt dizzy, but she managed to move into a sitting position.

"Where am I?"

"You are on the edge."

"Edge of what?" Suzie replied with irritation.

"Of death," the woman replied, still smiling.

Suzie's eyes flew open wide, "Am I dying?"

The woman laughed, "No, we are."

"Who?"

"Elam and I."

"But…" Suzie's words were cut short.

"Our time draws near. We have much to show you. You must be silent to understand what is being revealed to you. Your purpose will be known upon completion. Until then, you must trust and listen." She stood and walked up the hill. She motioned for Suzie to follow.

"Quickly. We haven't much time. They will return."

Suzie followed her through the pasture until they arrived at the top of the hill. Suzie immediately recognized the scene.

"I've been here before."

"Yes, at the beginning. This is my garden. This is where it began."

Suzie opened her mouth to speak, but the woman held her finger to her lips silencing her.

My name is Rebecca Elisabeth Kristol. In the year of 1863, I was a young woman of sixteen. My father, Nathaniel, was involved in a terrible business. It endangered the entire family. It was the business of freeing slaves.

My mother lost her life for her involvement, and I became the woman of the household three years prior. My father was a good man, though his business was very demanding, and I was left alone much of the time.

I spent many hours in solitude at the cemetery. For an unknown reason the cemetery was the only place I felt a part of something, of what I was unsure, but my desire to be there grew with each passing day. I mourned many a loss with others that I did not know. There I felt my life had meaning, and there it was revealed to me.

By the time I had become aged fifteen, stitching school and household chores had become distant memory. Most of the waking hours were spent alone in the cemetery. Many times I remained until long after the day's light had been spent.

Dusk was an enchanted time. My eyes played tricks on me, especially in the spring when fog blanketed the earth. As the thick mist moved over the ground, stable objects began to take on life.

Pine trees grew arms and walked above the gravestones. From the corner of my vision, spirits moved and gathered together. Their voices filled the air, though I was not afraid.

Many times, when I knew my father's business would take him away for the evening and deep into the night, I spent the night in the cemetery. I made my bed under a large oak tree, as I slept on the hardened ground. The roots cradled my head and wrapped themselves to protect me. Their murmuring lulled me to sleep.

At dawn's first light, before the sun chased the mist, the spirits gathered and took their places determined by the light of day. I watched them move into their places. Their bodies were tossed by the night's wind and their faces were drawn from sadness of leaving happier times.

I lingered on those mornings just a bit longer to watch the brightness of the sun return the day to what the living people see. The morning breeze stole the spirits' whisperings and carried them far away from listening ears. Their bodies slowly faded into their surroundings until they could be seen no more. The sun shadowed them, but they remained, watchful, and patient as they waited for the mist's thin line to beckon them to a more desired place.

Suzie listened intently without speaking. Rebecca's voice was mesmerizing as she told her story. Her voice was calm yet filled with sadness. When she finished, Suzie's desire burned for more.

Rebecca stood motionless with her face down turned. She looked as if she carried a heavy weight. Her eyes flooded with tears until they fell in narrow shimmers.

Suddenly, her eyes flew open. Her pupils dilated. She squinted toward the forest. Suzie heard no sound. In an instant, Rebecca ran down the hill, tripping twice over her dress. Her hair fell out of its knot and covered her face as she ran. She called to Elam.

Elam broke through the dense cover of the trees. The fog rolled behind him so rapidly it appeared alive. He bent for Rebecca with his outstretched hand. Rebecca glided onto Jasper's back with ease. Jasper's trot changed to an open gallop. They rode parallel to the edge of the forest.

From Suzie's view point, she saw a break in the trees. She watched as they approached the clearing. From within the forest she saw the band of riders. She tried to warn Elam and Rebecca but Jasper sensed their coming. He reared and kicked his front legs. The advancement of the riders was halted.

When Jasper's feet hit the ground, he changed direction. He ran toward Suzie. The riders and their horses stood at the opening. Their horses snorted and pawed at the ground waiting for approval to advance. It did not come. Nothing prevented their movement - no fence or ravine. Yet they did not move.

Jasper passed Suzie with incredible speed. Froth covered his coat. Elam clung to his mane. Rebecca's face was buried in Elam's back. None looked at Suzie.

She glanced back to the edge of the woods. The fog masked the edge from her sight. Suzie's heart raced. Her tongue felt thick and dry. Her throat closed from fear. The fog enveloped her. She felt their angry breath upon her. Hot anticipation spit from their nostrils. Their bodies obscured by the thickening fog.

Her feet felt nailed to the hard earth. She heard her heart pounding in her ears. Nervous laughter came from her mouth. She was startled by its sound.

She cried out, "What do you want from me?"

"We want the night rider," answered a voice from her left.

Suzie spun to address the speaker, but he could not be seen. His words held deep hatred.

In desperation, she gasped, "Why do you want the night rider?"

"He has seen that which he should not."

Another voice to Suzie's right added, "We have unfinished business." When he finished speaking, an iron rod fell at Suzie's feet. "Pick it up!" He sneered, "Take this to him. He will understand. He needn't run like the hunted in fear." The crowd burst into evil laughter. The horses snorted and pounded their feet.

"Take it to him!" the riders shouted.

Suzie wrapped her fingers around the rod. It was cold and smelled of death. When she stood, she was before Goldie Bell. The rain fell hard and she was chilled from her wet clothes.

She paused a moment before she moved. All seemed as it was before. Goldie was weather worn and the afternoon storm raged with fury. The wind bent the trees and tore their branches from their trunks. One crashed just to her right. It was then she noticed, her right hand held an iron rod.

29

Suzie drove to the inn without taking her eyes from the road. She replayed the scenes she had been shown over and over again in her mind. The tone of the rider's voices unnerved her. They were harsh, angry, and hollow. Their words were evil and their laughter haunting. The rain came in sheets. It was difficult to see. The weather conditions added to her uneasy feeling.

When she arrived at the inn, she sighed from relief. Quickly, she darted up the staircase to her room without speaking to anyone. The inn was eerily quiet and the floors seemed to moan as she rushed over them. Her only thought was to close her door and shake the feeling of dread.

She threw off her wet clothes and hung them over a chair. She turned on only the hot water for her bath. She heard something fall from the wet clothes and hit the tile floor. It was the pocket watch. She walked over to it, picked it up, and opened the cover. It was still. The time read 11:27.

"Another nine minutes."

She stroked the crystal and the gold cover with her thumb. She pushed the release and secured the cover in place. She admired the gold work on the front of the case. The back was identical. The memorial hair fob was soaked. As she ran her fingers over the blonde hair, she knew it had belonged to Rebecca.

She wondered why the riders chased them and what Elam saw. She closed her eyes to visualize the garden. Its significance was still unclear. She thought about Rebecca's gown. She felt certain it was for a special occasion.

With a push of a button, she started the gas logs in the bathroom. The orange glow reflected on the white tile floor. With her tub filled with hot, sudsy water, Suzie slipped in to warm herself. She allowed her thoughts to drift from Elam and Rebecca to Madeline and Patrick, refusing to harness them as they intermingled in her mind. There were uncanny similarities that encircled the two couples. Suzie smiled at how deeply involved she had become in both of their lives. She had only been in town six days, yet she felt a sense of belonging. She thought she should make it her permanent residence.

When her body felt warm, she dried off and dressed. She picked up her cell phone, which she hadn't turned on for days, and waited for a signal. She dialed Madeline and was not surprised when Patrick answered.

"Hello?" said the doctor.

"Well, good morning, or rather afternoon, I guess it is."

"Good afternoon, Suzie. We were just discussing you."

"Oh?"

"Attie and I were wondering what was on your schedule for the day?"

"Well, that was why I called. I have a date with my computer this afternoon, but I was hoping you were free for dinner."

"Perfect. We would like to cook for you. Say six o'clock?"

"Six would be great. What can I bring?"

"Just yourself. We `ave everything else under control."

"How about a bottle of wine?"

"We `ave a bottle of champagne chilling."

"My, you do have everything under control, don't you," Suzie laughed.

"We're anxious to see you."

"Me too. See you at six."

"Til then," Patrick said in his heavy Irish brogue.

"Until then," Suzie echoed.

Suzie listened to her voice mail. One was from her father, two from her editor, three from her friend, Carolyn, and two from her neighbor. All were normal except her neighbor. Suzie dialed her number.

After three rings, Joan answered out of breath, "Hello?"

"Joan, it's Patricia."

"Oh, Patricia, I'm so glad you called," she answered anxiously.

"Is everything okay?" Suzie asked, although she knew it wasn't. She could hear it in her voice.

"I hate to tell you this over the phone, but there was a fire in your studio."

"What? Is everything…?"

"It wasn't major, but you did have some losses." Suzie held her breath as Joan continued. "It started from an electrical outlet in the back. We got to it early. We were able to pull most of your work and materials from your studio before the smoke damage set in, but I'm afraid your apartment upstairs is a different story."

Suzie listened as Joan explained how she couldn't sleep and saw the ball of fire from the start. She quickly woke her husband and two of the neighbors. They carried out what could be saved. The men tried to put out the fire and had it fairly well contained before the fire department arrived.

The fire spread through the walls, and smoke filled her living area immediately. They carried out a few pieces of furniture, mostly antiques. When the water came through the roof, the rest was lost.

Suzie listened as Joan went down through the list of items that were ruined: her bed, one chest of drawers, sofa, coffee table, TV, stereo, kitchen table, and chairs, her clothes, and everything in her kitchen cupboards. It was odd to hear her belongings read off of a check list, but Joan was efficient. She made an excellent inventory of what was saved and damaged.

"I didn't call your insurance company," she continued, "because I wasn't sure which one you used, but I did file a police report."

Suzie sighed when Joan finished speaking. "Joan, I don't know how to thank you and all who helped. I feel helpless."

"Honey, we have everything under control. Bob and I have all of your work in our house. Not a piece of it has even a hint of smoke damage. We have your antiques in the garage."

"Thank you so much."

"I know you would have done the same for me."

Suzie's voice began to quiver. "It will take me fourteen hours to drive home…."

Joan cut her off, "Patricia, stay where you are. Finish your research. We have everything under control. There is nothing you can do here. Just call your insurance company and tell them to contact me. I'll take care of everything for you. After all, what are neighbors for?"

Suzie started to cry. "Thank you, Joan. Mom would be proud of you."

Joan's voice remained steady, even with the mention of Suzie's adoptive mother. They were old schoolmates and kept in close contact. In fact, Joan was the one who found the studio apartment for Suzie. She took on the role of looking after Suzie. She was a strong-willed woman with a warm heart, but not one to show a lot of emotion. She was the only family friend who called her Patricia.

"Your mother would have died in the fire trying to save her old sofa." They both laughed at the comment. "Anyway," Joan continued softening her voice a bit, "stay in Ohio. You need to finish what you have started. Your editor is counting on you for another book. Things will be fine until you are able to come home."

Suzie wanted to tell her about the past few days, but thought it would be better in person. She made Joan promise to call if she needed anything and gave her the telephone number of the Spread Eagle Tavern. She thanked her again and said goodbye.

Suzie dialed her editor. She was grateful to be greeted by his voice mail.

"Paul, it's Patricia. I have something for you to scan. Check your e-mail. Please call me with questions. My cell phone service is hit-and-miss down here, but we'll try to touch base. I know what I am about to send is incomplete, but it is finished through my research to date. I think the story line is as powerful as I promised. Tomorrow I will be at the library, so if we don't talk today, it will have to wait, unless you want to leave voice mail. Oh and Paul, one more thing, my studio apartment burned the night before last."

Without thinking, she hung up. She walked over to her laptop and turned it on. She turned off the fireplace in the bathroom, and returned to the desk.

She scrolled over the contents. She stopped at the poem 'On the Edge of Death'. As she reread her words, her body tingled from nerves. The very words she had written days earlier were the same that Rebecca spoke just a few hours prior. That coincidence was too strange for words.

Suzie scanned down to the end of the document and typed. Time slipped from all known reason and before Suzie finished, she had been working for over four hours.

The time was nearing five o'clock. She posted the information to Paul's email address. There was a knock on the door.

"Suzie, it's William."

Suzie tapped the send button and answered the door. "Hello there."

"Are you ready for a fire?"

"Boy, I needed you earlier. I came back from the cemetery soaked and freezing."

"Soaked?"

"Yes, it poured."

"It's been sunny here all day," he said with a question in his voice.

Suzie laughed, "Well, it rained in Salem." Suzie squinted from memory, "As a matter of fact, I drove through the rain all the way here."

"Nope," William added, "it's been sunny all day." He turned from her, knelt by the fireplace, and opened his tinderbox.

Suzie didn't want to question him, but it wouldn't be the first time that had happened since she came to town. She decided to keep it to herself. William knelt before the hearth and assembled his handiwork.

As he fumbled for his magnesium block, Suzie stopped him. "Wait. Don't light that yet. I'm going back into Salem to join my aunt for dinner. I will be late. How late are you scheduled to work?"

"I work until ten."

"Then light it just before you leave. I should be back by then." There was another knock on the door.

"Ms. DuVeau?"

"Yes," she replied as she opened up the door.

"Here is another bouquet from your admirer." It was David. He walked over to the bedside table and placed the vase in the center.

"No note this time," he added with a smirk.

He noticed the wood in the fireplace. "That looks like William's creation."

"Yes, he was just here. I told him not...."

David cut her off. "What did you say?"

"I said he was just here. I told him to light the fire just before he left work."

David looked at her puzzled and then began to laugh. He shook his finger as he spoke, "That was a good one, Patricia. You almost had me."

"What do you mean?"

"We all miss William. He took a special liking to you, you know. He made sure you had a wonderful fire and a few extra logs in case you worked late."

"Now you are toying with me. He was just here."

"That's not possible."

"He was just here!" Suzie insisted.

"I wish it were true and so does everyone else." David's voice cracked. "William passed away early Monday morning. I thought you knew. I'm sorry."

"But, I just saw him!" Suzie pointed to the fireplace.

"I don't know what you saw, but I wish it was William. I'm sorry to bring the bad news."

The moment was awkward. David felt just as uncomfortable as Suzie. He looked at her in question. Suzie did the same.

Just as he started to walk out of the door, Suzie asked, "David, what happened to him?" Her whispered tone was laced with sadness.

David hung his head. The only word he spoke was, "Fire."

30

Suzie thought of William her entire drive to Madeline's house. She was confused by the conversation and greatly saddened. She enjoyed her conversations with him. He was very protective of her. She missed him more than she was willing to admit. She fought the tears and tried to swallow the lump in her throat.

Madeline waited at the door. Patrick took Suzie's purse and wrap and hung them on the walnut hall tree. Suzie followed Madeline into the kitchen. They watched Patrick as he popped the champagne cork. It sailed toward the ceiling and bounced off the brass chandelier. It swung from disturbance.

Patrick lifted his glass and nodded toward Madeline, "I would like to propose a toast. To my dearest, Attie, may our life together be filled with much `appiness." All took a sip. Suzie never took her eyes off Patrick.

"And to sweet Suzie, may she find the desires of `er `eart and the love of `er life." He nodded and winked as he lifted his glass to his lips.

"Here, here," Madeline added. Everyone took a second sip.

"Come, dinner is ready," Madeline said as she motioned toward the dining room.

The table was set with fine linens and china. An oversized candelabrum filled the room with a soft glow. Charlotte's antiques shimmered with a worn patina in the dim light. The flicker of the candle swayed shadows on the walls. During daylight hours, this room appeared showy, but tonight it shone of amber hues. It exuded warmth of vision and feeling.

Patrick and Suzie sat through Madeline's insistence. "It has been too long since this house has entertained proper dinner guests. Please, relax and enjoy each other." She disappeared around the corner and reappeared with their dinner salads.

They talked and laughed through all four courses. Suzie noticed their anxious eyes.

Finally she blurted, "You two look like you are going to burst. What is going on?"

"Oh my," Madeline blushed, "are we that obvious?"

"Yes." Suzie replied coaxing for more.

Madeline looked at him, "Patrick...."

"We brought you `ere tonight to share some wonderful news with you. Attie and I are going to be married."

"Well, I'm not surprised except for the speed."

"Speed? My dear, I `ave been waiting for this woman to say 'Yes' for over forty years." The room burst into laughter.

"I guess when you put it that way..." Suzie stood and kissed them both. "Congratulations. When is the big day?"

"Next Wednesday," Madeline chimed, "if that is okay with you."

"Wednesday sounds great. What time?"

"In the morning, 9:30 a.m. at the little chapel in Hope Cemetery."

Suzie jumped with surprise. "In the cemetery?"

Madeline placed her hand on top of Suzie's. "I know it seems strange, but that is where we were brought together..." She smiled at Patrick, "...again. That place deserves some happiness."

"And besides, we want Charlotte to turn over in `er grave." Patrick added with a twinkle in his eye but not a smile on his face.

Suzie smiled, "Oh, I certainly understand that!"

Patrick walked over to Madeline. He placed his hand on her shoulder and knelt to one knee. He pulled a burgundy velvet box from his pocket.

He cleared his throat. "Attie. You `ave been my everything for as long as I remember. I never lost faith that this day would come." Madeline's eyes welled with tears as Patrick spoke. "The `ope that you would once again share my life `as carried me through many long nights. It `as been an eternity that I `ave longed to ask you, Attie, would you marry me?"

Madeline's tears fell down her flushed cheeks. She threw her arms around his neck and kissed him. She whispered, "Yes," and kissed him again.

It was difficult to fight the tears as Suzie witnessed the tender moment. Patrick removed the diamond ring from the box. It was a beautiful three-karat pink diamond, cushion cut, encircled with a row of white diamond marquis. It gave the appearance of a delicate rose. It was set in 18K gold and platinum. Madeline's face reflected the light as Patrick slipped it on her finger. She cried and so did Patrick.

Suzie threw her arms around both of them. She thanked them for allowing her to be a part of such an intimate exchange. She held Madeline's hand close to her face and admired as the light gathered and moved in the facets of the diamond. It's beauty was revealed from deep within.

"This is the most beautiful engagement ring I have ever seen. Where did you find it?"

"I `ad it made. It was one of the errands I tended to that made me so late the other day." Patrick wanted to swallow his words as soon as he spoke them. The only way to cover was to continue. "The designer was proud of `is interpretation of our love. `e explained each unique detail and I didn't want to rush `im. `e did a beautiful job."

"So you didn't waste any time, huh?" Suzie asked accusatorily.

Patrick took Madeline's hand and said to her, "When our first meeting went well, I met with `im that afternoon. I described your `air color, your skin tones, and `ow your eyes danced when we met." Patrick held up her ring finger and said, "And this was the result of our creation."

"Patrick, it's beautiful," Attie whispered.

"And so are you."

31

Madeline and Patrick's love was an inspiration. It was difficult to imagine spending nearly an entire lifetime alone, holding onto a hope that may never return. The loneliness in that longing had to be unbearable at times.

The only notion that surpassed Charlotte's control was the way Madeline and Patrick were able to forgive. Suzie questioned her ability and willingness to follow. She hated to call Charlotte 'mother'.

When she turned her car into the parking lot of the inn, it appeared most of the dinner crowd had left. The smell of wood smoke greeted her when she opened her car door. The inn had settled to an intimate crowd that surrounded the piano in the rathskeller. The chime of glasses drifted up the back staircase to the reception area. Laughter and song rose and fell as waves on the sandy shore. They slowly slid back from where they came, only to erupt again with renewed volume. The echo added to the feeling of calm.

She walked through the dining room toward the front staircase. As she passed the Asher Benjamin room, she noticed a couple sitting in the wingback chairs. They were involved in their conversation and took no notice of Suzie. She heard them mention her name, so she stopped. She searched her memory for the placement of this couple but came up blank.

"...staying here. She is working on her next book, I understand."

"I wonder what made her pick Ohio."

"Something to do with her mother, I guess. She lives on South Lincoln in Salem."

"Who is her mother?"

"I'm not sure."

Suzie chuckled to herself. It always amazed her how mixed up stories get. 'My mother lies in Hope Cemetery on North Lincoln,' she thought, 'although I wish she lived on South Lincoln. I would like to have a few words with her.'

Suzie listened to this couple as they discussed Patricia DuVeau. She entertained the thought of introducing herself, but she looked at her timepiece - it read 9:45 p.m. She wanted to see if William would visit her again. She slipped past the doorway and walked up the stairs.

When she opened the door to her room, the fire was just beginning to catch and William was kneeling on the floor. Suzie gasped when he turned and walked toward her. In the dim light she could see his face and neck had been badly burned. His face was unrecognizable, but she knew it was he when he whispered her name.

He held his hand out to her. She took it. When their hands touched, his peril was revealed to her.

She watched as he left the inn that Sunday evening. She saw him drive to his home. She observed as he slept. She noticed as the fire started in an electrical outlet. She could feel the hot flames on her face as they licked the walls with hunger. Smoke quickly filled his room. He never stirred. His bed became engulfed in flames. It rapidly spread to his face. The heat intensified. Its fiery fingers covered the ceiling in triumph.

Suzie dropped his hand and covered her face. Her knees buckled. She crumpled to the floor. Her sobs could be heard in the hallway as she cried William's name.

There was a knock on the door. "Suzie? Are you okay?"

Suzie rushed to the door and swung it open. William was standing there with his tinderbox. He was smiling. His face was perfect, but his eyes were filled with anxiety. Suzie rushed to him and threw her arms around his neck. She took his hand and led him into her room. The look on William's face changed from concern to confusion as Suzie stared at him. She smiled through tear-stained cheeks.

He brushed her damp cheeks with his fingers, "What's wrong?"

Suzie stood speechless. She turned from him and saw the wood William had left earlier still lying on the andirons, waiting to be lit. Her mouth moved full of words, but no voice was heard. She looked at William, toward the silent fireplace, and back to him again. William waited for her to speak. He held her hand firmly.

Finally, Suzie pulled her eyes from him and shook her head in disbelief. Which held the truth now or earlier? When she found her words, desperation filled her voice.

"William...I thought...I thought...you."

"Thought what?" William placed his tinderbox on the floor and held her close to him. He gently stroked her hair. Her scent was intoxicating. Suddenly he realized his forward move and placed his hands on her shoulders. "Suzie, you are scaring me. What's wrong?"

"I just had the strangest thing happen to me."

"Tell me." His eyes were kind and filled with concern. They pleaded her to continue.

Suzie tried to sort out the details in her mind - her conversation with David this afternoon, seeing William's appearance drastically different, and the fire in the fireplace. She moved toward the wingback. William knelt before her.

Suzie moved her face closer to his, "Is David still here?"

"David took yesterday and today off for vacation days. He'll be back tomorrow. Can I help you?"

The words he spoke were not what she expected to hear, though they made her happy. Her mind sifted through the details. She looked for the flowers David had delivered earlier. They were not there.

"David wasn't here earlier today?"

"No. He is in New York." William's face was grave, "Suzie, what is happening to you?"

"I'm not sure. I had a premonition about you. Something awful."

"What?"

Suzie shook her head and waved her hands in front of her, "I can't talk about it." Her voice trembled. "It was..." Tears dripped from her eyelashes. "Oh William!"

William squeezed her hand. "It's okay. I'm here. Nothing has happened." He smiled at her. His eyes settled on the silent fireplace. "How about that fire?"

Suzie's body tensed. She wanted to shout, 'No!', but thought better of it.

William understood. "You saw a fire, didn't you?"

"Yes." Her eyes flooded with tears. "It was awful."

He spoke softly as he stroked the back of her hand. He turned her hand over and tenderly kissed her palm. "Look at me. I'm fine."

All Suzie could do was sigh. The vision was difficult to shake.

"I have an idea. I'll get us some tea and stay until you feel comfortable. How does that sound?"

"Wonderful."

William kissed her forehead. "I'll be right back. I'll wait to start the flame. Okay?"

"Okay." Suzie watched him walk toward the door. "William?"

"Yes?"

"Thanks."

With his eyes lit from affection, he winked and closed the door. "I'll be right back."

Suzie heard his footsteps move farther from her room. She listened for the squeak of the third stair to groan beneath his weight. She sat in the dim light of her room and tried to process her thoughts. Never had her experiences been so powerful. She wondered why, but understood she would know when the time was right.

She blended thoughts of Elam with Madeline, Rebecca with Patrick, William and herself and suddenly, all became clear. Each story was its own, yet they were intimately entwined. Patrick's tenderness for Madeline was shown in William's toward her and Elam's to Rebecca. Their hands touched the same, kissed the same, and caressed the same. The resemblances in their movements were uncanny, blended, refined, yet uniquely different.

Suzie was lost in thought when William returned with a tray of teacups and a teapot covered in the signature cozy. He placed the tray on the empty bedside table. He poured two cups with the steeped tea.

"I chose Night time. I thought we both could use a little help with sleep tonight." He chuckled as he spoke. "How `bout that fire now?"

"I'm ready."

William knelt at the hearth. He opened his tinderbox and within minutes the flames caressed the kindling. The wood crackled from the heat.

The room was filled with a warm glow. They sat in silence and stared at each other. They whispered thanks for the other, yet unsure of their words. Their eyes were filled with longing, completing the circle of desire.

William sat cross-legged on the floor in front of the fire. Suzie sat comfortably in the wingback. They talked for hours. Suzie shared her experiences with Elam and Rebecca. He listened with wide eyes as she spoke. She told of Patrick and her Aunt Madeline. She spoke of their longing and desire for each other. Her eyes danced as she shared their story.

William opened himself to her. He told his own story. Although his experiences paled in comparison to Suzie's, he spoke of his own phenomena. He never permitted so much transparency in a relationship, but he felt compelled to share. His desire grew stronger, but he felt bound by their age difference.

With his inner turmoil too powerful to overcome, he tossed the last log on the fire. "Suzie, I should be going. It's late and you are a guest...."

She stopped him from finishing his thought, "William, I don't want you to leave."

He was surprised by her words and approached her hesitantly. He wanted to hold her, caress her, kiss her, but he questioned himself. Was he reading her correctly?

Finally he spoke, "It's late...."

"But the fire."

He moved toward her. His desire was strong. He moved the hair from her face and gently tucked it behind her ear.

"I'll be fine." His eyes searched hers for equal desire. "Really."

Suzie threw her arms around him and buried her face into his chest. There she stood a woman of forty-three, in her private bedroom, with a young man eleven years her junior. Her body quivered.

William felt her body shake. He pulled her to him and wrapped his arms around her. The log on the fire hissed. With a loud crack it spit coals at their feet. He brushed the hot embers from the wood floor. When he stood, Suzie moved into him.

Her words came in a whispered voice. “Please stay.”

32

She woke to a knock on the door. "Ms. DuVeau, your coffee is ready." Stumbling from the lack of sleep, she was slow to respond. "Just set it by the door, please. I'll get it in a minute." Her feet touched the floor and fumbled for her slippers, "Thanks," she added as an afterthought. As she chased the slumber from her mind, she was aware of William's absence.

Seated on the edge of her bed, she surveyed the room. The fire had burned entirely and the extra logs were gone. She remembered asking him to stay. She remembered their conversation and shuddered at the thought of her vision. She shook her head to remove the image of his charred face. She whispered his name. The room was silent.

Suzie opened the door and retrieved the tray from outside of her room. The smell of the coffee awakened her senses. She heard footsteps coming from behind her and her face flushed from embarrassment at being caught in the hallway dressed in a robe.

"Suzie," William spoke in a whispered voice.

She spun around. Her smile was warmed by the sight of him dressed in the same clothes as the night before.

"Where did you go? I was worried you went home."

"You were a bit hard to resist. When you insisted I stay, I couldn't refuse."

Suzie was relieved yet confused. She couldn't recall crawling into bed last night. William read her bewilderment.

"You fell asleep in my arms last night in front of the fire. I stayed with you until I could not stay awake any longer. You didn't stir when I laid you on your bed. I covered you with your robe." William's face flushed as he continued, "I kissed you goodnight and left your room about three o'clock."

Suzie watched his eyes sparkle as he spoke. He had a tender spirit and spoke softly. It was easy to become mesmerized with each spoken word. It was difficult to imagine him younger than she. His mannerisms and word choices were that of one much older. She found herself smiling at the thought of him kissing her goodnight.

"You're smiling." His fingertips caressed her lips.

Suzie's face flushed. She knew he was flirting with her. She heard the groan of the third stair and peeked around him. The waitress approached with her breakfast.

"Where would you like me to place this, Ms. DuVeau?"

Suzie held out her hands. "I'll take it with me." She smelled the aroma of fresh pancakes and real maple syrup. "Thank you very much. It smells delicious."

She carried the tray into her room. William followed. When Suzie closed the door behind them, it struck her odd that the young woman only addressed her and not William.

She spoke without thinking, "Do you know her?"

"Yes." He offered nothing else, nor did Suzie ask.

Suzie took the cover off the food. Her stomach ached from hunger. She pulled a second chair over to the fireside table. "Please, join me. There is plenty here to share."

William looked over Suzie's breakfast, "It does smell wonderful."

"Please, William, sit with me."

Suzie moved her chair and positioned herself closer to William. Her robe opened slightly and revealed the softness of her bare skin. When she arranged the table settings to suit her, she was aware of her gaping robe. She pulled the ends together and wrapped herself tightly with the belt.

She glanced at William as he smiled. "I don't mind."

Suzie bowed her head in embarrassment. She couldn't find the words. Her revealing was unintentional, at least consciously.

She slapped the back of his hand playfully."You shouldn't have looked." His reaction was unexpected.

William stood without a word. He took her hand in his and kissed the palm of her hand. He moved to each fingertip and kissed them, allowing the moisture from his mouth to arouse her senses. He moved one hand to her knee and gently brushed aside the fabric of the robe. His warm hand stroked the softness of her skin. He slid her chair to face him as he knelt on the floor.

His eyes never strayed from hers. "Suzie, I know our age difference could pose problems in the future, but that is a risk I am willing to take."

Suzie knew how he felt about her, but those words left her speechless. Her thoughts warned to be careful, to take it slow, to investigate these feelings for truth, but she threw caution aside and wrapped her arms around his neck. They held each other for a long while. Neither felt the need to speak.

Finally William whispered, "I must be going."

"I'll see you later?"

"I'll be waiting for your return from the cemetery."

'How did he know I was going to the cemetery?' she wondered. 'I didn't mention it to him.'

She smiled as he stood and kissed the palm of her hand again. He brushed her face with the tips of his fingers, kissed her forehead, and walked out of her door.

He whispered, "Until later." He disappeared around the corner.

Suzie listened for the familiar creak of the third step, but she didn't hear it. Curious, she rose from her chair and peeked out of her door. William was nowhere in sight. She closed her door and slipped into the shower.

Her thoughts of William and their previous conversations blended into the moments of desire and intimacy. She felt strangely close to him despite their brief time together. She hummed as she drove. It felt good to be happy.

When she pulled into the cemetery, she noticed the difference in Goldie's appearance. She was amazed how often the look on her carved face seemed to change. She dismissed the peculiar notion each time it crossed her mind. How could her expression change when she was forever carved in marble? But it was true, and today Goldie Bell Taylor was smiling.

Suzie approached the monument with reverence. The fresh bouquet of pink roses had fallen from her hands. Suzie knelt to gather them from the soft ground. As she lifted the tightly woven nosegay to their rightful place, she heard laughter of a young girl.

Suzie spun her body to see an image of Goldie Bell before her. Her laughter was muffled and distant, but her body stood only a few feet from her. She was dressed the same as the statue. The vibrant pink ribbon wrapped through her hair was the same color as her dress. The lace woven throughout was exquisite.

She looked at Suzie, smiled, and turned from her. She began to skip. She sang an unknown tune as she moved through the lawn. Suzie was mesmerized by this child's fluid movement. Goldie Bell stopped and glanced back at Suzie. Her eyes permitted Suzie to follow.

Suzie moved toward her. Her sweet song was a bit clearer. She followed Goldie Bell until her tiny feet suddenly stopped.

Fields of grain surrounded them. Long rows of corn stood in silent submission, ripe for harvest. The distant corncribs awaited their use. Goldie Bell cried out loud with glee as her swift feet carried her toward the farmhouse. She found her father bent over a large iron kettle, steaming with a thick dark liquid. Suzie watched as the man poured the dark syrup into a large pan.

They swirled the remnants of the sweet sauce with their hands. In unison they lifted their dripping fingers and licked the precious juice until they were clean, returning again and again. Their clothing was speckled with purple elderberry juice.

Their laughter was heard above all other noises. Her body fell into her daddy's arms and giggled with contentment. Her father cradled her as he sang to her and kissed her repeatedly. Goldie Bell threw her arms around his neck in adoration. Suzie's eyes filled with tears.

From the farmhouse porch came a call. "Goldie Bell…Jacob…" Her voice drifted on the wind.

Jacob walked toward the farmhouse. Goldie started to follow but hesitated and returned to the warm kettle. Jacob gave the large pan to Lizzie and called for Goldie again. She sat on the ground, cross-legged, and licked her fingers clean. Jacob laughed as he walked toward her. He scooped her up in his arms. She giggled and tried to break free from his grip. They laughed together and walked through the door.

In a moment the sky became grey. The overworked ground kicked dust into Suzie's face. She covered her eyes with her hands. It was difficult to breathe. The air grew thick with the swirling breeze. She rubbed her eyes to rid them of the debris. When her vision cleared, she stood at the foot of a small bed. Under a light layer of covers was a frail silhouette. She shivered with fever. A thunder jug was filled with blood-riddled spew. The smell of death filled the air. She heard hushed voices in the hall. Suzie peered around the door to see Goldie's parents as they talked to a man with a black leather bag in his hands.

Because of her conversation with Dale Shaffer, Suzie knew how this story ended. She watched Jacob comfort Lizzie as she cried. The doctor shook his head. He picked up his bag and walked out the door.

Jacob sat beside Goldie on her bed. He gently stroked her hair. Her innocent face was paste white. She winced from sharp pain as it moved through her body. No song or laughter was heard, only weak moans. Jacob wrapped himself around her small frame and sobbed.

Suzie wiped the tears from her own eyes. She searched her pockets for a tissue. Jacob brushed past her as he carried Goldie Bell's limp body. His face was drawn from pain. His cheeks appeared to be permanently etched by his own tears. She wanted to go to him and comfort him, but she knew she was only a bystander. She was not present in this time. She wept with him as he carried her.

In the next breath, she was returned to the cemetery. Jacob's face was buried in the fresh dirt. He filled his fists with the damp soil and sobbed uncontrollably. He was alone.

Suzie watched the months fade into years as time passed. She watched the grass grow over the mounded dirt in the cemetery. She saw the farm fall into ruin from neglect and depression. She watched Jacob's health fade from the will to continue. Suzie wanted to comfort him and tell him not to blame himself. How was he to predict that Goldie's fragile system could not purify itself from the iron she ingested? He could not have known.

Time passed as she watched the sale of the farm and the money paid to the Italian craftsmen for the commissioned monument. The statue was completed after much time and patience. The detail was exquisite - from the lace on her dress, the depth of her eyes, her little feet, the ribbon in her hair, to the circle of love her hands nearly completed.

Jacob was faithful to bring her fresh flowers daily. He placed them in her hands. The bouquets were mainly wildflowers that were gathered in season. In the spring, it was a gathering of daffodils nearly always alone, but occasionally they would be accompanied by some hyacinths or a pick of forget-me-nots. The summer invited varied flowers, cleomes, snapdragons, anemones, and daisies. In those days, the bouquets were mixed, but always laced with fresh colored leaves giving a grand show.

Autumn presented itself with field asters accompanied by an occasional gladiola. At times, when the flowers of the season were spent, the spray of carefully selected leaves bursting with their peak color was placed in her hands. When the season neared its close, a mixture of golden grain whispered the coming of winter. Her eyes seemed sad as she held them. Through the fallen snow on the brisk winter days, Goldie was adorned with winterberries, sprigs of ash berries, and the thorny twigs of multifloral roses laced with ripened rosehips.

Jacob struggled many days to travel the twenty-mile ride to Goldie's memorial. No matter how difficult the weather, or how his health fared, he rarely missed a day with his daughter. Many days, this was the only reason for his rising in the morning. Lizzie watched as her husband faded to a memory, but Jacob was determined to grace

Goldie's hands with a daily present of love and longing, wrapped in sorrow.

There was something innocent about the way her hands lay on her lap. Her fingers nearly touched, yet they were close enough to create a circle. They appeared to be fashioned specifically to hold a bouquet of flowers, given as a memory and as an expression of apology.

Occasionally, Lizzie brought flowers. She mostly brought pink roses. They had a large rose garden on the farm and a bouquet could be fashioned from May through November, at times even into December. If she visited on a day when the buds were light, she brought a single pink rose. On those days, Lizzie was filled with sadness, for that symbolized the coming of bad weather.

Suzie watched Jacob's health deteriorate. She counted the days he missed visiting his daughter. She wondered why she was not moving forward, why the story seemed to end. She seemed to be stuck in this part of the story.

Goldie's hands were empty and Suzie could bear it no longer. She had no idea how long it had been since she had a visitor. Goldie deserved to have her memory, as well as Jacob's loss, honored. She was a most loved child. The lengths that her father went to preserve her legacy would be difficult to match in any age.

With little difficulty Suzie took a step toward the statue. She had been unable to move in the previous scenes and this freedom of movement intrigued her. As she took her fourth step, she noticed a fresh bouquet lying on the ground. Suzie knew this was the final wish of Jacob, for the bouquet had his signature woven throughout.

It was a bouquet of lavender asters laced with black-eyed Susans, which were gathered from the fields. The flowers encircled the leaves and blossoms of alfalfa. Somehow, Suzie knew its symbolism. The asters represented innocence, the black-eyed Susans stood as a reminder of stolen life, and the alfalfa, known for its constant regeneration of life, was the promise from a father that his love would be shown through his life and the lives of many others. It was a public display of affection manifested in a flower bouquet.

Before she collected the bouquet to place in Goldie's hands, she picked a forget-me-not sprig. She saw Lizzie in the distance. She was visibly older than before. Several wrapped bundles surrounded her. They were placed in pairs on the ground before her. They were all different degrees of visibility, some nearly faded to memory while one pair was only slightly obscured. Among the twin bundles, lay one living child. This babe was only partially covered. Lizzie smiled through her tears as she gathered and cradled the baby in her arms. Suzie realized that after birthing five sets of twins, Lizzie finally had one child that survived, a son. She smiled and held the body of the naked child for Suzie to see. Suzie returned a smile. Lizzie turned and faded from view.

When Suzie looked back at the statue, a mound of dirt appeared at the base of Goldie's monument. It read simply:

Jacob Taylor
1820 - 1896

It seemed to her, at that moment, she understood why she was placed in this part of the story. Someone needed to fulfill Jacob's final wish and that someone was Suzie. She bent to lift the bouquet from the ground but just as she touched the flowers, she heard a voice from behind her.

"'Tis a circle that will never reach an end, nor will it ever be complete. 'Tis a circle of longing, of love, of desperation."

Suzie turned to find Rebecca standing before her. She held the bouquet in her hands.

33

"I'm a bit confused," Suzie confessed.

"All in due time," she responded through a smile.

"But, I thought..." Suzie's voice trailed off in thought.

"You have only a small part of the puzzle, the beginning. It will be shown. You must be patient. You must believe there is a purpose. Without it, all is lost."

Suzie felt her timepiece stir. It read 11:27 a.m. When she looked at Rebecca, she was smiling.

"Are you prepared?"

"Yes."

The sound of her 's' traveled on the wind. It swirled around them and became louder with each pass until the sound was deafening. Suzie lifted her hands to cover her ears, but Rebecca stopped her from doing so. She pointed to her left.

In the distance a stream appeared. It spilled over the rocks. It ran furiously, yet the sound soothed and soon drowned Suzie's resonating consonant. As they watched the stream, their bodies were drawn to its banks.

Peering over the steep edge, Suzie watched a young woman as she drew water from a calm pool within its rapids. Her clothing lay sprawled out on a flat rock to dry. She hummed to herself. High in the trees over Suzie's head a wood thrush sang. The woman looked up. It was Rebecca, though she was a bit younger. Suzie settled to absorb this next piece of the story puzzle.

Rebecca bathed herself and washed her hair. The pool was calm, yet the water rushed furiously around it. When she finished bathing, she stepped through the rushing water, careful to place each step to keep her balance. She dressed in her damp clothes and walked home.

Judging from nature's signs Suzie guessed it to be early summer. The daffodil leaves had turned brown nearly two-thirds from the tip and the forget-me-nots revealed their final color. The ground was littered with green maple leaves that promised another dry summer.

Suzie followed Rebecca as she walked. She spun her dress periodically to aid in the drying process. Her hat hung from its cord mid-way down her back. The weather was warm, dry and sunny.

They walked to a newly built Federal on the edge of town. It stood on a small lake and was complete with a summer kitchen and large barn. The dirt around the house was trampled hard from the carpenter's feet.

The porch surrounded the house in a full circle. At the north corner a gathering square was constructed. It was large enough for six rocking chairs that surrounded a knee table. Thrown over one chair was a hand-stitched quilt of red and white. A pitcher of fresh lemonade sat on the knee table. There was only one glass.

Rebecca walked through the back door into the receiving room. It was a long narrow room, which Suzie thought would make a great galley kitchen in the future.

Currently, the meals were primarily prepared outside or in the summer kitchen. The indoor kitchen was usually the final room completed. It was finished just in time for the warmth of the kitchen's wood stove to double as heat for the house.

She followed Rebecca through the dining room. It was a bright room with a full wall of windows. As the largest room in the house, it was obviously designed to entertain. The table was simply constructed and surrounded by twelve chairs. Only one chair boasted arms. It sat at the head.

The room to the right of the dining room was the parlor. It had a large fireplace with a raised hearth and was furnished with an intricately carved parlor set covered in dark leather. The front entry was set off to the side of this room. Its staircase, constructed of raised paneled oak, wound around twice as it stretched for its final destination, the drawing room. Only a small round table and a chair graced this room. Windows were set on all four sides and the view was far reaching in all directions. Suzie peered out of the windows. They were alone, one from this time and one from another.

Rebecca hummed to herself as she strolled through the house. She walked down the staircase to the second floor and continued down the narrow hall past the bedrooms. She paused at each doorway, but she did not look into the room. Her eyes were fixed on the narrow opening at the end of the hallway. She stopped at the dimly lit doorway and leaned her body past the entrance. She held her breath and moved her head from side to side as if listening for permission to enter. She ran through the entrance.

Suzie stood at the top of a narrow spiral staircase and waited for her vision to adjust to the dim light. When her eyesight adjusted she caught Rebecca's hem as it disappeared through a raised panel. The movement of the panel was flawless. Suzie followed Rebecca. They crawled on their knees past a series of rough pine panels, each with its own door. They were not larger than two feet square.

Rebecca counted out loud, "One, two...three," as she counted the doors they had passed.

She rapped quickly on the third door with a series of well-planned long and short knocks. Suzie noticed the doors were without handles. From the inside, the sound of a sliding lock was heard. The narrow door opened quickly. Inside the room were a man, a woman, and two young slaves.

"Father," Rebecca said as she pulled a piece of paper from her corset.

"Thank you, Rebecca. Now hurry," he added with urgency in his voice, "Time is not with us." He returned the piece of paper to her.

Rebecca closed the door and scurried back the cramped corridor. Her breathing was labored. When she arrived to the secret raised panel, she stopped. Once again she held her breath and moved her head from side to side as she strained to hear any sound. When she was certain it was quiet, she slid the panel, jumped out, and fled down the staircase.

Suzie was hard pressed to keep up with her. The more she tried to match her speed, the farther behind she fell. Exhausted, she finally gave up and sat on a dead tree stump. She noticed a wood thrush singing above her as it coaxed her to continue.

When Suzie rose, she stood in the middle of a clearing, deep within the woods. There were men hiding themselves behind every tree on the perimeter. When Rebecca burst through the brush into the clearing, one by one, the men presented themselves to her. Each face was grim. Their hands held an iron rod, like the one she had been shown with Elam.

Rebecca approached a man with grey hair and handed him a note she withdrew again from her corset. He opened the note and read its contents. He mumbled its contents several times to memorize it and quickly lit a match. The flaming paper floated to the ground and turned to a curled mass. Its edges glowed orange. The man stomped on the embers to snuff it out. As he ground his boot into the soft dirt, he motioned for all to go. Without a sound the men moved from the clearing. The sound of many hooves filled the well-trodden path. The men, dressed in dark clothing, carried their rods as they rode.

Rebecca watched them disappear with interest. The path grew silent. She walked over to the smoldering paper and covered it with her shoe until its glowing embers died. She knelt to gather the remains and scattered them among the leaves. She wiped her soiled hands on the meadow grass. She looked toward the men and whispered, "God speed." She hummed as she walked toward the house.

Suzie knew by the fluid motions this scene was familiar. It was made often, and with grave importance. She listened for the riders in the distance. All was quiet. She turned to follow Rebecca but suddenly found herself standing before Goldie Bell. Suzie held the bouquet of flowers in her hands. She was startled by the voice behind her.

"Aren't you going to give them to her?" Suzie turned to find William. His smile was wide and his voice was soothing.

She was overwhelmed with the desire to share this experience with him. For the next several minutes, she explained what she was shown. She offered in great detail her description of the house, Rebecca, the passageway, the riders and the mysterious pieces of paper. She skillfully described Goldie Bell, her father, Lizzie, and her babies. William understood why she was an accomplished writer. Her words radiated passion and excitement.

Out of breath, Suzie asked, "What are you doing here?"

"I came to see you," he answered.

Suzie blushed. She wasn't prepared for that response. "Oh?" was all she could manage.

"I came to ask you to dinner tonight."

Her face flushed red. Her throat tightened from excitement. She wanted to blurt out her answer, but she fought to gain control. Finally, she smiled and simply said, "I would love that."

William smiled at the positive response, "I'll pick you up at six."

"That's perfect."

William stepped closer to her, took her hand, and kissed her on the forehead. "I'll see you at six, then."

"Okay." She watched him walk away. His body was tall and firm. His dark wavy hair was tossed by the breeze as he moved farther away. Just before he moved out of sight, he turned back to Suzie and waved. She returned the wave and smiled at his thoughtfulness. As she blinked, he vanished from sight. She listened for the start of an engine but heard none.

She placed the bouquet in Goldie's hands. The feeling of watchfulness broke her thoughts. She spun around and found Elam standing there. He stretched out his hand. It held the antique pocket watch. Instinctively, she thrust her hand into her pocket only to find it empty. She was puzzled. Elam held out his hand to her. Without hesitation she took it.

When their hands touched, the surroundings again changed. Suzie did not recognize this place. It was dark and smelled of hay. The dirt floor was hard from much use, yet the wooden structure looked fairly new.

Slowly, the room was filled with filtered sunlight. The sun shone through the void in the opposing slats of the barn siding. The sky was filled with hues of orange and red. It would soon be dark.

Suzie looked at Elam. He was silent as he stared at the livestock door. The air sat heavy on their shoulders, waiting to expel its held energy. Suzie's heart pulsed in her throat. Her mouth became dry. She reminded herself to breathe. Elam's face was tense. His jaw was clenched and his eyes never left the door.

Just as the last bit of light was stolen from the barn, voices were heard outside. They drew closer, louder, and angrier. Many voices erupted, as others shouted to be overheard. Their footsteps were hurried, deliberate, filled with purpose. Their words were garbled.

The door flew open. In rushed twelve men carrying long metal rods. Their voices were angry. Many waved their rods in the air. It was obvious they voiced opposing opinions. They refused to listen to each other. Their voices escalated. One of the men struck another with his rod. Blood gushed from the wound. He lunged at his assailant and wrestled him to the floor.

The crowd gathered around them. They chanted their favorite's name. The fighters pranced around each other and swung their fists. One man connected. With a quick jab to the face, his eye split open. The swarm cheered. Blood littered their clothing. His wound was deep.

No one noticed the woman who entered the barn. In disgust, she clenched the door handle with both hands and forced it to close. The sound reverberated like a scoffing mother. The men immediately fell silent. All stared at the ground as she pushed her way to the center of the circle. With her hands on her hips, she scolded with her eyes. She spoke no words, but all knew her thoughts.

Her name was Hanna Prenstrum. She was a southern sympathizer, a Copperhead as they were nicknamed. She hated the anti-slavery movement and did her best to see its efforts thwarted. Her sister lived in Georgia on a twelve-hundred-acre plantation. Together they apprehended many rogue slaves and returned them to their "rightful" place in the South. The conflict between the Anti-slavery and the Copperhead movements was fierce.

"We have not the time for this nonsense." Hanna's voice was stern and unchallenged. The men conceded to her authority, all but one.

"But..." was all he could manage.

She held up her hand to silence him. Her stare was filled with intolerance. He did not attempt to speak again. After a few moments his eyes slid to the ground and she continued, "This is grave business tonight, men. The train is due at half passed nine!" She snapped, "It *will* be on time. The stop is not long. There are two slaves to be transported through false bottom buckboards. They will be released into freedom." The crowd groaned with her spoken words.

She smiled in triumph, but only for a moment. She regained her position of torrid hatred. "This must not happen! The slavery sympathizers must be stopped." The men stood as stone idols. The earth fell silent.

When her words hung long enough, she gave them their charge. "You have your rods which will cover you for a while. Your luck will not be long. They are taking the men to Kristol's new Federal. You must lie in waiting." The men clung to each word -- their faces writhed from their deep hatred.

"The attack must be a surprise." Her voice escalated, "Kill no one! I want those slaves returned to me unharmed." She stomped the ground and added under her breath, "They belong to my sister."

The men grumbled. She held up her hand again, "Silence!" The men obeyed. Through clenched teeth she hissed, "They will be returned to me unharmed, or I will see to your own hanging!"

As the men absorbed this threat, the woman stomped her foot on the hardened earth. The men snaked their faces toward her. Her shoe rumbled the ground, but not a cloud of dust was stirred. The earth seemed to moan from her request, yet would not yield a speck of dust in defiance. She pounded her foot again. The ground refused to comply.

"GO!" she shouted in a voice not of this earth. The men scurried to leave her presence. As the last man mounted his steed, she added, "Do not disappoint me again!" They rode into the blackness, each one swallowed by the evil which held the night.

Elam's face was void of color. His words were hushed and solemn. "Wickedness has been shown here tonight."

Suzie knew the rest of this story was not pleasant. She tried to comfort Elam. He turned his face from her. She knew he longed for another. She heard the sound of Rebecca's voice whisper in her ear, "`Tis a circle of longing, of love, of desperation." Her voice was soft and sweet. It sounded so real. She listened again but heard only the song of a wood thrush.

Her eyes returned to Elam. His face was upturned. He was smiling. He turned his face to Suzie and held out his hand to her. She didn't understand why this was revealed in short stories - all interwoven somehow, but seemingly, unconnected to her. Her eyes were full of questions, but she spoke none.

After a long while, Elam stood, Suzie took his outstretched hand. They arrived at Rebecca's home. They walked silently to the back yard. Elam's stride was quick and with purpose. Suzie struggled to keep up with him. She heard cries long before they found Rebecca. Her body was bent over another. The ground was wet with fresh blood. Elam's face mirrored her pain.

Suzie's body writhed at the sight of Rebecca hovering over her murdered mother. The dirt surrounding her limp body was ripped apart from many horse hooves. Without asking, she knew who was responsible. Her heart hardened with rage. She moved to comfort Rebecca, but Elam held her back.

His eyes flooded with tears. He whispered, "We are not of this time. It is only being shown. The pain is great, but naught can be done." He hung his head in defeat.

Suzie's vision became blurred. She lowered her eyes to the ground and found herself standing in fresh mown grass. At her feet was the gold pocket watch. Its cover was open. The hands were still. It read 11:36. Their time had stopped.

34

Patrick drove quickly to his house. He struggled to contain his excitement. He wanted to scream out loud. Today he felt lucky and blessed. His car turned into the drive and he thrust it into park. It leapt forward and rocked as if it shared the excitement.

He raced up the sidewalk and threw open the front door. In three strides, he ran across the living room into the kitchen. He lifted his hand to his chest to calm himself. After a deep breath, he picked up the receiver and dialed Attie. It seemed an eternity before he heard her voice.

"Hello."

"Oh, thank God you are `ome." His breaths came in short bursts.

"Patrick, what's wrong?"

"Nothing, absolutely nothing. As a matter of fact, everything is right, so very right! I need to see you immediately."

The urgency in his voice left her with no doubt, "Come on over. I'll be waiting for you."

Patrick was so charged he didn't say goodbye. He grabbed his car keys and headed for the door. He moved in such a flurry, the very piece of news he wanted to present to Attie floated out of his leather notebook, fell to the floor and skirted under the sofa. Only a tiny corner of the paper was visible. He was unaware of its absence.

Attie hung up the phone in anticipation. Patrick's excitement was obvious. Her mind filtered through the morning.

They woke at 6:30 a.m. and shared coffee and tea in the front parlor. He had been preoccupied all morning. When Attie questioned him, he simply replied he had an errand in Boardman this morning. He mentioned an old associate. He didn't appear agitated, only anxious.

They laughed as they talked about their plans for the late afternoon. They had a two o'clock appointment with a travel agent to book their honeymoon trip. After much discussion, and Patrick's persuasion, they agreed to spend three weeks in Ireland, Scotland and the English Cotswolds. Attie had been to England with Charlotte but never to Ireland or Scotland. They were excited about the trip. She glanced at the wag-on-the-wall. It was 10:40 a.m.

She stood at the front door and counted cars as they raced down the street. She daydreamed of their new life together. She couldn't remember the last time she was this happy.

She was startled when the telephone rang. Just as she touched the receiver, it stopped ringing. She picked it up anyway and heard only a dial tone. She drummed her fingers on the stand. She glanced at the clock again -11:04 a.m. Where was Patrick? He should have arrived by now. A growing feeling of dread shrouded her.

Suzie left the cemetery at 11:45 a.m. She was anxious to return to the inn to type her new experiences into her computer. She drove in a mental fog until traffic suddenly came to a halt. She saw flashing lights ahead of her and strained to catch a glimpse of the accident. An ambulance sped past her. She turned off her engine and opened the door.

The air was cool when Suzie stepped out of her car. Spring had unveiled itself in its usual show. The leaves were still dressed in their sap green shawls and the ground was clothed with their feathery casings. Daffodils, hyacinths, and tulips competed for the best award of color and stature. The wind carried a crispness that twirled in hurried fashion. She found herself enveloped in the beauty of the morning until she saw the accident scene. The rush of people around the crumpled automobiles stole the serenity.

The policeman held the crowd at a distance. An ambulance silently closed its doors and pulled away from the scene. The absence of the siren spoke volumes. The lump in her throat hindered her breath.

The crowd muted as the second ambulance moved into position. The emergency personnel moved hurriedly. Suzie whispered a silent prayer for those involved as the crew lifted the gurney into the back. Within a few well-rehearsed seconds, the vehicle sped down the street. The crowd watched in reverence as it disappeared around the corner. Its siren screamed.

The low murmur rose in volume. People shouted their eyewitness accounts of the accident. The policeman struggled to hear over the sound of the wrecker's back up signal. The local news crew had arrived for their 'And this just in...' story. A young woman gave her tearful account when the noise subsided:

"...was traveling west on Franklin. She made a hurried left hand turn onto Lincoln. Our light just turned green. We were traveling the same rate of speed. Oh, I'd say about 25 - 30 m.p.h. There were three of us, the blue pickup truck behind me, myself, and the silver car in the front. She," continued the young lady as she pointed toward the red car involved in the accident, "turned right into him. I don't even think he even saw her. I swerved to miss both of them and ran up on the sidewalk. The blue pickup swerved the other direction. I think my car is still drivable."

"How fast was she driving?" asked the officer as he was scribbling in his notebook.

"I don't know, but she was going fast, too fast. And her light had to be red."

Their conversation continued, but Suzie's attention was drawn to the reaction of a woman who stood on the opposite side of the street. She cried as she crumpled to the ground. It was difficult to watch. Suzie turned her head as her eyes filled with tears.

"How quickly life can change," she whispered to herself.

Suzie walked quietly back to her car. She chastised herself for joining the circus. The last car was loaded onto the flatbed trailer. She glanced at the wrecked vehicles as she drove past them. She never made the connection.

Madeline stood nervously on the front porch. It wasn't very often an accident happened on South Lincoln. She listened for the approach of the emergency equipment. The moan of the sirens surrounded her veranda. She knew something was wrong.

"Oh, Patrick. Where are you? You should've arrived by now," she whispered repeatedly. She glanced at her watch. It was 11:46 a.m.

Patrick rushed out of the driveway. His heart was light. The news he had to share with Attie bubbled out of him. He rehearsed the words he wanted to say. He anticipated her reaction.

The drive seemed to take an eternity. He lost entire blocks from his visual memory as he drove. By the time he turned onto State Street, it felt as if he'd been driving for an hour. Traffic was heavy and everyone seemed hurried.

He caught the light at South Lincoln Avenue just as it turned red. He was the second car. He moved into the left turn lane and sighed with impatience. Once again, his mind drifted to Attie and her reaction to his news. It was difficult to contain his giddy laughter. The light turned and he moved through the intersection quickly.

Without warning, the vehicle directly in front of him, slammed on the brakes. Patrick's reaction was quick and precise. He managed to stop his car only inches from its back bumper. The driver yelled obscenities to the young boy as he darted across the street on his bicycle.

"Kids," he sighed.

Patrick continued toward Attie's. He approached Franklin Avenue when the traffic light turned green. He counted the seconds to Attie's drive. A smile lit his face.

He never saw the young woman in the red sports car. He didn't see her punch the accelerator when the light changed. As he entered the intersection, he glanced over to the leather notebook lying on the front seat beside him. His whole life was about to change. His thoughts drifted to

Attie as his body was enveloped in the distant sounds of metal and glass.

He felt no pain.

35

The next few days were a blur. Madeline struggled without medication. Suzie tried to hold herself together, but anger controlled her thoughts. Her aunt's suffering was impossible to comprehend. Simply stated, it was not fair.

They made it through the funeral plans, flowers, and the newspaper article, but choosing Patrick's casket was most difficult. Madeline collapsed under the pressure of this decision, as Suzie listened to the funeral director's rehearsed speech. She wanted to scream. She walked away in mid-sentence and knelt beside her weeping aunt.

"Please tell me what to do," Suzie begged.

Madeline glanced at the choices and pointed to the one on the end. "That one," was all she could manage. Her hand fell from the air and hung limp at her side.

Suzie walked over to the oak casket. It had simple lines and boasted a hand carved cluster of oak leaves. The overall feeling was simple.

Suzie pointed to the casket. "This one will be fine."

"Excellent choice," the funeral director declared.

Without a word Suzie walked over to Madeline who sat slumped in a wingback. She touched her and Madeline stood. They went through the door in silence.

At the calling hours Suzie felt agitated. She wanted to be alone and the constant flow of people overwhelmed her. The number of lives Patrick had touched was a true testament of his life.

She listened to their stories of his influence on their lives. Men and women of all ages stood together to say goodbye to him. Many of these visitors knew each other, and by the way they embraced, much time had passed since their last meeting. This seemed to help Madeline with her grief and calmed Suzie's nervousness at the same time.

One gentleman caught her attention as he walked through the arched opening. He was a very dark-skinned man, nearly seven feet tall, dressed in African attire. The colors of his robe were refreshing in a room filled with dark suits. He wore a box hat graced with a wide band. The ribbons hung to his mid-back and swayed to music that only he heard. He held a book in his hands.

His demeanor captivated more in the room than just Suzie. Several conversations came to a halt when he took Madeline's hand. His eyes were soft brown and full of compassion. His accent left no doubt he was from South Africa.

"My lady," he caressed her hand. "Patrick was a good man. He loved you very much and spoke of you often." Madeline's eyes flooded. "My name is Navarei Tambattu. We practiced medicine together in the Congo." His eyes flickered with fire as he spoke. The words rolled from his lips in a well-polished fashion and their rhythm captivated. Madeline's expression was empty.

"We met in New York at a convention. It was my first time as a volunteer to my mother country. He took great pride and helped ease my apprehension. We spent many years volunteering as a team, he with the healing of the body and I with the mind. The native people loved him and mimicked his accent often. His cheerful countenance was a great comfort to all people." He placed his hand on top of Patrick's folded ones as he lay in the casket, "Brother, you will be missed. May you rest well in the comfort of fresh grass in the desert's oasis."

He turned to Suzie and smiled. "Soon, very soon, when my lady is ready, spend time with this." He handed her a book. Its cover seemed to be some sort of canvas dipped in a waxy substance. The paper inside was handmade with bits of leaves, bark fragments and flower petals. The pages were tattered and worn, but the grace of Patrick's penmanship gave elegance to the crude construction.

"One of the natives stole this from him many years ago, when he was a child. Patrick was filled with sorrow for it held much of him within the covers. We thought it to be lost forever, but a changed heart of a now young man proved otherwise. It was returned to me only last week. I had hoped to give this to Patrick myself and witness his joy in its recovery. I now surrender it to you." His smile was great.

Suzie took the well-loved journal from Dr. Tambattu and managed a smile. He gently squeezed Suzie's hand as she received it.

He placed his hands on both of their heads, and with an upturned face, spoke words in another language. An indescribable feeling of peace settled on them.

He smiled as he looked at them. "May your road be lined with down from those who traveled before you, their footprints close and your pebbles small."

The room was silent as all eyes held this stranger. Madeline and Suzie stood motionless as he walked through the crowd, bending slightly to clear the arched opening and disappearing through the open door. It seemed as if the crowd breathed a sigh simultaneously and then filled the room with excited chatter. The solemn mood became a celebration. Suzie was happy for the change. It helped her through the next visitor.

She was a young woman, in her early twenties. She had a bandage on her face and walked with crutches. Her appearance paled in comparison to Dr. Tambattu.

"I'm very sorry," her voice quivered uncontrollably. "I came to say I am sorry," she repeated. "I…I…" Her body shook as she stood before them. Her words were lost. Tears streamed down her face.

Suzie tried to cling to the feeling of peace Navarei had placed on them, but she struggled with the equal pull of anger. Before she could respond, Madeline took the young woman's hand.

"It was an accident. You mustn't blame yourself." Her voice was sure and strong.

Suzie's ears betrayed her. Did she hear that? She shot a disapproving glance to her aunt, but the look in Madeline's eyes left no doubt that Madeline forgave her. The foreign words of Dr. Tambattu were heard again in Suzie's mind. Peace regained control. She placed her hand over theirs and squeezed with a show of affirmation. The young girl nodded her head and smiled weakly. The people watched as her body moved through the crutches.

The rest of the day passed without any more surprises. Suzie and Madeline felt renewed strength from the unexpected travelers. Suzie recalled the warmth of their gestures and how their selfless acts reflected Patrick's legacy of love and forgiveness.

On the morning of his funeral, the earth and sky mourned with them. The air was cold. The sky opened with a downpour that flooded the streets. The mood was solemn yet celebratory. Several people rose to speak of how their lives were touched by Patrick. Their stories were inspiring.

Many approached Madeline and placed tokens in her hands. The items quickly overflowed onto her lap. She was given carved animals and birds, a hand-made belt fashioned from animal hide, pieces of cloth, a scarf, diamond cufflinks, photographs, drawings, paintings and many pieces of jewelry, including rings, bracelets and a necklace -- all with a specific story. One seemed especially personal to Madeline. It was the necklace.

Suzie watched Madeline's face as a young man rose from the audience. He approached the front of the chapel slowly with a slight limp. He was a handsome man, in his mid-thirties. He had a young girl by his side. She held his hand while he spoke. He had a thick accent, but his English was well schooled.

"I met Dr. McCelvy when I was a lad of eight. He was in our village in Angola for nearly three weeks when I had an accident. Our soccer fields long ago were used as a field for land mines. The villagers located and detonated all without incidents, all but one. It was my foot that found it, but thanks to Patrick McCelvy I can stand before you today. The limp will serve as a reminder of his skilled hands. Had it not been for him, my foot, as well as part of my leg, would have been amputated. Only an act of God brought us together."

The young man wiped a tear from his cheek. He looked at his little girl and smiled. He drew in a deep breath.

"Patrick inspired me, even as a child. I saw him several times over the years. We kept in contact through letters and telephone calls. He helped me as I entered college and again through medical school. He visited me in Pittsburgh when I completed my residency. He surprised me this past Christmas with an unannounced visit to my home in New York. It was there he met my daughter, McCelvy." The room fell silent after a deep unison sigh. Madeline's smile was filled with pride. He continued, "I am who and what I am today because of the unselfish sacrifice of a man named Patrick William McCelvy."

He held up a gold necklace and looked at Madeline, "This was made as a reminder of you. He spoke of you often and held you in his nightly prayers. His faith was strong and his love for you was deep. He held this in his hands as he spoke of you. He gave it to me to carry me through my recovery. He told me to keep it, for it brings strength and holds power within its stone." He walked to Madeline and handed her the necklace.

"Now it has made its way back to you." He smiled as he gave it to her and kissed her on the cheek. McCelvy hugged her in the shadow of her father.

Madeline took the necklace and covered it with both hands. She ran her hands over the fine gold chain, which gathered together in the center and dropped as a single thought. A gold circle held the clear blue oval stone. It was smooth and concave in shape and hung like a locket, though it did not open. Madeline rubbed her fingers over the stone as the minister rose from his seat.

After no others stood to speak, he began his summary. The methodic tone in his voice, blended with his soft undertone, made Suzie's mind wander to distant places. His words comforted her, but her thoughts moved in a different direction. His voice rose and fell in beat to a distant drum and announced a call of arrival. The stories consumed her and she longed to visit these places and walk where Patrick had been. She watched as Madeline fondled the necklace's stone.

The service seemed to end before it began. Suzie remained lost in thought and Madeline drank in every word. The smile seemed etched on her face. When the pastor finished, many followed to the cemetery. As the door closed on the hearse, the finality of the day seemed to weigh on Madeline. They rode through town without speaking.

The rain fell hard as they entered the cemetery. The windshield wipers raced furiously. It was impossible to halt heaven's tears. Suzie noticed the void in Goldie Bell's hands as the long black car crept past her. She turned to speak to Madeline, but the sorrow on her face stole the words. The silence continued.

The crowd huddled to shelter themselves from the angry wind and driving rain. The ground was soft and riddled with fresh mud. The wind ripped at their coats and hats. The tent poles moaned from the weight of the gathering water.

The pounding rain drowned out the pastor's final words. He extended his hand to Madeline and Suzie. They rose as commanded. They pulled a rose from the arrangement and placed it on the top of the closed casket. Madeline's face was pasty. She stumbled as she walked from the crowd. Suzie held her arm to steady her. They walked in silence to the car. Madeline's fists were drawn tight over the necklace.

They were wet and chilled. Suzie turned to Madeline and placed her hand over hers. Madeline shook, her hands frozen with grief.

Once again, the car passed Goldie Bell. Suzie nearly missed the elaborate bouquet in her hands. The flowers were steady in the wind.

"That's odd," Suzie spoke quietly. Madeline remained unmoved, the plastered smile molded on her face.

Suzie drove her aunt home and stayed with her for several hours, trying comfort her with the wonderful stories they had heard. Madeline stared out of the window, unmoved.

In desperation Suzie read from Patrick's journal to her aunt. Nothing stirred a change in her demeanor. At four o'clock Suzie called Madeline's doctor.

A knock broke the silence at 4:45 p.m. The doctor was quickly ushered through the front door. He checked her vitals, opened his black bag, and withdrew a syringe. He asked Suzie to assist him.

They led Madeline through the kitchen to her bedroom. Suzie changed her aunt into her nightgown. When Madeline was placed on her bed, the doctor administered the shot. Madeline never flinched.

"She will sleep now. Don't be alarmed if she doesn't stir until late morning. She has been through quite an ordeal today and given her medical history, she may take a while to respond normally to the effects of the sedative." He patted Suzie's hand. "She'll be fine. Try not to worry."

"I plan to stay with her tonight."

"I think that would be wise. If there are any changes, don't hesitate to call me."

"Thank you," was all she could manage.

"I'll show myself out." He turned and walked out of the door.

Suzie held Madeline's hand. She appeared peaceful. She felt sorry for her. She released her tears.

When Suzie brushed a strand of hair from Madeline's face, she noticed the necklace hung around her neck. She hoped the stone would heal a broken heart.

She whispered, "Sleep well," and turned to go.

Madeline's eyes flew open. She sat straight up in her bed and grabbed Suzie's arm. "Did you see Patrick's flowers?"

"What?"

"The flowers Patrick brought. Weren't they beautiful?"

Suzie thought the sedative created a hallucinogenic effect. She patted her aunt's arm.

"Try to sleep, Aunt Madeline. It will be better in the morning."

Madeline did not acknowledge Suzie's comment. She mumbled about Patrick's bouquet. The medication finally forced sleep. Suzie helped her head to the pillow.

She kissed her forehead and whispered, "Good night."

As Suzie walked through the doorway, Madeline spoke "...the flowers ... beautiful ... roses ... forget-me-nots ... beautiful ... my Patrick ... gave them to her ... I watched him ... she smiled."

"Who smiled?"

"Goldie Bell."

36

Patrick had prepared for this day unbeknownst to Madeline and Suzie. He completed a new will and named Madeline and Suzie as his beneficiaries. He had purchased two cemetery plots, side by side for Madeline and himself. The headstone with Patrick and Madeline's name inscribed was ordered, paid in full, and the delivery date set for May 26th. All seemed to be in order.

When Suzie walked through his front door, an eerie feeling passed over her. Her throat tightened from restrained tears. She tried to focus on something that would not make her cry, but as she glanced around the room, memories flooded her eyes. She remembered the bee sting, his physician's bag, the cup of coffee, his smile and tender touch. She stood surrounded by the gifts that had been given to Patrick in appreciation of his kindness and skill.

At the funeral, she listened to many stories that seemed to dance with life. She focused on each token displayed in the room. She sat on the sofa and held her head in her hands. Her sobbing continued until her tears were gone.

She glanced out the window. The daylight slid into twilight. She sat motionless and watched the world cover itself in shadow. The rain stopped, but the foliage bowed in reverence and dripped away the day's tears. The lamp beside her sprang to life from an automatic timer. It startled her.

She drove in silence to Madeline's house. The house was dark. She had never noticed the groan of the front door hinges until this evening. The entire attitude of the house seemed to echo her feelings. She walked slowly to not wake Madeline.

She heard the rhythm of her aunt's breath. Suzie watched as she slept. Her body was unmoved. She drifted to Madeline's words about the flowers. She decided to unwind by taking a hot bath.

She sat naked on the edge of the tub and swirled the hot water with her fingers. She slid deep into the water of the old claw foot bathtub and allowed the water to caress the bottom of her chin. She soaked until the water cooled.

It felt strange to sleep in her mother's bed. Within minutes, however, she was sound asleep. The only sound that filled the room was the soft rhythm of an antique clock. Suzie heard nothing until morning.

When she woke, sunlight streamed in the east window. It cast shadows of tree branches that swayed in the morning breeze. She stretched and climbed out of the antique bed. She dressed and headed down the stairs. The house seemed to hold its breath as Suzie tiptoed into Madeline's room. Her bed was empty.

She felt a nervous twinge as she went to the kitchen. She called out her name and listened for an answer, but none came. Her thoughts scrambled as she ran through the house. Madeline could not be found.

She burst through the back door in a panic. "Attie! Where are you?" Her heart raced and her breathing became more labored. She ran to the garage and was relieved to find Madeline's car. She took a deep breath convinced her aunt was out for a walk. She returned to the kitchen and expected to find a cup of unfinished tea. There was none.

"Now that's odd. She always has a cup of tea before her walk and her second one when she returned."

She walked back into her bedroom. Her nightgown was not in her bedroom. Her robe was stretched across the bottom of her bed, untouched. Her walking shoes were in her closet. Her apprehension rose. She scribbled a few words on a piece of paper and darted out of the front door.

Don't leave. I'm trying to find you.

Even as she penned those words, she knew Madeline would not read them.

She pulled into Patrick's drive and left her car idling. As suspected the house was empty. She jumped into her car and rushed to Hope Cemetery. She didn't notice the small crowd of people who stood near Patrick's grave. Her attention was focused on Goldie Bell and the bouquet.

She flung the car door open and ran to the statue. Her strides were long and deliberate, but the harder she ran the further from the statue her body moved. She was weary of the riddles this place held for her. She was irritated by the way her mind and body were held captive by forces unknown. She screamed and fell to the ground.

The group of five people that gathered around Patrick's grave heard a scream, but by the time they faced her direction, her body had crumpled to the ground and out of their sight. They turned their attention to the woman with a tear-stained face. She was dressed in a thin nightgown which was drawn to her knees. Her eyes were open and empty.

The ambulance pulled into the lower drive. People from The Flower Loft were drawn to the scene and the crowd quickly grew. They moved out of the path of the gurney. They gently gathered the woman onto the stretcher, placed her in the back of the ambulance, and closed the door. The people watched the silent vehicle as it left the cemetery. The murmur of the crowd was heard as they disbursed. In a matter of a few minutes, the cemetery was empty, but for Suzie.

She lay on the ground for a few minutes, long enough to be shielded from Madeline's death. She woke to a gentle touch on her arm. It was Elam.

"I can't do this anymore," she exclaimed. "I'm exhausted!"

His smile continued. He knew she was close. He knew she would understand. It would only be a short while. He held out his hand for her.

She sat up in frustration, "Did you not hear me? I can't do this anymore!" Her voice was elevated and agitated. His expression remained unchanged. "Elam…I...I…" His calm eyes spoke to her. She took his hand.

Suzie watched as he gathered daffodils from a patch that would one day hold his body. They walked alone in the cemetery and stopped before a less-worn statue of Goldie Bell. Elam pulled the pink roses from her hands and replaced it with his spray of yellow daffodils. He held the bouquet of roses tightly in his hands. His hands trembled as he stood motionless. A wood thrush sang. Elam turned around, and smiled as Rebecca walked toward him.

She moved through a soft mist that cleared as she drew closer. She was dressed in a long pink gown and held her hands out to receive the bouquet that Elam presented to her. He brought his hands to her face and moved his fingers through her hair. His thumbs caressed the outline of her lips. She smiled at the romantic gesture. Neither of their lips moved as they spoke.

"It has been too long, my love," Elam whispered softly.

"Too long indeed," Rebecca responded. "Need it be much longer?"

"No. It will be soon. Very soon." He kissed her forehead.

She closed her eyes, kissed her own fingers, and touched them to his lips. They held each other without speaking. The songbirds sang in chorus around them. The only sound that broke the enchanted serenade was the pounding of distant horse hooves.

"Until then," Rebecca said. Her body faded into the thickening mist until it was no longer seen.

The galloping of the horses became deafening. Suzie placed her hands over her ears to ease the resounding noise. Elam stood erect and faced the gathering dread. Soon the assembly of men broke through the fog. They stopped and surrounded Elam with their ring of fury. The horses pounded the earth with their hooves, anxious to ride. The noise covered the men's voices. One man held up his hand. All fell silent, even the horses.

"We have come for you," his words cut.

Elam stood silent. Suzie tried to speak, but her words were silenced. Again, she felt trapped by the mystery.

Finally Elam spoke. His lips moved at the words, "At what charge have you sought me?"

The men laughed. The leader spoke again, his body swayed as he spit his words toward Elam. "You need to ask this?"

They scoffed and erupted in cruel laughter. Wickedness choked life's beauty.

Suzie held her breath. She had been with Rebecca and Elam as they rode from this angry crowd. It was obvious they were driven to finish evil deeds. Suzie's thoughts drifted to her past visions.

She thought of the journey she traveled with Elam. She remembered the house, the men, the iron rods, the bloody body, the shackled men, and the angry mob that chased him. She knew these men were the same. The cold voice of the leader could not be mistaken.

She drifted to the barn. Her thoughts were snared by the sound of the woman's voice, evil and cold, the same qualities as in this man's voice. Their laughter was haunting and bound her thoughts. She forced her mind to move from this vision.

She focused on Rebecca's beauty and innocence. She saw her in the clearing of the woods with her own group of men surrounding her. She managed a smile as Rebecca gathered the charred paper and tossed them in the air to cover her involvement.

Her thoughts were moved by the background voices of these evil men. She saw Rebecca hovered over her slaughtered mother. Her mind retraced the silent trip down the hall, through the passageway, and into the hidden room for the smuggled slaves. She sought the faces of the slaves as she compared them to the ones in shackles. She gasped when she realized they were the same. She forced herself to look upon the one hidden by a pool of blood. His face was difficult to see from her angle. The leader kicked his lifeless body and rolled the man onto his back. She felt dizzy when she recognized him. It was Rebecca's father.

The world spun from confusion as her thoughts moved to make sense of her visions. The sound of the horses mixed with angry voices pounded in her ears. She grew dizzy from the movement and her world lost all color. She fell to the earth in slow motion. She heard a sweet voice that called her name. It sounded like William.

37

When she woke, she was alone. Her head pounded from confusion. She sat cross-legged on the soft green grass and cradled her head in her hands. Her eyes were closed. She listened for the sounds of anger, but heard or felt none. She placed her hands on the ground to steady herself, and as she tried to stand she felt something cold. When she opened her eyes, the gold pocket watch lay on the ground The hands were still and read 11:45 a.m.

She held the watch in her hands and tried to piece the puzzle together. She felt she was missing pertinent information. The nine-minute time intervals confused her the most. She stared at the watch. The hands jumped. Time had called her attention.

She heard her name from the distance. It was a voice she recognized. It was Madeline. Standing, she saw her aunt wave in the distance and motioned for Suzie to follow her.

Madeline was dressed in a pink chiffon dress, its length nearly to her ankles. The bareness of her shoulders made

Suzie shiver from the cold. The thin spaghetti straps of the summer dress didn't cover much of her youthful skin.

Suzie stopped a few steps from her aunt. She was confused by what she saw. All of her visions had been people who had passed on before her, people that had something important to share with her, something that involved her. The idea that Madeline stood before her as a youthful young woman stirred foreboding feelings within her.

"Suzie, I'm so glad you came. I knew you would." Madeline made a motion to Goldie Bell's hands. Suzie noticed the same bouquet she saw earlier. The lavish one that Goldie Bell held yesterday was placed on the ground in front of the statue.

"He said you would come." Madeline giggled. "All of the time you spent in this place, I never understood why until today."Her aunt appeared to be in her early twenties. She was beautiful. Her long, dark hair bounced on her shoulders as she walked.

"But..." Suzie began, "I came here to find you...you look so different...."

Madeline laughed, "You mean younger."

"But this means..."Suzie stopped herself from continuing.

Madeline held out her hand. Suzie took it and they returned to her house. They stood as they watched Madeline sleep in her bed. The wag-on-the-wall clock chimed four o'clock. Madeline's eyes flew open wide. She threw off the covers and walked out of her bedroom. She paused for a moment as she stood before 'Lunar Dream'. She kissed her fingers and brushed Suzie's signature with her moistened touch and walked out of the back door. A smudge of her lipstick could still be seen on the glass over Suzie's signature.

Madeline's bare feet crossed many streets as she walked in the dark toward the cemetery. She gathered flowers in the shadow of the streetlights. She lifted the lavish bouquet from Goldie's lap and replaced them with the ones she had just picked. She carried the bouquet to Patrick's fresh mound of dirt. She threw herself onto his grave and wept until her tears were dry. A fist full of the dry earth filled each of her small hands. Her face was flooded with grief and stole her breath. She was left with empty eyes.

Suzie's face was filled with horror and her eyes with tears. No words came.

Madeline gathered both of her hands. Her eyes were filled with spirit. "Watch," was all she said.

Suzie wiped the tears from her eyes, "I don't want you to go."

Madeline didn't reply. She stood still as the stolen breeze and waited. Her smile was thick in anticipation.

They looked to the east as the first light turned the sky to a pale shade of wine. A familiar hand gathered the bouquet from beside Madeline. A gentle voice spoke her name. She sprang to the sound. Patrick stood beside her with his hand outstretched.

"Attie, I knew you would come."

Madeline threw her arms around him. Neither seemed aware of the lifeless, crumpled body of an aging woman that lay at their feet. She squealed from excitement. They walked together toward the statue of Goldie Bell.

Rebecca's voice could be heard in the wind, "'Tis a circle that will never reach an end, nor will it ever be complete. 'Tis a circle of longing, of love, of desperation."

Suzie watched as they faded into the morning mist. They never looked back. She touched her face in disbelief and felt the dried tears on her cheeks. She was unsure if what she saw was real or like the others. She walked mechanically to Patrick's grave. The impression of two fists and the missing dirt were clearly seen. She pulled the watch from her pocket. It was silent. The time was 11:54 a.m. She felt a hand on her shoulder. She turned to see a young woman standing there.

"We found her early this morning," the woman said. "She had fallen onto his grave." Her finger pointed to Patrick's mound. "I ran back to the shop and called the ambulance. They came quickly, but she was gone." Suzie stood in disbelief. The woman continued, "I didn't know who to call…I'm sorry."

Suzie found no words.

38

Suzie was alone once again. The conversation left her heart burdened yet she was filled with brilliant memories of Madeline and Patrick. She walked to the sculpture of Goldie Bell.

Yesterday's rain had cleansed the world of its leaf casings. The water, which rushed like a mountain stream over the roads, had long disappeared. The breeze was crisp and carried a freshness that only comes after a spring rain. Suzie drew in a deep breath of the new life. It soothed her.

She passed the patch of daffodils growing on Elam's grave. She knelt to pick one, just one, and planned to give it to Goldie Bell. Their fragrance seemed especially sweet this morning. She smiled as she watched their faces bounce in the gentle wind. Her hand selected a large yellow jonquil and plucked it from the ground. With it, she gathered the two adjacent leaves.

She followed the narrow road until it led to Goldie's memorial. She pulled Madeline's bouquet from Goldie's hands and gently positioned it on the ground beside the one Patrick had placed the day prior. She slid the single daffodil and the two leaves into the gathering place. She smiled before she turned. She held out her hand to him. He smiled as he took it. He knew it was time.

When their fingers touched, Suzie felt something she hadn't noticed before. His hand warmed hers, yet it felt strangely cool, disconnected. It was an odd sensation. Only a few would ever experience it or be able to describe it.

Elam took her to a place within the cemetery grounds that she hadn't noticed before. It was parallel to Goldie Bell and hidden by several large trees. They grew in a tight circle and surrounded a small group of markers. He placed his hands over Suzie's eyes and when he removed them, time had moved backwards.

Rebecca knelt on the ground, humming to herself. Fresh dirt mounds were strategically placed in a circle. Each marker had its own sapling planted in memory. She finished the final planting, a pin oak, on her father's grave. The small stone marker simply read:

Nathaniel Kristol
October, 1864

To the left of Nathaniel's grave was another small marker. Its inscription read:

Love lies here

Abigail Wentworth Kristol
May, 1860

They watched Rebecca water the young trees. Her faithfulness was rewarded by their growth. She planted daffodils near her father's marker and tended to the rambling pink rose, which gathered around her mother with a show of blossoms. Many hours she sang and talked to them.

The movement of time, forward and back again, and the disheveled seasons held Elam and Suzie captive. The wind whispered through hollow eyes as it moved through the growing branches. The harsh weather consumed all bitterness and spit at Rebecca's health which seemed to fade with each visit. Her skin grew pale, transparent in nature. Even in the warmth of spring, her countenance remained. The beauty of the patch of jonquils did not bring a show of pleasure to her face. The summer's dry breeze was kind to the plantings and autumn brought the only fresh color. Her long pink dress never soiled or wore. It was difficult to know when she passed from the living. The only constant was her age. She appeared to be in her late teens.

They watched Rebecca cut a small shoot from the climbing rose and unwind it from her mother's grave one autumn. She snipped the opening bud from the top. It floated to the ground. She pulled the cluster of leaves from the bottom three nodules. Carefully she split the bottom two inches of the stem and placed it in a jar of steeped willow branches. She carried the present to Goldie Bell and planted it at the base of her statue as a memorial. She dug a tiny hole and planted the split stem. Only two clusters of leaves appeared out of the ground. She poured the willow growth hormone on the cutting and covered it with the jar. It grew into a beautiful climbing rose. Suzie's mind recalled her penned words:

Pink roses smother her name
Etched in mind and granite.
She waits for the waning moon
Lives on the edge of shadows.

She gathered another puzzle piece and placed it in her mind.

Time passed and the circle of trees grew. The roots of her father's tree took hold and gathered its strength from him. It consumed his marker and hid his face from onlookers. Her mother's rose stretched until it wound around the tree and attached for support. A small patch of ground in the center of the circle never yielded life. Not a single blade of grass grew there. It seemed to forever lie in turmoil.

Rebecca never left the cemetery. She wandered day and night. The only time her face held light was in the presence of Elam. Suzie watched their love mature. She wondered how this could be.

After their initial meeting in the towne center, they met only in the cemetery. Suzie watched with curiosity as they called for each other with a show of flowers. Elam picked daffodils in the spring, usually alone, but occasionally mixed with hyacinths. In the summer, his arrangements were field wildflowers full of the life and promise which the season brings. The autumn daisies and asters were laced with branches of brilliant fall leaves. In the long winter months he brought a bouquet of dried grains intertwined with fresh pine branches and winterberries.

Rebecca's bouquets were always fresh picked pink roses. Unknown to many from where she came, flowers grew all months, all seasons. She brought them to Goldie Bell, silently calling to Elam, out of the sight of all. Only Elam saw her, for it was his destiny. Her coming was announced by the song of a wood thrush.

Her thin frame appeared through a fading mist. As she glided closer to him, the vision became full. They touched as normal, embraced, but never kissed. This puzzled Suzie, but she did not ask. Much of their life was revealed in small fragments of time until their final day.

It was late spring, of what year Suzie could not tell for many seasons had passed uncounted. Elam traveled by the cover of night. He rode hard as if in pursuit though Suzie saw no one. He had an iron rod in his hand. He rode to a farmhouse northwest of Salem, jumped from Jasper's back and tied him loosely to a tree. He had learned his lesson well. He leaned the iron rod against the side door of the house, tapped twice, and quietly ran back to Jasper. He leapt onto his back and rode back toward towne.

The gentleman of the house opened the side door. Suzie recognized him to be one of the men Rebecca met in the woods. Without a word the man snatched his black cloak and walked to the barn. He held the iron rod in his hand. He rode in the same direction. Within minutes, Suzie witnessed the gathering of the group. They came in silence, called by an innocent iron rod that rested against the funeral door.

The scene changed to a place along a single set of railroad tracks. The night was dark. The only light was from a lone Dietz lantern that glowed from a post hook. It swung from anticipation. The night held its breath. No breeze was felt.

Several men moved about. One uncoiled a hose from a container of spring water. Another held the handles of a wheelbarrow heaped with coal. The leader stood on a small platform. He stared at his timepiece.

"Five minutes!" he shouted. No sooner did the words come from his mouth than the rumble of an approaching train was heard. Its steam engine grew louder. The whistle blew before it rounded the bend.

The men sprang into action when the train settled to a stop. They filled the train with fresh supplies to carry them through to their next stop. Suzie was so busy watching the men carry out their hurried duties that she nearly missed the group at the ninth rail car.

One by one, five men slid from the trees that covered their bodies. All held iron rods in their hands. They ran to the rail car and placed the narrowed end of the bars in the slight opening of the door. When the workers in the engine car dumped the load of coal into the bin, the men pried the rail car door open. The crack of the jarred door was camouflaged by the tumble of coal.

As soon as the door opened, two black men jumped out. With the fall of the second load of coal, one man swung the door closed. It slammed closed with a loud bang. The timing was off and the sound was unmistakable.

The watchman on the platform sprang into action. He ran to the blind side of the train and surveyed the cars as he ran past their metal doors. He ran past the ninth car without hesitation. When he neared the caboose, his attention was drawn back to the middle of the train. He followed the sound and found Elam. He sat on a pile of rocks and threw them at the train. The crack of rock on metal was deafening. The only sound that rose above it was the jingle of Elam's drunken laughter.

The man shook Elam to his feet. He reeked of alcohol. "What the hell are you doing?" he shouted angrily.

Elam played the part well. He slunk to the ground and bobbed in a stupor. The man grabbed the empty bottle of liquor and threw it to the ground. It shattered in the rocks. Elam never flinched. He kicked Elam in the chest and he rolled onto his side. He drew back his foot for a second blow, but the train whistle blew. The steam released the brakes and the train rolled forward. Five minutes had passed. He ran to the front of the engine. Elam jumped to his feet. He ran through the woods to join the others.

By the time Elam arrived at the buckboard, only the driver could be seen. Bales of straw were piled high behind the wagon seat. Elam jumped in beside the driver. Not a word was spoken. Elam held his ribs.

The wagon followed a trail to the back of a house. Closely planted trees lined the well-used path. It was nearly impossible to peer through them. Suzie recognized this place as the one Dale Shaffer had described in his story about slave smuggling. Elam's involvement came as no surprise.

When the buckboard came to a halt at the back door, Elam tapped four sturdy knocks, equally timed, on the wagon seat. A latch hidden from view slid open. Out from the false bottom jumped the two black men. Another sympathizer took the horses and the wagon into the barn. While he and the two others unloaded the straw, Elam and the driver led the slaves through a narrow opening in the back of a fireplace. Elam went first, followed by the two slaves and last crept the wagon driver. Only the driver crawled out.

When the men returned from the barn, they toasted with a shot of whisky, tipped their hats, and rode back to their homes. The iron rods stood stacked in the corner of a horse stall and waited for their next freedom call.

Folded in one corner of the narrow room was a fresh set of clothing for the men. Three bowls of hot soup, warm rolls and coffee were beside them on a tray. Elam pulled a bottle of liquor from his pocket, lifted it in the air, and whispered, "To freedom." He took his second swig from that bottle for the night and presented it to the men. They echoed the whisper of freedom as they drank the remainder of the liquid. It soon warmed their veins and soothed their nerves. The sound of the roaring fire which covered the hidden seams of the passageway lulled the three of them to sleep.

Not one of them stirred as a band of men pounded on the front door of the house. The owner opened the door. They burst past him with their accusations. They trampled through the entire house and searched for the smuggled slaves, but found none. They shouted their questions. The owner, sleepy-eyed and dressed in pajamas, stood before them in denial. After they searched the barn, they left without notice. Jasper hid the iron rods. Sleep came easy.

39

Suzie glanced at the antique timepiece. The hands still moved. It read 11:57 a.m. She glanced back to Elam. His face was grave. The men slept with their bodies propped in a corner. Elam woke to three gentle taps on the fireback. A small brass lantern lit the opening.

"It's time."

The two men rubbed their tired eyes from the short nap and crawled out through the warm ashes. The time neared morning though at least two hours of dark cover could be found. The men leapt onto Jasper's back and followed the guidance of the rider before them. The two horses disappeared in the darkness. Elam left on foot.

He walked for nearly two hours until the early morning light stretched thin across the eastern sky. He was filled with hope at the sight of the coming day. He was anxious to report to Rebecca of another successful mission. As he crossed the field that boarded the cemetery, Jasper ran to Elam's side. He threw his head skyward in agitation. Elam tried to calm him, but Jasper jumped and pawed at the air.

Elam jumped onto his back and rode hard through the cemetery. Jasper stopped at the usual place and pawed at the ground while Elam picked a daffodil. His breathing was labored. He needed to see Rebecca. Jasper's erratic behavior made him uneasy. He ran to Goldie Bell.

He quickly gathered the bouquet from Goldie's grasp and placed the single jonquil in its place. He listened anxiously for the arrival announcement. Rebecca's obscured body moved closer to him. The sound of galloping horses and many voices moved closer. His body tensed from anxiety.

He glanced at his timepiece and held out his hand to Rebecca. She extended both hands to him, but she was still shrouded in a heavy mist. Just as their hands would have touched, the band of riders broke through her essence scattering forever its image.

"No!" shouted Elam. He collapsed to the ground. Rebecca was gone. The daffodil in Goldie's hands shriveled.

Suddenly, Suzie understood. Her time had come. She would be the instrument to break the cycle of Elam and Rebecca's continuous struggle.

She ran to the place where Elam would rest in time. She snatched a handful of daffodils. Her chest was tight. She clutched the bouquet and ran to Goldie Bell. Jasper flew past her in a panic. She glanced in Elam's direction as her feet pounded the earth.

The men surrounded Elam in a tight ring. Their horses snorted and pawed at the ground. Vibration from their hooves wound around the sound of crashing metal and pounded within her ears. Their voices were filled with hatred. Elam was defenseless. The men struck him with the stolen iron rods. His hands covered his head from their blows. Suzie knew it wouldn't be long.

Her lungs burned from the denial of oxygen. Her body was drenched in nervous sweat. When she finally came to the statue, she yanked the withered flower and tossed it to the ground. With thoughts of restoring Rebecca, she thrust the fresh bunch of flowers in Goldie's hands. At that moment, the pocket watch began to chime the noon hour. Never before had she heard its song.

The sound of the small timepiece filled the void that surrounded her. Time seemed to slow and the earth rejoiced. The sky flooded with the sweetness of birds sharing their songs. The pitiful shriveled daffodil floated to the ground in feather fashion. When it finally touched, the last note of the noon chime rang. The world fell silent.

Suzie lifted her head. What she saw surprised her. Standing just a few feet from her was Goldie Bell. The softness of the eyelash lace of her dress echoed her innocence. Her hands held a cluster of blue flowers, her signature flower, forget-me-nots. She giggled as she stared past Suzie. Her feet moved with excitement. Her face lit with love.

Suzie turned to see Jacob walking toward Goldie Bell with a fresh-picked spring bouquet. His eyes never strayed from his little girl. He gave her the bouquet of daffodils laced with hyacinths. She drew in the fragrance and whispered something to him. Their laughter joined. She carefully selected a stem of her blue forget-me-nots and presented it to her father. He bent to rest on one knee, kissed her forehead, and took the stem of remembrance. They smiled and turned their attention beyond Suzie.

Before she had a chance to move, Lizzie strolled past her. She, like Jacob, had a bouquet in her hands. Her tribute was always the same, pink roses. The flowers gently swayed with her movement. Their long stems boasted of multiple layers of soft petals. They scented the air with a thick damask perfume laced with a hint of green apples and ripened apricots.

Lizzie's smile broadened as she neared her daughter. Goldie's tiny hands presented a sprig of forget-me-nots. Their color was sky blue with yellow centers. Lizzie embraced Goldie.

Suzie watched as they conversed and laughed. After only a few minutes of precious conversation, they turned to face Suzie. All were still as they waited. Suzie looked over her shoulder and saw no one. Confused she turned in all directions, waiting for something to happen. The Taylor family's excitement overshadowed her bewilderment. Rebecca stood before them.

She was dressed in a flowing pink gown wrapped with silk ribbons. Her golden hair was drawn to one side. A wide pink ribbon was woven through the curls. She knelt beside Goldie Bell and accepted the forget-me-not gift with a gentle kiss on the cheek. As she stood, Goldie whispered something to her, which brought a smile to her face. Lizzie selected a pink rose from her bouquet and gave it to Rebecca. She brought it to her nose and drank in the heady fragrance. She presented it to Goldie and all turned to face Suzie.

Elam brushed past her as he hurried toward the gathering. His last few steps quickened to a sprint. He picked a daffodil from Jacob's bouquet and knelt on one knee as he held it up to Rebecca. When she accepted it, he gathered her in his arms and lifted her in the air. His long black coat and her gown entwined as he swirled her in a circle. Jacob, Lizzie and Goldie joined their laughter.

When Elam gently placed Rebecca on the ground, he held her face in his hands and kissed her. His tenderness was refreshing. Rebecca threw her arms around his neck and they held each other in a long embrace. They were set apart by separation, in their lives and in time. Only moments in history were shared on this cemetery ground. For it was here their destiny came together. It was here

Elam vowed to join her family's plight and smuggle slaves to freedom. It was here they planned their escape. It was here they both died. It was here they called to each other through longing, desperation and love. It was here in this place, a normal cemetery filled with thousands of stories. Stories rich with emotions, many too powerful to lie in the ground, left unsaid and unable to rest. It was difficult to fight the tears.

Suzie was so wrapped in the moment that the steady footsteps approaching from behind her went unnoticed. All of her questions were about to be answered, her apprehensions soothed, her mind to rest with this next visitor. When he touched her shoulder, she turned to him.

He wiped the tears from her face and whispered. "I have something to show you."

40

Patrick stood with Suzie in Hope Cemetery, a much younger man. His hair was light brown and wavy, not white, as she knew. His build was modest, but toned. He stood about 5′9″ in height, nearly eye to eye with Suzie. His mischievous eyes sparkled as she stood before him.

He placed his hand on Suzie's shoulder. Instantly, they were together in his home. They stood in the front room in silence. Patrick seemed anxious. Tears flooded her eyes. Patrick held her until her body went limp and her sobs faded to silence. He whispered softly. "My dear little girl. This is not a time for sadness but of rejoicing for I `ave wonderful news to share with you."

Suzie hardly felt like rejoicing. Unable to hide her sarcasm she said, "I don't feel happy." She hung her head, "We didn't get to say goodbye…I didn't say goodbye."

"I am `ere before you now, not to say goodbye but to bring clarity."

"I am sorry Patrick. I'm not following you."

Patrick sighed deeply and began to tell his story, "I `ave to take you back to the day the bee stung you, remember?"

"Yes, but…."

Patrick continued through her question, "When I looked into your eye, I saw something which excited me. I noticed a design in your iris, which was the same as Attie's. I `ad spent so many hours staring into those beautiful eyes of `ers that I `ad no doubt, but I needed to be sure. When you left, I gathered your coffee cup and placed it in a sterile bag. I took a teacup from Attie's later that day."

"The day I left this earth, I was on my way to share this information with Attie, but fate `ad other plans for me." His face grew grim. "I never saw `er coming. I should `ave been more careful. Just moments before, I was nearly in an accident. As I approached the light at South Lincoln and Franklin, it changed to green. I continued through without slowing. I glanced down at the notebook on my front seat and allowed my mind to wander to the blissful conversation about to take place. My `eart was filled. I drifted away without pain."

Suzie's face was twisted with confusion and sadness. He took her hand and assured her all would be fine. He continued his tale with music in his voice. His smile would not waiver. "The comedy within the irony was the fact the very proof I needed to show Attie `ad slipped from my notebook as I ran out of the front door." He knelt to his knees and slid his arm under the couch. He withdrew a single sheet of paper, glanced at it, and handed it to Suzie.

Her hand trembled as she accepted the document covered with graphs. Slowly she read the contents, careful not to miss a word. Much of the medical language she did not understand, but she knew enough about DNA to know its meaning. Patrick was her father and Madeline her mother. She held out her hand and felt for the arm of the chair. Patrick helped her land softly. He spoke no more.

Suzie stared at the paper for several minutes without speaking. Several times her lips parted, but no voice was heard only deep sighs. How could she have missed this? Her mind screamed questions, but she simply couldn't find the words, any words. All Patrick did was smile.

Patrick stood before her with his hand outstretched. Without hesitation Suzie took it. She stood in disbelief as she watched the lives of Madeline, Charlotte and Patrick unfold before her.

Madeline and Patrick held each other a long time before speaking. Madeline's eyes were rimmed in red and Patrick's soothing voice spoken in soft whispers calmed her. She was dressed in a hospital gown. The shades were drawn, a warning to the sun its presence was not permitted. He held her trembling hands within his own. His love for her was obvious. After a few minutes he walked to the window and opened the blind. Madeline squinted from the brightness of the sun. She shook her head in rejection but conceded to its warmth. Within minutes her dark mood passed. Her voice, as well as the room, was lit with life.

"I guess you are right," Madeline whispered. "I don't want to see her, but I will go."

"It will be good for you, Attie. Maybe, the visit will `elp your memory."

"Maybe...."

"You must think positively. Your memory will return. You will be released from the `ospital. We will marry and `ave children. We `ave our whole lives to be together. For now, patience and `ealing is of what we need to pray."

Madeline jumped from her bed and threw her arms around Patrick. He held her close as they walked down the hall to visit Charlotte. When they entered the room, Madeline's mood changed. The anger and resentment that surrounded Charlotte felt like an oppressive weight. The ceiling moved closer and the sunlight appeared to sour in

Charlotte's presence. She turned her head from Madeline. Madeline wanted to dart out of the room, but Patrick stood firm.

"Attie, my dear," he whispered to her, "Your sister loves you. You'll see."

"But..." Madeline lowered her head, "she is mean to me, Patrick. Her words are ugly. She can't be my sister. She's evil."

Madeline ran from the room. Charlotte's laughter echoed in the halls. Patrick felt conflicted. He understood the resentment Charlotte held against her sister, but had he known the future, he would have left town with Madeline without regret. His thoughts were read by Suzie and she understood his strength and conviction.

In the next moment, they stood again in Madeline's room. She witnessed firsthand the awakening from Patrick's journal. She watched Madeline's face as she screamed for help. She watched the pain strangled by fear. Patrick was unknown to her. All they had shared was lost.

The moments flew at a rapid pace. The ache of loss was unbearable to watch. Each visit became more volatile. Patrick became more confused until a chance meeting occurred.

He was ushered from Madeline's room by security and warned not to return. He held a restraining order in his hands. He could not continue his life in this place. He decided to accept the position in Arizona. As he left the hospital, he overheard two interns discussing Madeline. He hid himself and listened closely.

"I tell you, I caught her."

"Caught her what?"

"Placing this tape in a recorder."

"Oh don't be ridiculous."

"I'm telling you, that woman gives me the creeps. She holds power over people."

"You watch too many scary movies." He laughed.

"Go ahead and laugh, but I'm telling you she is brainwashing her sister."

"Brainwashing? You're grasping at straws."

"Don't you wonder why all of the sudden she wants nothing to do with Patrick? Doesn't that seem strange to you?"

"Although I will admit, it does appear odd, Patrick explained what could happen if her memory returns. He said she could lose some if not all current events."

"Yes, but what caused it?"

"The medication, the trauma, the series of events, who knows?"

"Her sister. Her sister caused it. She made this tape full of old memories, family memories, to jar her memory..."

"Well that's hardly evil."

"In and of itself, no. But listen to it. Listen to how it is presented. Charlotte plays it while she sleeps. She asked the nurse to play it for her. The first five minutes is innocent and sweet...

"Madeline, it's me, Charlotte, your sister. Listen to my voice. You know it well. We live together in our parents' house in Salem, Ohio. We lost our parents in a terrible accident. You are all I have left. Please don't leave me. I need you, Madeline, especially now. The car accident has left me hurting. It's so bad that I need your help. I know I might sound angry about the accident, but I will get better. Please promise me you will..."

"That sounds innocent enough, but listen to this. I'm going to fast-forward a bit. This part played long after the nurse was gone."

"...Don't you remember? We used to take turns on the swing daddy made for us. I always insisted that you swing first, don't you remember? After a while, you would let me swing. Daddy would laugh at us. Sometimes our dog, Giza, would chase us. Well he was really your dog, but you would let me play with him sometimes. My daddy bought you that dog, don't you remember? I was the one who wanted that dog, but you always got what you wanted. Daddy loved us both, but he loved you more. You were his favorite and I was mommy's favorite... Your dresses were always prettier than mine. That's because daddy always bought yours on his trips. He bought me other things, stupid things, things I always hated. He never bought me a dress...Daddy always hugged you first, sometimes just a bit too long I think. He would kiss you too, not me. I got a kiss on the cheek. He always wanted you to sit on his lap, sometimes in his private chair in his study. Sometimes the door would be locked. I don't know what he was doing to you, but you liked it. You always laughed and asked for more. Sometimes I would sit and wait for an hour before Daddy would unlock the door. Usually I would find you sitting on his lap on those days. Men always liked you more, Madeline. It's because you did what they wanted, whatever they wanted. Mommy said you were a bad girl and that I shouldn't do the things you do, but you always seemed to have more fun. All the boys liked you and so did their daddies. Did you do things with their daddies too, like you did with our daddy? You are a bad girl. I can fix you, but you must stay away from the bad boys, especially older boys, because you will just do bad things with them and then you will be ashamed...I'll help you not be ashamed, Madeline, but you have to listen to me...I love you...no one loves you like me...I can help you not be bad with the boys, but you have to listen to your older sister, Charlotte. Listen to my voice...Remember it well...I'll help you be a good girl..."

Patrick had heard enough. He walked around the corner. The two interns were so involved in the tape they didn't notice him. Without a word, Patrick held out his hand. The intern stopped the tape and dropped it into his palm. All were silent as he walked away.

He went to his house that evening and made his own tape. One that wasn't full of lies, one that would hopefully undo some of the damage that had been done.

He knew Charlotte was a master manipulator, but he had underestimated her. It was clear his position with Madeline had drastically changed whether it was in part because of this tape, he couldn't be sure. He had studied Madeline's illness and others like her. He was sure another trauma was the cause for the drastic change. He was heartbroken, but he couldn't win at Charlotte's game. She played dirty. She played to win, no matter who got hurt. Since she was Madeline's legal guardian for the next year, he felt it was in Madeline's best interest if he stopped fighting. He truly thought it was the best thing for Madeline. His reason made sense to Suzie.

Suzie watched as he reentered her room that night. He hadn't mentioned the tape in his journal. He obviously felt so conflicted that he couldn't admit it to himself and wanted to keep it secret.

He slid the recorder from under Madeline's bed. He was relieved to find it empty. That meant only one destructive tape had been made.

He pushed the play button, and whispered, "I love you, Attie. Hear my voice. I am the man who loves you."

He bent to kiss her and felt her acceptance. His soft voice echoed in the background. Words of love and encouragement filled the room. This final gift gave him the strength to walk out of the door.

Once again Patrick held out his hand to Suzie, but in it this time was a mini reel tape. The word "Madeline" in Charlotte's writing was scrawled on it. Suzie knew this tape was the one Patrick made for Madeline. He attempted to conceal its identity by disguising the label.

"Do not feel sorry for me. I `ad a rich life and was fulfilled by the love Attie `ad for me through all the years. We may not `ave walked side by side, but that love carried both of us through some difficult years and brought us together in this place."

When he finished speaking, they stood in the presence of five others at Hope Cemetery. Goldie Bell, Jacob and Lizzie Taylor, Rebecca and Elam stood in a single line touched by the shadow of Goldie Bell's statue. Patrick accepted a spray of forget-me-nots from Goldie. She giggled as he took them from her. He handed her a bouquet of florist flowers, in the center was a dozen pink cabbage roses. It was the same bouquet she held on the day of his funeral.

Suzie did not hear Madeline behind her. She placed her hand gently on Suzie's shoulders. Suzie spun from surprise.

"Mother!" she exclaimed. "I didn't know, yet somehow I could feel it. I wish…."

"Child, there is not time for wishes of things past. There is only time for this." As Madeline moved her hand, their surroundings changed. They stood in Madeline's home.

"All you see is yours. We are sorry we left you the way we did, but I know in time, you will understand." Madeline's face was rich with radiant light. She never looked so content.

"It's not fair. I just found out the truth and now you are gone."

"Suzie, you as well as I, have felt it all along. The bond between us can never be severed. The truth is a beautiful thing even if it brings pain."

"But, Charlotte…."

Madeline held up her hand to silence her. Suzie obeyed. "Not today. Those memories are long swept away since the day Patrick came back into my life. I have heard his voice in my dreams, calling me, longing for us to be together. I knew that I must wait for him so I spent a lifetime serving my duty to an ungrateful soul who could not be comforted. Her life was not her own and she will spend eternity paying for it."

Madeline walked Suzie through her house. She pointed to a box on a shelf in her library. "Bring that to me dear, please."

Suzie slid the rolling ladder to the spot where the box was placed. When she wrapped her hands around it, she felt the layers of dust on the box. She thought it odd, for everything that surrounded it was free of neglect. This small wooden box was regarded as inaccessible. Suzie heard the rattle of the contents as she held out the box to Madeline. Her mother stood still.

After moments of long stares, Madeline sighed. "Open it."

Slowly, Suzie opened the lid of the box. Inside was a mini reel tape. The writing on the label was from Madeline. It simply read: "Charlotte." Madeline motioned for Suzie to place it in a recorder, which was sat on the partner's desk in the center of the room. As the tape played, Suzie recognized Madeline's voice. She spoke in soft, but firm whispers.

The words floated around the room and enveloped them as it spun. Suzie felt herself move. What she witnessed disturbed her. The calmness in Madeline's voice, recorded long ago, continued to play.

Madeline and Charlotte stood in the threshold of Charlotte's bedroom door. Charlotte screamed as she waved a mini reel tape. Madeline's guilt-riddled face was down turned. She opened her mouth to explain but was silenced by Charlotte's anger. Her flushed face drew closer to Madeline. Her hot breath came in panicked bursts as she spit her venomous words.

Charlotte's voice shrieked the words "traitor, liar, manipulator," while the soothing sound of Madeline's recording continued to play

.

"... forgive you... won't hold you responsible... Love you through your faults... know what you've done... aware how you control me as well as others... hear what others have said... sorry for you... pathetic... sad... time to mellow with age... can you forgive... let go of your anger... you can be a good person... have witnessed this first hand... your husbands loved you... you can be thoughtful... why are you so angry... let it go... show your good side...."

As Suzie watched Charlotte lose control of her emotions, a strange thing occurred. She walked without her cane. She did not limp or hesitate when she took a step. In her tantrum, she pounded her foot on the floor several times and lunged toward Madeline, all without a single hobble. Madeline never lifted her eyes. Suzie wondered if she knew.

"You are so worthless, Madeline. Your life is a waste. You can't even lift your head from your life's shame." Charlotte's words gurgled in a demonic voice. Its sound was chilling.

Madeline made a move to the top of the steps. Without looking at Charlotte she said, "I'll get your medicine."

Madeline started to walk down the stairs, but before she stepped on the third stair tread, Charlotte lunged at her. The tape she clutched in her hands hit Madeline's face. Madeline brought her hands to her face to shield herself from future blows. Charlotte lunged at her again and lost her footing. She tried to catch herself and screamed in horror as she plunged.

Madeline's anger and moment of hatred prevented her from extending her hand to help. Instead, she moved back along the wall and watched her sister tumble down the entire flight of stairs. When Charlotte stopped on the bottom riser, her body was strangely contorted. Her legs were wrapped around each other. Her left arm was clearly broken from the way it was positioned and her right arm was under her body. Her eyes remained fixed on Madeline.

"Charlotte!" Madeline fled down the stairs. "Oh my God! Charlotte."

Madeline dared not move her. She felt for a pulse. It was weak. "Hang on Charlotte. I'll call for help."

She ran to the telephone in the kitchen and called for an ambulance.

"...it's my sister. She has fallen down the stairs. Her pulse is weak...hurry..." Madeline dropped the phone as she heard her sister cry. The telephone swung from its cord.

When Madeline turned the corner, it was obvious her sister was dying. Madeline knelt beside her and cradled Charlotte's head in her hands. Tears flooded her eyes.

"Hang on. They'll be here soon."

Charlotte moved her mouth to speak, but no words were heard. Madeline moved her face closer and strained to hear. Charlotte's mouth moved but still no voice.

"Shhh...It will be okay. Try not to speak. They are coming."

With her final breath Charlotte forced the words to come.

"...always...hated you...."

Madeline stood in shock. Charlotte's head hit the floor. Did she just hear her sister say that she always hated her? She tried to dismiss the notion. She tried to form other words that Charlotte must have said. She stared at her dead sister in disbelief. In that moment, it struck her.

Madeline glanced at the top of the staircase. Charlotte's cane or walker could not be seen. She ran up the stairs. She tried to recall the series of events which had just occurred. She tried to remember when her sister used her cane. She walked the length of the railing back to her sister's bedroom. Both of her walking aids were there.

Madeline felt betrayed. She replayed her sister walking freely as she bantered. She watched Charlotte lunge at her twice without faltering. She remembered her running down the hall. She replayed her hot breath that spit words of hatred. She remembered turning to walk down the stairs and as much as she would like to forget, she now remembered positioning her foot to trip her sister as she struggled to catch herself.

In hind sight, Madeline watched her sister roll from step to step. Her body slammed against the hard cherry banister. She watched in horror as Charlotte's arm wedged itself between two spindles. As her body continued to tumble, her arm bent backwards and snapped with a loud crack. With each roll Madeline replayed Charlotte's darkest moments.

She watched as Patrick was served a restraining order. She heard Charlotte's cruel laughter as an officer escorted him from the hospital. She saw the confrontation on their front porch when Patrick came for her five years later. She heard the evil lies on the subliminal tape. She watched Charlotte destroy every letter Patrick sent. She watched Charlotte sign for the abortion. She witnessed her temper tantrum when it couldn't be done. She watched as Charlotte manipulated and confused Madeline forcing another memory loss. She watched her sign the adoption paper as Suzie's mother. She watched as Charlotte belittled her husbands into submission.

The visions stopped with the echo of her final words. Madeline stared down at her sister's lifeless body. Without thinking, she walked up the stairs into her sister's room and grabbed her cane. She placed it at the top of the staircase and waited for the paramedics.

Moments before the ambulance pulled into the driveway, the mini reel tape landed on Charlotte's chest. Instinctively, Madeline looked up from where it came. She saw nothing, but quickly snatched the tape. She shoved it in her pocket as the paramedics came to the front door.

Suzie stood speechless at what she was shown. She wondered why Madeline chose to show her these series of events. No one suspected or would have blamed her for what happened to Charlotte, especially Suzie.

Madeline read her thoughts. "I needed to show you the truth. So much of my life has been based on lies and manipulations. I just couldn't have that for you." Tears stained her cheeks as she continued, "My darling daughter, I have sensed you all of my life. I knew not of our connection until this day, but I sensed it. Charlotte did an excellent job of keeping us apart. I made many promises to her over the years involving you. I was the one who felt the heart tug, not her. I always thought that strange, but knowing my sister as I did, nothing surprised me. She was a mystery in many ways." Madeline sighed and added, "She suffered much, but much she caused."

"I just wish we had more time together. More time as a family, out from your sister's shadow."

"The time we shared was precious, was it not? Many families can't boast of that. Be glad, Suzie for what we have shared. Life is too short to dwell on the 'what ifs'."

Madeline collected herself gracefully, "Now come with me. I have something to show you."

Immediately, they were in another house. Suzie knew from its description that they stood in the study of Madeline's childhood home. The opening was a wide arch. There were no doors.

Madeline never looked back. "That room never had doors."

Suzie made no reply. She knew why her mother revealed this to her. It was one more confirmation of Charlotte's empty soul.

Suzie followed her mother through the house. When they turned the corner from her father's study, they were back in her home on South Lincoln. As they walked together into Madeline's living quarters, she held out a key. "This will open the safe that is located behind the painting of your grandparents in the keeping room. It has all of the pertinent papers you will need for estate purposes." She moved closer to Suzie and took her hand, "I would love to see you make this your home. You have business in Salem. You'll need to live close."

"Close to what?"

"The cemetery, of course."

As Madeline's lips formed the words, their bodies were moved back to the cemetery to join the others. Suzie was aware of the weight of the antique watch in her pocket. She wrapped her hand around it. She didn't want this moment to end.

Suzie cried out, "No!"

Jacob was the first image to fade. His face was focused on Goldie and her innocent smile. Goldie tossed him a kiss and he was gone. Lizzie was the second. She also was focused on Goldie Bell as her body faded into the background. Her colors were completely enveloped by those that surrounded her. Rebecca followed as the third. She extended her hand to Elam and as he took it, he became the fourth to fade from view. Suzie caught a glimpse of his wave to Goldie just as his hand blended into the swaying tree branch behind him. The final cry of the wood thrush was heard over the wind.

Suzie's cheeks were damp with tears as she watched this group of people move through this life to one of rest and completeness. They no longer longed for the love they had lost, no longer lived their lives stuck in their hell or filled with desperation for what they had lost. They finally had peace. Their journey was complete, fulfilled, finished.

She looked to Madeline and Patrick for some sign of permanence although she knew there would be none. Patrick and Madeline stood hand in hand and smiled at Suzie. Their bodies were barely a watery mist, but their faces and eyes remained clear. Madeline extended her hand to Suzie, but time was stolen from them. With Suzie's final blink, they were gone. Suzie gasped. She wanted them to stay, but she couldn't find her voice. She was left alone with Goldie Bell, the only one of the seven who remained.

Suzie made a step toward the little girl, but Goldie's feet started to move. Her tiny feet were quick and no match for Suzie. She stepped behind a nearby fir tree. When Suzie neared the base of the tree, Goldie was gone. Behind Suzie came a girlish giggle. Quickly she turned around. What she saw shocked her.

Goldie held a bouquet of spring flowers. The large gathering held a circle of trilliums surrounded by late blooming daffodils. In the center were tall spikes of flowering quince in full bloom. As Suzie walked closer, she saw a cluster of forget-me-nots woven throughout the bouquet. Goldie Bell held out the last cluster as an offering to an unseen guest. She giggled as Suzie approached her.

"Who do you see, Goldie Bell?" she asked as she knelt on one knee. Goldie made no reply. She stared into the air. Suzie focused on the flowers until they vanished from her hand. Suzie held her breath until her lungs burned. She dared not to breathe. One by one, bands of forget-me-nots bloomed under Goldie's feet. She giggled as she skirted among them. Her body swayed to unheard music. She placed her bouquet on the ground and danced with her unseen partner. In a moment she stopped. Suzie felt a strong desire to join her. She stooped to pick a spray of the magical blue flowers. When she gave them to Goldie Bell, William appeared beside her. She gasped from excitement and ran to him.

William moved closer to her. She felt the warmth of his breath against her skin. Her body moved with strong desire. She quivered. When he touched her cheek, she leaned into him.

When their lips touched, Suzie felt her body move. For a moment, love and desire spanned the chasm of time. Their bodies and souls merged as one embracing the waves of passion, bringing two lives together in history. She felt as if it were happening in the present and she hoped it would never end. She opened her eyes. She felt his touch. She heard his voice call her name.

In the sudden moment that he appeared, he was gone. Only the longing on her lips and the desperation in her heart remained. Suzie stood frozen in time, uncertain if she was in the present or the past. She was afraid to move, fearful to break the spell. She longed for William. As her thoughts cleared, she realized what she needed to do. She knelt and picked a cluster of forget-me-nots that bloomed at Goldie's memorial.

The face of this small child, with whom she had become so intimately involved, smiled at her. She sat on the marble pillar as a living child. Suzie held out her gathering of the delicate, yet significant flowers. The little girl took them from her hands and smiled. Her face lifted to the west.

William walked toward her. Although Suzie wanted to deny what she saw, she knew his life on earth had ended in the fire she was shown. Her mind raced back to all of the signs she had refused to see - the young woman who walked past him without acknowledgement, the missing creak of the third stair at the Spread Eagle Tavern, how he appeared when she thought of him, but most of all, his absence in the past few days. She was elated to see him but brought to tears knowing the man she had fallen in love with was not a reality. She fought self-pity.

Her thoughts drifted to her mother and father and the heartache they endured as they lived apart from each other their entire lives. The same longing, choked by desperation, felt by Elam and Rebecca. Their situation was not too dissimilar. Although William was alive when Suzie first met him, Rebecca was not. Their love spanned time and history as they clung to each other for support. She shuddered to think of the hell Elam had endured until she came to his aid to break his incessant curse.

"His aid!" she exclaimed out loud. Suzie saw the mist that surrounded her began to lift. She finally understood why she was called.

Nine visions - nine people - Goldie Bell, Jacob and Lizzie, Elam and Rebecca, Patrick and Madeline, William and now herself, were all connected to this statue. All called to continue a celebration of life and love manifested through a gathering of flowers given to this innocent child in longing and desperation. Eight people had been placed before her. She was the ninth.

Nine-minute intervals, all represented by a tale of reason and mystery, to show each other the role they must play in its continuance. The gold antique pocket watch was only an instrument to illustrate. As Suzie pulled it from her pocket, the hands slowed and stopped. It read 12:03 p.m. She smiled as she watched it fade from her palm into a memory. It had served its purpose. It was no longer needed.

She knew when she lifted her eyes, the world would be as she had always known it. She stood in Hope Cemetery beside the statue of Goldie Bell and listened to the sounds of life in Salem. The sky was speckled with white cumulus clouds surrounded by a sea of blue topaz. An unusual sight for early spring in Ohio but welcome nonetheless.

Suzie turned her face to the sun, permitting its force to envelop and penetrate her core. She felt energized by its warmth. With her head clear of its own cloudiness, she moved with purpose to the base of Goldie Bell Taylor's memorial statue. Innocence and foresight sparkled in her eyes, as her weather-worn face seemed softer to Suzie than ever before. She decided to repaint this image to illustrate her new vision.

She gathered her striped vintage blanket and spread it on the ground at the base of Goldie. The colors she chose seemed to fit the aura of the day better than the ones she had used prior. The antique hues of the gum Arabic pigments, wrapped themselves around the purity of her facial expression. The transparency of the paint opened to brilliant hues, creating crisp results that suited Goldie Bell's innocence.

Suzie finished the details of her face in record time. When she reflected on the results, she remembered the words of Dale Shaffer, "Take time with her mouth. No one ever seems to get it right." She smiled at the results, perfectly captured. The corners of her mouth were slightly upturned and her cheeks pulled from a grin.

Her skilled hands moved quickly over the cold-pressed paper. She added the embellished lace dress that Goldie had worn for more than a century. She was pleased with the results. She now focused on the details of William's bouquet.

The sun hid its face behind a cloud, allowing the details to be drawn without the distortion of direct sunlight. When she swirled her brush around in the water, the sun reappeared. It cast a bright glare on the bouquet. She moved for a better position, but the brilliance would not subside. Woven throughout the bouquet was a necklace.

The sun shone off the gold ring that encircled the pearled chalcedony stone. She recognized it immediately as the one given to Madeline at Patrick's funeral. She pulled it from the bouquet trying not to disturb the arrangement. With the final tug, the necklace and a sprig of forget-me-nots pulled from the center. The flowers which had been wrapped around the gold chain floated to the ground. She held the necklace tight in her hands.

"Thank you, mother," she whispered.

A slight breeze blew across her face and on it a periwinkle sulfur moth. It flew past her cheek and caressed it with its tiny wings. Suzie touched the spot on her face as she watched the moth float on the breeze. She wiped away her tears.

She looked at her mother's necklace. On it appeared a written word, in cursive, all lower case:

believe

She smiled as she whispered. "I do...***believe***."

With those spoken words, the letters on the stone faded until they disappeared. Suzie clasped her hand around the stone and smiled. It was warm to touch. She knelt to pick up the sprig of forget-me-nots from the ground. With the skill from an artist's hand, she positioned it in the bouquet. She heard footsteps brush the soft spring grass behind her. She smiled before she turned around. She knew who it was, and she knew how to bid him to come.

Her life, her destiny, her reason for being walked towards her, his face flooded with anticipation. William held his arms open for her. She laughed out loud.

It had begun.

www.ingramcontent.com/pod-product-compliance
Lightning Source LLC
Chambersburg PA
CBHW020555310726
48979CB00008B/1222/J

* 9 7 8 0 9 8 0 0 3 3 2 5 0 *